The Lost Heifetz
and Other Stories

MICHAEL TABOR

For Nathan
with best wishes

Michael Tabor

The Lost Heifetz and Other Stories

ISBN: 978-0-9986778-0-4 (paperback)
ISBN: 978-0-9986778-1-1 (hardcover)
ISBN: 978-0-9986778-2-8 (eBook)

*The Lost Heifetz and Other Stories is a work of fiction.
Names, characters, places, and incidents are the product of
the author's imagination. Any resemblance to actual persons,
living or dead, events, or locales, is entirely coincidental.*

Printed in the United States of America

Cover and Interior design by 1106 Design

For family and friends, past and present.

CONTENTS

THE LOST HEIFETZ

My study is suffused with the autumnal glow of late afternoon sunlight. It would almost be a crime to turn on my desk lamp and disturb the golden tranquility of the moment. I sit back and listen to my daughter practicing the violin in the next room. She has just started to learn the Bach sonatas and partitas, and although it is early days in her lifelong musical journey to the mountaintop, I can hear—or maybe it is just a father's pride that hears—a certain warmth in her tone that tells me the music is already starting to speak to her. When I hear her play Bach on his violin I often wonder what he would think if he could hear her. When I gave her the violin for her last birthday, I simply said that it belonged to a man I once knew who gave it to me and who would have wanted me to pass it on to her. It will soon be time to tell her the whole amazing story.

It all began on a Sunday afternoon in October, about twenty years ago, when I had dropped by the old HMV store on Broadway and 72nd Street to look for a recording of Bach's *Well-Tempered Clavier* by Andras Schiff. I had the Glenn

Gould recordings, but after hearing some of the Schiff at a friend's home, I was very interested in buying the Schiff for myself. After a few minutes of idly flipping through the racks of CDs I went to the desk at the back of the store where they kept a selection of music guides and reviews. I picked up the *Penguin Guide to Classical Music* and flipped it open to the section on Bach. At that point an irritatingly campy voice loomed over my shoulder.

"Can I help you find anything?" I turned to find a smug-looking sales assistant with curly ginger hair and a loudly colored sweater.

"No. I was just browsing."

"Well, you certainly won't find anything in *that*," he said pointing at the book in my hands. "Those guys are just a bunch of English armchair music critics. They're not practicing musicians. They don't know *anything*." He suddenly plucked the book out of my hands. "I see you're looking at the Bach section."

The guy was really starting to annoy me but I remained polite. "Yes, I was looking at their discussion of recordings of the *Well-Tempered Clavier*."

"Well, that just proves my point. *See*, there's no mention of those *divine* ..." and he said "divine" with a little shudder, "Glenn Gould recordings. Obviously those self-proclaimed experts just don't know how Bach should be ..."

At that point it happened: out of the corner of my eye I noticed an elderly man, just a couple of feet away, wearing an old beige raincoat and a battered brown hat, listening in on our brief exchange. He suddenly spoke up in a thick European accent.

"So tell me: who knows how it really should be?"

He came right up to us. He took off his hat revealing a head of thick white hair. He had a very lined but clearly once handsome face and twinkling gray eyes. The sales assistant stared at him angrily, obviously irritated that his profound commentary on the contemporary music scene had been interrupted. The old man spoke again.

"So tell me: who knows how Bach should be?" His eyes seemed to fix on me like some ancient mariner. "Let me tell you. Years ago, before the war, I was in Vienna at a Bach recital by Szigeti, and I was there with my good friend Max Aldinger …"

This was amazing. "You knew Max Aldinger?" I burst out.

He ignored my question and continued. "At the end of the recital the audience stood up and applauded, and the lady standing next to us turned to Max and said, 'Very nice, but it is not Bach.' And my friend Max—and I remember his exact words—turned to that foolish lady and said, 'But excuse me, Madame, did Bach *himself* tell you how it should be?'"

The old man was very animated and repeated the story. "That lady, as she clapped her hands …" and here he imitated a little hand clap, "she turned to Max and said, 'Very nice, but it is not Bach' and Max said, 'But excuse me, Madame, did Bach *himself* tell you how it should be?'"

The assistant shrugged his shoulders and minced off to another part of the store in search of easier prey, leaving me with this amazing old man. I was bursting to ask him a million questions.

"When exactly was this? How did you know Max Aldinger? Were you a professional musician in Vienna before the war?"

He gave a sad little smile and seemed on the verge of answering my questions when the opening bars of the slow movement of Bach's double violin concerto started playing over the store's sound system. His face seemed transformed—as though the music had wiped away the lines of old age—and a small, almost seraphic, smile started to form on his lips. But only for a split second: at that instant, the store door was pushed open by a departing customer just as a police car with blaring sirens roared past on 72nd Street. The harsh sound penetrated the store like a blast of ill-tempered wind accompanied by a momentary flash of red and blue lightning. To me this was no more than mildly irritating: a typical occurrence in a New York day that a New Yorker scarcely notices. But to my mysterious stranger it was clearly much more. The look of other-world serenity that had just started to spread across his face instantly changed into one of fear. His jaw clenched and his body stiffened. He quickly put his hat back on and tightened the belt of his raincoat.

"Excuse me, sir, for interrupting you. I wish you good health and good luck with your search for Bach," and he walked briskly out of the store.

4

The whole encounter, for all its brevity, was incredible: Bach, Szigeti, Aldinger. I had to know more. I ran to the exit to catch him, but by the time I had got outside onto the street he had disappeared.

Only in New York, I thought to myself as I made my way home. The old guy was most likely a member of that community of elderly European Jews who populated the Upper West Side. Maybe he had been a musician in prewar Vienna. But Max Aldinger? How could he have known him? The great violinist, teacher, and humanitarian had held court in Vienna until the Nazis kicked him out for helping Jewish musicians escape. Maybe he was one of them. But what really stuck in my memory of our encounter were those final moments when the Bach concerto started playing, only to be interrupted by the braying of the police siren—a hideous counterpoint to the lyricism of the violins. Although it was only for an instant, that initial look of serenity on his face somehow suggested—and I couldn't really have said why at the time—a deep and special intimacy with the music. By contrast, his fearful reaction to the sudden blast of the police siren was far more than the shudder of anxiety often displayed by the elderly when startled by an unexpected noise or intrusion, and I wondered if the siren had stirred up some dark memory.

Whoever he was, and whatever his story, the incident would make for a wonderful anecdote, and I looked forward to telling it to my old friend Peter, a violinist with the

5

Metropolitan Opera orchestra. Peter had briefly studied under Aldinger and might even know who the old guy was. Over the next few days I practiced his accent. I just loved the line, "But excuse me, Madame, did Bach *himself* tell you how it should be?" In fact, it all rather haunted me: in those few lines he had really got to the essence of musicianship. As a talented teenage violinist I had set my heart on a career as a soloist and, in those fantasies permitted in adolescence, dreamt that I would become a pupil and protégé of the legendary Max Aldinger. However, my teacher, a former assistant concert master under Ormandy, finally had to put me straight: "Colin, you are indeed a very talented young man. If you wish, you could become a very good violinist. But I have to tell you now, before it is too late, you will never be a great violinist. It is difficult to explain: you play with great precision, and you can play with some feeling, but the music itself never truly speaks to your heart. Without that, you will never be able to communicate the deepest meaning of the music to your audience." It was, at the time, a shattering blow. But he was right. I eventually overcame my disappointment, decided to make music my hobby, and embarked on a career as an independent software developer. Over time, I was able to persuade myself that I had the best of both worlds: a rather successful business and the ability and opportunity to play chamber music for fun with professional musicians like Peter. To him and his friends I was the "exceptional amateur" and, over the years, that made up for not being the "unexceptional professional."

Music was Peter's life: when not playing professionally, he was either teaching or playing for fun with his friends. I had first got to know him when he married a distant cousin of mine, and although he was quite a bit older than me, we stayed firm friends even after they divorced. We usually met up in a small group every few weeks to play. At our next meeting it was just the two of us, and I told him my story. I expected him just to have a good laugh. To my surprise, he became uncharacteristically serious.

"This is absolutely the most incredible thing. Can you remember if he put an exact year on when that happened? Was it 1937? This is amazing, absolutely amazing."

"Come on, Peter, it was just an old geezer reminiscing, maybe even fantasizing. It's certainly rather unusual, but why is it so absolutely amazing? What's the big deal?"

Peter explained. He reminded me of his brief period of study under Max Aldinger. During one class, Max told them the story of how in Vienna, around 1937, he had attended a Bach recital by Szigeti in the company of his then-favorite pupil Isaac Berg. At the end of the recital, as the audience applauded, a lady standing next to them said "Very nice, but it is not Bach," and Max recalled how he had turned to her and said, "But excuse me, Madame, did Bach *himself* tell you how it should be?"

"So the old guy was this Isaac Berg?"

"No. That's simply not possible. Berg was killed during the war. Your guy must have heard that story from someone. Maybe even from Max himself. That's certainly possible:

Max had a huge circle of friends in Vienna. But your guy couldn't have been with Max at that Szigeti concert. Simply not possible. If you ever run into him again, try to find out who he is. Berg … my goodness, I haven't thought about that name for quite a while. Now there's a story for you: Isaac Berg, the lost Heifetz."

"The lost Heifetz?"

"You don't know about Berg? Well, I guess not too many people today would have reason to. I only heard about him in detail from Max once. Dear old Max, how he loved to praise and promote his pupils. But, for some reason, in Berg's case—and by Max's account he might have been the greatest of them all—he was rather reticent. At a party about ten years ago, just before he died, I found myself sitting next to the great man. I think he already knew that he was dying and he suddenly held forth about Berg. I remember it rather clearly. It was as though he wanted to pass on a secret before he left us."

Peter poured himself a large glass of whiskey, held it up for a moment as though toasting his late teacher, and told me the story.

"In 1935 Max was on a concert tour in Poland. While visiting the Warsaw Conservatory he heard a student named Isaac Berg practicing. Max, with his legendary ear for talent, was immediately taken with the young man's playing and invited Berg to study with him in Vienna. As you know, Max was famous for his 'stable'—some say it rivaled Leopold Auer's—and Berg joined Max in early 1936.

Apparently Berg was in a league of his own, and Max was determined to launch his young protégé onto the Viennese music scene. It all happened in a rather sensational way. Max was scheduled to play the Bach D-minor, but the day before the concert the other violinist became very ill and Max persuaded Furtwangler to let him bring in Berg as a substitute. Apparently it was an absolute sensation. At the end of the performance the audience gave them a standing ovation, and Max remembered Furtwangler grinning from ear to ear as he patted Berg on the shoulder. The Viennese music critics—probably taking their cue from Furtwangler—gave the performance, and Berg's playing in particular, a glowing review. Well, you know how it is: everybody loves the sensational debut of an unknown, and Berg became quite the rage. Max then arranged for him to give some solo Bach recitals, and it was after those that everybody started to realize just how incredible Berg was.

"Max also went on about Berg's violin. Berg told him that he had found it in an old music shop in Warsaw. It was very old. Probably late seventeenth century, but no maker's name. Max recalled that on the bottom was carved a tiny crescent moon. He made a little joke about Berg 'making the moon shine' because Berg could draw the most gorgeous sound out of it. Max talked a lot about that: claiming that when he played it he simply couldn't match Berg's tone. I never really believed that, but that's what Max said."

Peter paused for a moment, stretched out on his sofa, and sipped on his whiskey.

"I don't think I've ever told you this, Colin, but after Max told me the story I just couldn't get it out of my mind. A few years later, when we were on tour in Vienna, I tried to check it out for myself and dug up as many of the music reviews from that period as I could. Sure enough, Berg gave a number of recitals during 1937 and at the beginning of 1938. The reviews were amazing. One critic, after a Bach recital, wrote—and I still remember his words exactly—'It was if Bach himself had spoken to the young soloist and he, in turn, communicated the immortal message to his audience; most particularly so in his playing of the chaconne of the second partita.' Imagine if somebody got a review like that today in the *New York Times*. They'd have every recording studio in town knocking at their door.

"Anyhow, I even tried to track down the critic. He had died at the end of the war, but his widow was still alive and I went to see her. She must have been in her late 80s and seemed a bit demented. But she remembered going to some of the Berg recitals with her husband, and suddenly became quite lucid as she reminisced about Berg. His technical brilliance, richness of tone, sensitivity of interpretation—you name it, Berg had it. Apparently her husband told her, although he never dared put it in print, that Berg was destined to be the greatest violinist of all time and already made Heifetz look quite pedestrian.

"She went on about what a handsome young man he was: his twinkling gray eyes, his luxuriant head of hair, his elegant mustache, and how all the women in Vienna were crazy

10

about him. And then she said that if it hadn't been for those International Zionists starting the war everything would have been so very different. God, those Austrians, they just never got it! Berg himself was Jewish, but because he was a protégé of Max, well regarded by Furtwangler, and perhaps because he didn't look Jewish, they found it convenient to overlook it, while still spouting their virulent anti-Semitism. After hearing a few more minutes of sick historical fantasy from the old bird I was glad to end the visit."

"Apart from the written accounts of his playing were there any recordings?"

"No. That's the tragedy. There was nothing other than the reviews and word of mouth. In its way, it makes the whole story even more romantic."

"But what happened to him?"

"Well, according to Max, in February of 1938 Berg's father became ill and Berg went back to Warsaw to see him. A few weeks later the Nazis were in Austria, and that was pretty much it. Max almost immediately lost contact with him. He tried to enlist Bronislaw Huberman's help to use his Polish contacts to find Berg and maybe get him a visa to Palestine, but it was all too late. As you know, Max spent the next year helping Jewish musicians get out of Europe until the Nazis decided to go after him too. But he got a tip-off and escaped to the States."

"And Berg?"

"When I asked Max about Berg's fate he looked extremely sad and just said, 'Poor Isaac. Those damned Nazis.' So that must have been it: Berg was trapped in Poland and presumably rounded up at some point and sent to the gas chambers."

"Would he have been the greatest?"

"According to Max, probably yes."

Peter poured himself another glass of whiskey before going on.

"Of course, maybe we're just seduced by the romance of the old story of a young genius being cut down before his time. We have Cantelli and Lipatti, but at least we have some of their old recordings that reveal their exceptional talent. But with Berg we have nothing but a few old memories. Now there's probably only a handful of people left who would even recognize the name Isaac Berg, let alone have heard him play. Sad, isn't it? Within a few more years he'll just be a lost memory, let alone the lost Heifetz."

We sat in silence for a few moments and then Peter clapped his hands, as though trying to break a spell, and looked at me with a grin.

"Colin, it's just the two of us this evening. Do you want to play anything?"

"Yes. This may sound a bit crazy, but since that incident in the record store and the way the old guy reacted to the Bach concerto, and what you've just told me about Berg and his sensational concert debut playing that piece, I'd like us to play the largo together."

Peter smiled. He understood. And so we played that piece—one of the greatest and most beloved compositions in the violin repertoire. As we played, perhaps inspired by the tragic story of Isaac Berg, we both seemed to feel its immense beauty. Although Peter and I played together as friends—there was never a formal teacher-pupil arrangement—he was, to all intents, my teacher. That evening was no exception. He conducted with his bow and hummed out loud as needed, and through his direction and masterful playing helped me reach into the depth of the music: a piece in which the violins compete with each other, circle each other, and then sing to each other. In its way, to me at least, it is one of the greatest love duets ever written, and that evening I felt it in a way I had not felt before.

"Well, Colin, I don't know if Bach *himself*," and here Peter could not resist parodying my rendition of the old man's accent, "spoke to you this evening, but you played beautifully." As I left to go home he gave me a paternal pat on the back, "I have the feeling that you won't rest until you find him. So, my young friend, find him!"

Peter's story haunted me in the same way that it must have haunted him when he first heard it from Max Aldinger. The idea that such a brilliant talent could be forgotten was very distressing and I was determined to find the old man. I was convinced that he must have somehow known Berg and in all likelihood had heard him perform, and I wanted to hear the account of a witness to Berg's playing. Maybe a little story could be published somewhere—just to keep the memory of Berg alive a bit longer. I went back to the

HMV store a few times on the off-chance that the old man might be there. That irritating assistant and his outlandish sweaters always seemed to be on duty and, on my third visit, I overcame my distaste and asked him if he had seen the old man in the store again, or if he knew who he was.

"Never seen the old fool before or since," was his reply.

Peter was right: I had to find him and find out who he was, but it seemed like an impossible task. What was I to do: plaster "lost-dog" notices without a picture all over the city's record stores asking for information about an old man with gray eyes who might have attended a Szigeti concert in Vienna in 1937? My only option, at least to start with, was to follow my hunch that he lived somewhere on the upper West Side, and I decided to go back to what was once my old neighborhood. Elderly residents could often be seen walking along Riverside Drive or in Riverside Park and maybe I would spot him there. My rational side told me that patrolling Riverside Drive in the hope of finding the old man was ridiculous with practically no chance of success, but my desire to resolve this mystery was too strong to be discouraged by logic. However, going back there also meant revisiting my own past: stirring up carefully buried memories of my short-lived marriage when my ex-wife Emma and I, seemingly having it all, had an apartment on Riverside and 94th. I liked to think that I had moved on from my divorce, then almost two years past, but I hadn't.

We had first met at a reception after a private chamber concert organized by Peter for a major donor. Although

Emma was not a practicing musician, her job as a fund-raiser for the Met meant that she was very well-connected with the New York music scene. We both came from successful families, we both had Ivy League degrees, we both had promising careers, and we both had that self-assurance and streak of arrogance so typical of successful and well-connected young professionals living in the city. At first we competed with each other, then we circled each other, and before too long we started to sing to each other. We had a lot going for us: a shared love of music, a great social life, great sex, and a common fear of being single in New York. A simple tune that sang the song of marriage, but it was not the greatest love duet of all time. Our marriage started off with a brief crescendo followed by a slow and stealthy diminuendo. At first, a long loving kiss when she left for work in the mornings, then a kiss on the cheek, then a "must run," and finally the silence of absence as her business trips become more frequent and longer. And then one day she quietly announced that she had met someone else and wanted a divorce. Our duet had run its course.

My quest for the old man and what was now, in my mind, the legend of Isaac Berg soon had me walking up and down Riverside Park, revisiting my own past and in search of another's. Despite the apparent hopelessness of my task I found myself enjoying my solitary walks. In the past, when I had walked in the park I was usually in a rush to get somewhere with my mind often preoccupied by work. Now I noticed details of the scenery, and the people around me, that I had once taken for granted. A young couple pushing a pram: that might have been Emma and me; but starting a family had been pushed to a future chapter in our carefully drafted marriage script by the practical concerns of raising young children in Manhattan. An elderly couple—impeccably dressed in smart overcoats and neatly tied wool scarves—walking slowly along through the golden fall leaves and holding hands in a way that spoke of both love and physical support. That, too, might have been Emma and me in another universe. I wondered if the old man I was seeking had a wife to go home to, or if he lived the life of a lonely widower in a dusty, dimly lit, apartment with piles of old *New York Times* stacked on a Formica-topped kitchen table, listening to ancient LPs, and treating himself to lox from Zabar's. A couple sitting together on a park bench in total silence: was it because they didn't have a single word to say to each other, or because they didn't need to say a single word to each other? I certainly knew which case would have eventually applied to Emma and me. A solitary man of my age sitting on a bench, staring out over the Hudson: was he lost or at peace? I didn't yet know.

Then, one day, I caught a glimpse of the old man. He was too far ahead of me to catch up to him, but I saw him turning off Riverside Drive into 87th Street. By the time I reached there he had disappeared. Now I knew where to concentrate my search. The next weekend I saw him again and followed him, at a distance, up 87th Street and identified the building he entered. There was a doorman on duty and I decided to go back another time, armed with a suitably concocted story, to see if I could find out who the old man was. A few days later I was again on the Upper West Side, this time to meet a friend who worked at Columbia, and afterward I stopped by the building. There was no doorman on duty and the main lobby door was locked. However, in the entrance, I could read all the names of the residents by the buzzers. I didn't really know what I was looking for until, under 3E, I saw "I. Goldberg." I felt a chill run up my spine. Could "I. Goldberg" really be "I. Berg"? Could that old man, with his twinkling gray eyes and once handsome face, who claimed to have been with Max Aldinger at a Szigeti recital in Vienna in 1937, actually be Berg himself? The more I dwelled on it, the more I was convinced that I had made the most amazing discovery, and that Berg was still alive and living in New York under the name of Goldberg. It all seemed too fantastic, but it only served to fuel my curiosity. Somehow I was going to have to confront him and find out who he really was. The next Saturday afternoon I stationed myself near 87th and Riverside and saw my quarry walking along the Drive. He sat down on a bench a few yards away from me. I walked over to his bench and sat down at the other end. He briefly glanced in my direction, tightened his coat belt, and then resumed his reverie over the Hudson.

I tried to strike up a conversation. "Nice afternoon, isn't it?"

Of course that was hopelessly naive of me. Total strangers who try to strike up conversations on park benches in New York are the last people one wants to talk to. He did exactly as I would have done: ignored me, got up, and walked away.

The next weekend I again saw him walking along Riverside Drive. I caught up with him and tried the direct approach. "Excuse me, sir, I don't know if you remember me, but we met in the HMV store a few weeks ago and we talked about the violinist Max Aldinger."

"Young man, I do not remember talking to you at any time about any subject. You are mistaken," and he turned to walk away.

However, I had caught a glimmer of recognition in his eyes as he spoke to me, and I was determined to persist. But instead of trying a diplomatic approach I suddenly blurted out, "But Mr. Berg, I know who you are."

His face paled for an instant and then he regained his composure. "Sir, my name is Goldberg, Isaac Goldberg. I do not know any Mr. Berg. You have been following me for the last few weeks. Nobody likes to be followed in New York. If you do not leave me alone I will call the police," and he looked in the direction of an NYPD patrol car parked a few blocks away.

"Look, I'm really sorry, but you see …"

I was just about to tell him the story Peter had told me when he turned away and walked briskly toward the patrol car; but just before he got to the car he turned up 84th Street. I knew I had completely blown it. There was now no way the old man would ever talk to me again, let alone not call the police. I sat on a bench and stared out across the Hudson. I was very angry with myself and sat there for quite a while stewing over my stupidity and for losing what was probably the one opportunity I might have had to find out who he was. I don't know how long I had been sitting there when I heard a slight rustling. To my utter amazement, the old man was now sitting at the other end of the bench.

He smiled at me. "Excuse me, young man, I did not mean to be rude. Yes, I do remember talking to you in the record store and … do not worry, I did not call the police."

"God, no—I should be the one apologizing. I was following you and must have seemed incredibly rude just now. But after we met in the store and I told my friend Peter about what you had told me, I just had to talk to you again."

"So, who is this Peter? A friend of yours?" he asked.

And so I told him everything, and once I started it was difficult to stop. There was something in his twinkling eyes and benign smile that made me feel that I could tell him anything. I told him about Peter, about me, about Emma and me, about my walks along Riverside Drive and in the park in search of him, and about the story Max Aldinger had told Peter about Isaac Berg. I told him that since our meeting in the HMV store I had become foolishly obsessed with the idea that he was really Berg himself. That I felt a total idiot because I knew Berg had died during the war, but that I had wanted to hear about Berg—who he obviously must have known—and that I hoped he would forgive me for upsetting him so much. When I finally finished, he chuckled.

"Yes, when I was in that store and heard that very stupid young man say how Bach should be played something in me just snapped and I had to speak. But to think I told my story to a fellow musician and even one whose friend was a student of dear old Max!"

"So, please forgive me for asking: who are you, how did you know Max Aldinger, and did you know Isaac Berg?"

He looked deeply into my eyes as though measuring me up and estimating my worth. He took a deep breath. "Yes, I was a student of Max Aldinger in Vienna. I was … I am … Isaac Berg."

He saw my look of amazement. "So now I shock you, young man. I know everybody in New York is meant to be crazy, but I am not a crazy man. I did not die in the war, but after what happened to me I never wanted to play the violin again. But maybe it is time I told my story. So, if you please, I will tell you the story of Isaac Berg.

"I will not comment on what your friend Peter told you about my playing in Vienna all those years ago—history must judge that. But it is true that in February 1938 I went back to Warsaw where my father was very ill with cancer. When the Germans took control of Austria in March of that year I knew it was not safe for me to go back to Vienna, and I lost contact with Max. My dear father struggled on and although I was desperate to find a way out of Europe, to

England or to America, I could not leave him to die alone. He survived much longer than my brother and sister and I expected, and he didn't die until August of 1938. A few weeks later, the Nazis invaded Poland, destroyed my country, and started to round up us Jews. A small group of us ran away into the countryside and hid in the forests."

I nodded. One of Peter's colleagues had somehow survived the war as a boy in Poland by hiding in the forests, and I had read about groups of partisans who had done the same. Berg sighed and continued his story.

"There was just my brother and sister and two close friends of ours. It seems incredible now but somehow we managed to stay alive for more than two years. But then one day I had gone off looking for food, and when I came back to our campsite I found it deserted. There were tire tracks and a few cartridge cases on the ground. My brother's hat was lying nearby, stained with blood. A patrol must have found them and taken them away. I was shattered. I knew that I would never see any of them again and that it was only a matter of time before I would also be found and shot. As I wandered around that scene of desolation I found something remarkable. A few yards away, near the tire tracks, I saw my violin lying in the dirt! For some crazy reason I had carried it with me during our years on the run but never dared to play it, of course, for fear of being heard. For some reason the patrol hadn't found it, or they had taken it and it had fallen off their jeep when they left. For the next few days I hid deep in the forest, scarcely daring to move in case another patrol came by. But, at the same time, I wondered why I was even trying to live. I was so tired and hungry and heartbroken it would have been easier to die. After a week of living off berries and mushrooms—some of which I ate in the hope that they would poison me—I decided that I should give up. I would walk out of the forest and let fate do with me what it willed.

"After several days, I came to the edge of the forest and found a road that I followed. I still hid among the trees, and sometimes a few jeeps and tanks would roll by. One evening I saw a large building by the roadside. It looked a bit like a farmhouse, and in the distance I could see the outline of a small town. As I got closer to the building I could see bright lights on inside, and I heard the sound of a violin being played. Outside I saw a cluster of black automobiles with swastika flags and some German soldiers standing guard by them. Then I heard German songs being sung from inside the building. It was obviously some sort of club that the Nazis were using.

"Although I was still hidden by the trees I was no more than fifty feet from the front entrance. Suddenly there was a lot of shouting, and a big man came out of the building dragging another man by the collar. He kicked the man in the backside and shouted in Polish, 'Get out of here you drunken fool,' and throwing a small object after him, yelled 'and take your goddamned fiddle with you. Don't ever come back here again.' A few soldiers had come to the door and, roaring with drunken laughter, threw beer mugs at the

22

ejected man who ran off down the road. I then heard the big man say in German to the soldiers, 'Many apologies, sirs. I promise you that drunken peasant will never play in this club again.'

"That night I hid in the woods near the club and decided on a crazy plan. I tried to clean myself up as best as I could and shaved with a piece of broken glass. The next morning I walked up to the front door of that building with my violin in my hand. A big man came to the door. By his profile he must have been the same one I had seen the previous night.

'What the hell do you want?' he demanded.

'Excuse me, sir, I am looking for work. I heard in the town that you need a musician to play to your guests.'

'Who told you that?'

'Your club is famous, sir.'

'Well, fiddler, this might be your lucky day. Play me something.'

"So I played him a few little waltzes and caprices. He obviously liked what he heard but was still very suspicious.

'What's your name and where do you come from?'

'My name is Bezinski, sir, and I come from the next town.'"

Berg paused as though reliving that moment, and then continued. "That was such a risk! I had no idea where I was, let alone the name of the next town. This man suddenly stuck his face very close to mine and said, 'Tell me Bezinski, you're not a Jew are you?'

'No sir,' I said.

'Well, Bezinski, I don't know who you are, or what your game is, but you can certainly play the fiddle. Be here at six o'clock tonight. I won't pay you, but if our honored guests …' and here I noticed a slight edge of sarcasm in his voice, 'like what they hear, we can talk business.'

"So that night I found myself in the devil's lair, as it were, playing the violin for a roomful of Nazis as they drank and laughed. I played them waltzes, and when they sang their horrible songs I accompanied them on the violin. They liked that. A few gave me tips that the host immediately took from me. I had nowhere to go and when the last German had gone I volunteered to help clean up. By the time we were finished it was so late that nobody really noticed me anymore, and I slept in a chair at the back of the kitchen.

"After a few days, it became clear to the club owner that I was good for his business, but I was also homeless. He struck a tough deal: I could work in the kitchen during the day and play the violin at night as well as help serve drinks when they were busy. In return, I could sleep in a small shed at the back of the club and get two small meals a day. The owner, whose name was Stanislav, told me, 'If you work here Bezinski, you do exactly as I tell you. You see nothing and you say nothing.'

"Occasionally, very late at night, I would see through a crack in my shed door shadowy figures slip out of the nearby woods and sneak into the club. Of course I saw nothing and said nothing, but I suspected that Stanislav, for all his

24

fraternizing with the Germans, was also working with the Polish underground.

"Stanislav was a rough diamond. He quickly guessed that I was a Jew on the run, and after a few weeks I found a set of identity papers made out in the name of Bezinski lying on my bed. Nothing was said. I continued to play the violin and help around the club. The weeks turned into months and things seemed to be going quite well as I entertained the soldiers. They were mostly young officers stationed at a large garrison near the town. Best of all, nobody took any notice of me anymore. I just became part of the club furniture. I was just the little Polish fiddler who played the soldiers their favorite tunes and served them drinks.

"Then one night there was an unusual air of excitement and, quite late, a small group of young SS officers who I had not seen in the club before walked in, fawning at the side of a senior officer. I overheard a few whispers among the club regulars about 'Berlin'. I performed my usual routine, but as the evening wore on I noticed the special visitor staring at me. The next night he reappeared with his entourage. After a while he summoned me to his table. He looked at me as though I was an insect.

'You play well, fiddler. Where did you learn to play?'

'From my school teacher, sir.'

"He looked at me with piercing gray eyes and then got up and left. The next evening he was there again. After about an hour he motioned to a young officer sitting at his table. The officer pulled some papers from a briefcase and walked over to me. 'Here, fiddler, the colonel has brought you some music to play,' and he handed me some sheets of music. The whole thing made me very nervous. I fumbled with the scores, pretending to have difficulty finding a place on the bar to put them. The colonel motioned to me to start playing. I quickly glanced through the first few pages of music. They were simple folk pieces. I played them pretending to struggle a bit with the unfamiliar tunes.

'You can do better than that, fiddler,' the colonel called out. 'Play them faster.'

"Stanislav nodded at me, clearly anxious that I should please an important guest. So I played the tunes again. This time more fluently.

'That's better, fiddler. Now play them even faster.'

"I felt trapped. But I had no choice and played faster. The colonel laughed and his group laughed with him. 'Bravo, fiddler,' he called out and then motioned to the officer who again brought over some more sheets of music for me to play. They were again simple tunes and, as I played them, the colonel seemed to lose interest in me and became engrossed in conversation with his entourage. He had given me many sheets of music and I turned them over one after the other without thinking.

"Then something remarkable happened: as I turned to the next sheet of music I noticed that the score was much denser, but I was in such a daze that I started to play it anyhow. As I played the first few notes, I realized—and it was both thrilling and terrifying—that I was playing my beloved Bach! I froze. That sheet of music was no simple German folk tune. It was a page from the second Bach partita. I had been trapped. The colonel suddenly looked up at me with a cold, penetrating look and called out, 'Play on, fiddler, play on.'

"At that instant fate intervened. The waiter who had been serving the colonel's table tripped over and dropped his tray of drinks. It made a tremendous noise and mess, and as he fell he also knocked the sheets of music off the end of the bar. A couple of drunken young soldiers roared with laughter and threw their beer mugs at the waiter as he lay on the floor. Stanislav immediately ran forward to clear the debris and pulled the man up by the scruff of his neck. He motioned to me to continue playing and I quickly reverted to my usual repertoire of folk tunes. While all this was going on, the colonel left. I went to bed that night with my mind in turmoil.

"Obviously, the colonel suspected something. He had laid a trap for me by slipping that sheet of Bach in among the other tunes. Had he recognized me even though I was clean-shaven and had lost a lot of weight? Vienna had been full of Nazis working out of the German Embassy in 1937. Maybe he had heard one of my recitals. But my nightmare had only just begun. Suddenly my shed door was pulled open and two German soldiers were standing there.

'Come with us. Colonel Beckendorf wishes to see you.'

"I froze with fear, and one of the soldiers grabbed me by the shoulder.

'Come fiddler, come. You can't keep the colonel waiting all night.'

"I staggered to my feet, and suddenly one of the soldiers
laughed.

'And fiddler, bring your fiddle.'"

Berg stopped and gave me a little smile. He looked
very tired. "So, now that I have got this far, I must tell
you the rest."

I nodded to him to continue. But in that brief pause
before he resumed his story I was struck by how very quiet
it had become around us. I could have sworn that there
was no traffic noise, that the birds had gone quiet, and that
even the leaves rustling in a mild breeze had become still.
It was as though everything nearby had become mesmerized by what they were hearing. Berg took a deep breath
and continued.

"I cannot describe how frightened I was as I was pushed
into the back of one of those dreaded black automobiles and
driven into the German garrison. In a daze, I followed the
soldiers along seemingly endless, dimly lit corridors lined
with forbidding steel doors and finally found myself being
pushed into a large, dimly-lit office. One wall was draped
with that cursed swastika flag and on another hung a big
picture of The Devil himself. Sitting behind a desk was
Colonel Beckendorf. He dismissed my escort and beckoned
me over to his desk.

'Welcome, fiddler. Welcome.'

"I bowed, still dumb with fear.

'Do you have any idea why you are here, fiddler?'

'No, sir. No.'

"He gave a tight-lipped little smile.

'Well, fiddler, I thought we might talk about music.'

'About music, sir?'

'Yes, about music. You play very well, fiddler. Far too well for a nightclub waiter.'

'I'm just a waiter who plays the fiddle, sir.'

'Yes, but a waiter who plays Bach.'

'Bach, sir?'

'Don't play the dumb fool with me, fiddler. Tonight at the club, you started to play Bach from the scores I gave you before that idiot waiter fell over.'

"I pretended to catch on. 'So that piece of music was by Bach? It looked very difficult.'

'You do know who Bach is, you fool?'

'Yes, sir. My schoolteacher told me about him. He wrote church music.'

"The colonel looked disgusted. 'Bach was the greatest composer of all time and, of course, a German—like all the greatest composers.'

"I knew he was playing with me.

'So, fiddler, have you ever been in Vienna?'

'Vienna, sir? I have never traveled outside Poland.'

'A great city, Vienna. A home of German culture. I was there in 1937 and heard many fine concerts. If it hadn't been for those International Zionists starting this war, I might still be there. Do you know who Max Aldinger is?'

'I have never heard of him, sir. Is he a general like yourself?'

"That little piece of flattery didn't work.

'I'm a colonel, you fool. Aldinger was a violinist. Really a very good one, and he had many fine students. But Aldinger was also a fool: he liked the Jews, you see,' and here the colonel looked at me very hard. I said nothing and let him continue.

'He had one favorite pupil, a Jew called Berg, who played in Vienna that year. Some said he was going to be a very great violinist. But of course that would not have been possible. Jews have inferior genes and can never be great artists.' Again the colonel looked at me very hard. 'You look a bit like Berg.'

'I'm Bezinski, Colonel.'

'That's what your papers say, Bezinski.'

"Suddenly the colonel seemed to relax. He poured himself a glass of schnapps and settled back in his chair.

'I play the violin myself, you know.'

'I'm sure the colonel plays very well.'

'Well, when I was a young man I wanted to be a concert violinist. But my teacher told me, 'Beckendorf, you are indeed a very talented young man. If you wish, you could become a very good violinist. But I have to tell you now, before it is too late, you will never be a great violinist.' For a young man, that was a terrible blow, but now I serve a greater master,' and he looked up at the picture of The Devil on the wall."

Berg paused. There was anger in his eyes. "That was what was so terrifying about those Germans. On the one hand they could be so intelligent and cultured, but when all that intelligence became perverted by Hitler they became the greatest monsters the world has ever known."

Berg resumed his story. "Beckendorf looked at me with a smile like a wolf about to eat a rabbit. 'So now Bezinski, we play,' and he pulled a violin out of his desk.

'Play, Colonel?'

'Oh yes, Bezinski. So now we play together. It is sometimes good to play to forget the problems of war—which we are winning, of course. Tonight I thought it would be good to play with another musician. Not a single peasant in this wretched garrison can play as well as you, so that is why I brought you in. I even have some music for us to play.'

"He took out a thick score from a drawer, turned to about the middle of it, and tossed it across the desk to me. It was Bach! He had given me the score of the D-minor concerto and had turned it to the sublime largo. I knew he was trying to trap me. It was a trick worthy of Machiavelli. He must have heard my first concert in Vienna when Max and I played that piece, and he was now trying to make me reveal my true identity by forcing me to play it.

'This music looks very difficult, Colonel.'

'I think you can play it, Bezinski. Take some time to study the score. We wouldn't want to disgrace Bach, would we?' He picked up a file from his desk and started flipping

31

through it and writing notes in it. 'Tell me when you're ready, Bezinski.'

"I cannot tell you how I felt at that moment. It was as though God himself was punishing me for trying to stay alive. Beckendorf clearly knew that I was a much better musician than I had pretended to be at the club. I couldn't play too badly: he would know that I was faking it. But if I played well he would be suspicious of me, having in his mind that I might be Berg. So I decided to play him at his own game and although it caused me indescribable pain, I resolved to play Bach badly!"

Here Berg stopped and looked at me with tears in his eyes. "Can you understand what that meant to me? Bach *himself* had told me how it should be and I was going to deny it. And so we played. I have to say that Beckendorf was a fine musician. An exceptional amateur. He conducted with his bow and hummed out loud as needed. I played just well enough to keep him happy but just badly enough to show him that I was no true musician. In some passages he tried to tease out of me the deeper meaning of that immortal piece, but I was too good for him and he never trapped me. Toward the end I heard him mutter '*Dummkopf*' under his breath. Never has an insult sounded so sweet. When we finished the colonel looked enormously pleased with himself. For him it must have been great sport. For me it was an absolute torment.

'Indeed you play well, Bezinski. Who knows, if you had had a German music teacher you might have become a good violinist. You may leave now.'

"He pressed a button on his desk and two soldiers stepped inside his office and took me back to the club in that evil black car. I was sure that the colonel would be back for me. Even if he didn't think I was Berg anymore, he must have suspected that I was a Jew. I knew that he would toy with me a bit more and then have me stripped and beaten and shot. But again, fate intervened. He never came back to the club. It was suddenly deserted, and I learned from Stanislav that the Germans had just invaded Russia and many of the garrison soldiers had been sent to the front."

Berg stopped. "A pretty story, no?"

I felt absolutely drained and had no idea how Berg himself must have been feeling, but I was insatiable for more.

"What happened then?" I asked.

"So many things: the Germans, the Russians, the camps. I am too tired to tell you all of it. But yes, I survived the war and came to America soon afterward."

"But your music? If you had gone to Max Aldinger he would have helped you start your career again. He said that you would have been the greatest of them all."

Berg became very animated. "No, never! The day I landed in America I swore that I would never play the violin again. You have to understand that I had made a pact with the Devil in order to live. I sold my soul. I denied my faith. I denied my God-given gift. I prostituted my talent. I pretended to be a little country fiddler. I entertained the Nazis. I played Bach badly to trick that cursed colonel. Never could I have gone on stage and played again. I had denied what Bach *himself* had told me and I could never, out of respect for him, play him again."

"You have never played again?"

"Not since the end of the war. I did meet Max in Central Park in 1949 and he, bless him, begged me to resume my career. I told him my story and why I would never play again. He was very sad, but he understood and promised to keep my secret. Since then my life as Isaac Goldberg has been very quiet and simple. I earned a living as a proofreader for a small publishing house. I married a wonderful woman who had also lost all her family during the war. I never told her of my previous life as Isaac Berg. She died of cancer five years ago. We loved to read to each other ..." His voice tailed off for a moment as he watched a golden fall leaf drop to the ground by his feet. "We had a daughter who lives in Pittsburgh now. To the rest of the world I was an unknown man: just another old man queuing up for his lox at Zabar's. And then I met you in that record store!"

I don't how long we had been sitting on that park bench but the sun was setting over the river, and it was starting to become quite cool. The traffic noise on Riverside Drive had suddenly returned, as had the singing of the birds and the rustling of the leaves. Berg got up.

"So that is the story of Isaac Berg. Thank you for listening, my young friend. Maybe sometimes when you play Bach with your friends you will think of me." With that he walked away and was soon out of sight.

I was overwhelmed by this incredible tale and sat on the bench for quite a while, thinking over what he had told me. I had learned from the reminiscences of other Holocaust survivors that you survived the war only if you had such a story to tell. Berg's story was no more incredible than some of the others I had heard. But there was a special difference, of course. Because Berg had survived and sworn never to play again, the world had missed out on an amazing talent. Yet if he had died in the Holocaust that talent would also have been lost. It was all so tragic. It also put my own privileged life, my concerns and disappointments, into stark perspective. In his case, the most brilliant career had been cut short. The Nazis had murdered his brother and sister. He had suffered immense physical hardship and danger during the war, and his beloved wife had died five years ago. All I had to complain about was the fact that I wasn't a good enough violinist to have had a career as a soloist, and that my shallow marriage had failed.

Eventually it became too cold to sit around any longer and I got up to leave. I was seized by the desire to see Berg again and decided to go to his apartment on 87th Street. In a few minutes I was outside his building but now in a state of indecision of what to do. Then, from around the side of the building, I heard a violin being tuned. There was a barbed-wire gate between his building and the adjacent one, but for some reason that evening it was open as though beckoning me, and I crept around to the back of his building. There was a light on in an open third-floor window. Out of it I could hear scales being played: at first slowly and then evermore quickly. The virtuosity with which the scales were being played was breathtaking. I recalled Heifetz's little joke about how students were often afraid of practicing scales when really it should have been the other way around. Then there was a pause, and then it happened: through the window came the immortal sounds of Bach's second partita. Apparently Berg hadn't touched his violin for decades and now he was playing again. The beauty of his playing was indescribable, and when he reached the chaconne I found tears running down my cheeks. It was, indeed, as if Bach himself had told Berg how it should be and he was communicating that message to me. Perhaps for the first time I truly understood, deep within my heart, what my music teacher had told me all those years ago.

Why after all these years was Berg playing again, and for whom was he playing? Had he guessed that I would follow him home and by playing would prove to me beyond a reasonable doubt that he was, indeed, Isaac Berg? Was he playing for his father, his brother and sister, his late wife, and all the others he had lost? Or was he playing, perhaps for one last time, for Bach himself? And why was I crying? Had his playing released an outpouring of bottled-up emotions that I had been denying for so long about my limitations as a player and my failed marriage? All absolutely nothing compared with Berg's losses: the opportunity for a truly historic career, the loss of everybody he had loved and now, because of me, he had even lost his secret. Or was I simply moved to tears by the sublime beauty of his playing that only I was qualified to appreciate at that moment?

I wanted to run up to Berg's apartment and tell him that he really was the greatest of them all and that if he wanted, even at his advanced age, he could play again and the world would welcome him with open arms. But I also felt like a terrible voyeur listening in on an intensely private moment that Berg needed for himself. I suddenly felt very humble and crept back onto the street. As I made my way home I felt great sadness, but I also I felt strangely at peace. It was as though many feelings I had been unwilling to confront for so many years had now somehow been resolved.

Nonetheless, the excitement and emotion of that incredible encounter was too much to keep to myself. I phoned Peter late that night. He must have thought I had completely lost it as I tried to explain to him that I had found Isaac Berg.

"Are you sure you haven't been smoking any exotic substances this evening?" he asked, his voice tinged with irritation at having been woken up at such a late hour.

"No, Peter, you have to believe me."

"Come on, Colin. It sounds like a great story but you don't need me tell you that New York is full of wackos with fantastic tales."

"But, Peter, *I heard him play.*"

At that point Peter's tone completely changed. We both joked around a lot, but when it came to music he knew I was deadly serious. He agreed that Berg/Goldberg, whoever he really was, had a story to tell and we arranged to meet outside the 87th Street building at nine o'clock the next morning and try to visit with this mysterious old musician.

We met as planned, and when we went into the building's lobby there was a doorman on duty. His name, Powell, was stitched on his blue jacket.

"We are here to visit Mr. Goldberg."

Powell looked at us suspiciously. "There ain't no Goldberg here anymore."

"But look …" and I pointed to the name by the 3E buzzer, "there is I. Goldberg. I met with him yesterday."

"Yeah, that was yesterday, but he ain't here today."

"When will he be back?"

"He ain't coming back."

I took out a small wad of bills I always kept in my jacket pocket for taxi fares and tips. Anticipating a reward, Powell started to talk. "Man, I tell you, it was quite some business last night. Old Goldberg started playing the violin and wouldn't stop. Never knew he played. His neighbor, Mrs. Maisky in 3F, came down to the lobby and said, 'Powell, tell that old fool Goldberg that we don't need no Mr. Hifritz playing in the building all night,' and I said, 'Mrs. Maisky, there ain't no Mr. Hifritz in the building as far as I knows, and I knows *everybody* in this building.' And she said, 'Hifritz, Schmifritz, just go and knock on Goldberg's door and tell him to shut up'. Man, she was one mad old lady, and she kept going on about this Hifritz dude."

"Heifetz," suggested Peter helpfully.

"Yeah, that was it, Heifetz."

Powell looked at Peter suspiciously. "So you know this Heifetz too?"

"Sort of."

It was obviously Powell's pride to know everybody. "So who's this Heifetz dude?"

Peter got Powell's measure perfectly. "Heifetz, he's just a dude."

That seemed to satisfy Powell who continued with his tale that had obviously been a huge relief from the monotony of his job. "Well, I went up to Mr. Goldberg's apartment and knocked on his door. I don't think he heard me with all his violin noise. The racket stopped for a bit and then he started up again. Reckon he must have played the whole night. When I came back on duty this morning, old Goldberg was siting in the lobby with two big suitcases. He said, 'I'm leaving Powell. I'm going to stay with family in Pittsburgh. God bless you.' He gave me a hundred dollars, and before I could say anything a taxi came up and away he went. Just like that. Man, that was a big surprise. He was a nice old dude and to suddenly leave like that. A big surprise."

I could see Peter looking at me with arched eyebrows, probably suspecting that I was playing a gigantic practical joke on him. I felt pretty foolish, and we started to leave.

Just as we got to the entrance Powell called out to me, "Say, are you Mr. Jackson? Mr. Colin Jackson?"

I turned back. "Yes, that's me."

"I almost forgot. When I was helping him put his cases in the taxi he said that a young man called Colin Jackson, a white dude, would be coming by today to see him and that I was to say goodbye for him and give you this," and Powell pulled out a bundle from under the reception desk. "He said I should tell you that he wouldn't be needing it no more and that he wanted you to have it."

With that, he handed me something wrapped up in a soft black cloth. I unwrapped it. It was a very old violin. Peter snatched it up and looked at it. His mouth dropped open as he pointed to the tiny crescent moon carved on the bottom.

THE PAWNBROKER

The neon sign flashed on and off with a seductive wink that beckoned me in. I was short of cash, behind on deadlines, and late in love. I had no choice, and into the pawnshop I went. I was the only customer. There were shelves of electronics—mainly boom boxes and small TVs—a heavily fortified cabinet of firearms, a padlocked display case of chunky rings and gold pendants glistening with false promise, and a rack of old guitars.

"Can I help you, buddy?"

I turned around to find a man who, to my writer's eye, presented a rich menu of stereotypes: trailer-park white-trash, a redneck, an ex-marine, my high school gym teacher, the guy sitting next to you at the bar who you don't want to talk to. He was a little above medium height with a strong brawler's build, black jeans, and a tropically patterned shirt. The shirt was untucked and concealed a bulge on his hip that I could only assume was a handgun. His face was strangely difficult to describe other than a coarse complexion, a trimmed goatee beard, a baseball cap with a team logo I didn't recognize, and a pair of large, orange-tinted glasses that hid his eyes. It was difficult to estimate his age: maybe forty, maybe fifty. His voice hinted tones of a Texas good ol' boy, a southern drawl, a mid-western hick, the twang of a New Jersey mobster. He was, in short, all my favorite characters rolled into one.

"You must be a writer."

He could clearly see the look of amazement on my face. "You guys are in here all the time. Are you here for a loan?" He immediately held up his hand. "Before you start, I have to tell you that I've got more voices, tones, moods, and plot lines than I can handle at the moment, so it'd better be good."

"I've a narrative voice that I'd like to pawn."

"And what sort of voice is that?"

"It's a first-person narrator, but it's really a parody of," and I named a celebrated writer of the day. To my surprise, this drew a grin of recognition.

"Hmm … first-person parody. That's a nice change. It's usually stories about my father's Alzheimer's, my battle with cancer, my son is gay. You know, the usual boring stuff."

Despite the camouflage of his glasses, I could sense his eyes boring into me and holding my attention as he continued to speak. This was not the voice of some bearded loon.

"Man, I have to tell you, it's all so predictable with you writers these days. Only this morning I had a blonde chick in here wanting a loan on a rape story. 'Sorry honey,' I said, 'nobody is interested in those anymore.' Then she told me it was a rape *and* incest story. 'Dime a dozen,' I told her. Then she got really upset and said it was a rape *and* incest *and* murder *and* suicide story, and that she was really desperate for the money. I took her into the storeroom and showed her that I had racks and racks of them and, sorry cupcakes, no deal. She burst into tears and told me that it was *her* story and ran out of the shop. I almost felt sorry for her. Cute chick, though. Nice tits." He gave me a sly look. "I'm more of a leg and ass man myself. What about yourself?"

I didn't know what I disliked most: his familiarity, or the fact that we shared the same taste in women. He grinned and took on a friendly, confidential tone. "Let me show you something," and he motioned me to follow him through a door behind the shop counter. "As you know we are required by law—and, yes sir, we are a law-abiding outfit here—not to display pawned goods for sale for at least thirty days. This is where we stash it all." And there, beyond the racks of TVs and boom boxes and sports equipment, were long shelves, seemingly extending to infinity, marked Murder, Incest, Insanity, Suicide, and so on. I noticed one long shelf covered with a black screen.

"What's on that shelf?" I asked.

He laughed, "I hope you never find out, old buddy."

I wanted to investigate the contents of the shelves and delve deeper into the darkness but, sensing this, he quickly ushered me out of the storeroom and back into the shop.

"What do you do with all the plots and narrative voices you can't sell?" I asked.

He ran his hand lovingly over the rump of a large paper shredder on a table by the storeroom door. "Now this here shredder," and he pointed to the insertion slot that revealed a vicious row of shining teeth, "can shred even the toughest material at the rate of a thousand lines a minute. I send it all off to a recycling company that sorts it all out and sells refurbished ideas to a certain publishing house. I get a good deal. In fact, it's what makes me able to do business with you guys. To be honest, a lot of what gets brought in here sucks and rarely sells, but there's enough of a profit margin from the recycling to keep me afloat." He gave a wolfish grin. "But every now and then, I get a masterpiece in the making and make a tidy profit." He gave me a penetrating look, measuring me up and pinning me down on his butterfly-board of struggling writers.

"So here's the way it works: the recycling company sends the publishing house characters and plot lines, and they sell them online to the customers who use their story-writing program. Look …" and he flipped open a laptop computer on the counter, "it's a really neat program: you pull up the dials for Tone and Mood—the basic package has the range of one to ten, but you can download more range for a few bucks. Then you click on your choice of Characters and Plots and the program writes the story for you. It comes with the usual sex and violence basics, and you can buy more voices and plot lines from their website. Here's an example of something I wrote the other day: a zombie time-travels to Tibet to meet the Dalai Lama, gets kidnapped by extraterrestrial aliens disguised as Somali pirates, is rescued by Navy Seals, has group sex with them in the back of their pounding Blackhawk helicopter, and then gets home and wins American Idol. Maybe not *War and Peace,* but I've already sold a few copies on Amazon.

"Now the thing I really like is this editing tool called the F-bomber," and he clicked on the menu bar and scrolled down a long list of expletives: fuck, shit, cocksucker, mother-fucker, motherrrr-fuckerrrr, and so on. "See, you use it to click in your favorite F-words to spice up the story. There's even an option that suggests the best places in the story to use it. Brilliant, don't you think?"

What could I say? "Absolutely brilliant."

"I knew you'd like it. Well, enough of that. Now let's see what you've got."

At that point he took off his glasses to rub his nose. I could now see his eyes: they were dark, so very dark, while his pupils seemed to have a slight reddish glow to them. I had just read an article about crocodiles and their incredible night vision—far superior to the best military technology available. There was a picture, taken in the dark, of a crocodile's head. One could just make out the lethal jawline and teeth, and the eyes staring back at the camera with a dull red glow. Maybe my pawnbroker was the crocodile whose mouth was the armor-piercing paper-shredder and whose eyes could see into the darkest regions of my mind. As writers we need those dark corners of our imagination: we project them onto blank sheets of paper to create the light and shade of our stories. But where does that dark matter come from? Some of it is already within us. Some of it we need to find, sometimes the hard way. And for those writers who contrive it, it is merely a false shadow across the pages of their stories. God knows what darkness he had hidden on that screened-off shelf in his storeroom … Suddenly a pair of fingers snapped across my eyes.

"Wake up, buddy-boy. I can't hang around all day while you daydream about your Pulitzer Prize."

I handed him my manuscript and he started to read it out loud.

Last Night
By
Sam Taylor

Where does one go at this time of night? Perhaps to the bar where the bartender, who might remember my name, will call me "Bud," and offer me the latest mixology. One shot or two? And maybe, in a moment of daring, I could make a mock toast— flirtatiously acknowledged—to an unknown woman perched a few seats away, her tight skirt riding up her smooth tanned thighs. At this time of night all women look desirable to me.

46

The pawnbroker smiled to himself. He looked like the veteran of many a barstool encounter.

But no, I could go instead to the all-night diner and banter with the good-natured waitress who does not know my name, will always call me "Honey," and will ask how my day is going even when my day is all but done. Quite how done my day is she will never know. Through the brightly lit diner window, I see a solitary, thickset man feeding his loneliness with a gigantic burger. He turns toward the window and I can see a small splatter of ketchup on his T-shirt—his stigmata.

"Hmm ... good imagery, I like it."

But no, the place to be on this night is the dimly lit coffee shop where the barista will call me "Man," and earnestly discourse on the tasting notes of his precious brews. One shot or two? More choices, more shots. How many times can a man be shot before he knows he's had enough?

The pawnbroker chuckled, "Nice ... I'm a Dylan fan too. One shot or two? I know the feeling, old buddy," and he patted the shirt-covered bulge on his hip, but I couldn't tell if "old buddy" referred to me or to his gun. He read on.

This is my place, my way station: a theater in the small with bit players on display. Some with faces tinged by the silver glow from their computer screens—kabuki-masked actors at digital play—while other nighthawks silently sing their lonely arias. A young couple, pale-faced and tense, sit across from each other separated by mugs of coffee and a plate with the debris of a half-eaten cookie—communal fare without communion. He takes her hand. She pulls it away. Breakup or breakdown? I wish I could tell them it isn't worth it.

He gave me a penetrating look. "I see you're writing from the heart, old buddy." I blushed with embarrassment. He grinned and continued reading.

Old Mr. Prufrock, sitting alone in a dark corner, is eating a piece of cake that he shares with the ghosts of his past. I could go over and lend him my coffee spoons, but by now there is probably nothing left for him to measure. I know the feeling.

"It's difficult to resist old J. Alfred, isn't it? You know, the story-writing program I just showed you even has a Prufrock option: it will scan through your story and suggest places where you can make a Prufrock quote. Quite useful when you're writing highbrow stuff like this. Why, only the other day I tried it on a story about a surfer dude who's a frustrated poet and it gave me: 'Let us go then, you and I, when the surf is riding high'. What do you think?"

On the one hand, I was amazed that a pawnbroker would know Eliot. On the other, I had the feeling that I was being mocked and just gave a small, noncommittal smile. However, he must have picked up on my hurt feelings and gave me another big wolfish grin. "I have to say, old buddy, this really is very nice. Lots of potential. OK if I read on?" I nodded.

I'm sitting at the corner table by the window—my window on the world. Looking through the window onto the brightly lit street I can see my reflection and, at the same time, I can see the people come and go. They are walking through my head—two worlds interconnected by a trick of light that does not illuminate. The nocturne of the outside world plays its oft-repeated tune: a young couple, confident in their immortality, rush by hand-in-hand with carefree laughter; a middle-aged couple walk by in robotic routine, and even through the window their silence is deafening; an old man, slightly stooped and warmly shrouded in a duffel coat packaged with a colorful scarf, walks a small gray-muzzled dog—his best friend. Three successive and perhaps inevitable acts passing by. And what do they see through the window? The young immortals will not even notice me. The silent couple might sneak a quick glance at the stone face in the window and contrive a crumb of conversation out of me, while envying my solitude free of any human obligation. And the old man might recognize a kindred spirit and tip his hat toward me, and I would salute him back with my coffee cup.

It is time for me to go.

The pawnbroker looked serious and frowned. "You know, Sam, you really have something here, but I hope you won't mind if I make a suggestion?"

I was completely mesmerized. "No, please do."

"It's this carefree young couple running by hand-in-hand. Sure, it reminds you—I mean the narrator—of what he doesn't have. But let's face it: it's kind of obvious … lonely hearts and all that. My story-writing program cranks out lines like that all the time."

I was just about to explode with indignation at his criticism of what I thought was a line of great poignancy, but he was one step ahead of me.

"Now don't get me wrong, old buddy. It's a great piece. Plenty of potential. But just suppose you—I mean the narrator—sees the young couple arguing, and the girl runs into the coffee shop and sits at the table next to his. Think of the possibilities: eye contact, a conversation starts up, a revenge fuck, who knows …"

Just as my anger was about to boil over, he gave me a friendly smile. "Buddy, you really do have a great piece here. It was only a suggestion, just a suggestion. I'm happy to give you top dollar for it."

My curiosity outweighed my anger, and I nodded for him to continue.

"Well, before you tell me what you want, let me tell you how we operate here with writers. Unlike that stuff …" and he waved his hand dismissively toward the TVs, guns, and guitars, "the laws aren't very precise and we can be flexible. We can offer short-term loans, and we don't have to fill out the usual police forms. All you have to do is sign a form that says that, to the best of your knowledge, the material isn't stolen." He laughed, "I have to say, most of what gets brought in here is such crap it would be difficult to believe that anybody would want to steal it anyway."

Maybe he was in a good mood; maybe he liked me; maybe he knew something about my work that I didn't. And he seemed so confident about the loan amount that I wondered if he had a Blue Book of literary values hidden away somewhere. We negotiated a five-day loan of $1,000. Although I didn't want to run the risk of losing my latest creation, I was fairly confident that my overdue royalty check would arrive any day, and given the apparent lack of customers there appeared to be little chance of anybody coming in to buy it, even if I missed the deadline.

Just as I was about to leave the shop, a big Rottweiler came out from behind the counter and yawned at me. He had a metal-studded black leather collar. I've always found that if you praise a dog for its good looks, even if it's as ugly as sin, their owner will always warm to you. "That's a very fine dog you have."

"Yup, that's Wag. He's the sweetest puppy. If he likes you, he'll love you to pieces …" Wag looked up and gave me a slobbery grin. "And if he doesn't, God help you." Right on cue, Wag bared his enormous fangs and growled.

"Had him long?"

"Not long. My old German Shepherd, Bruiser, died about a year ago. Great dog: retired military K-9, two tours in Iraq. Man, I have to tell you, we see it all in here. Soon after Bruiser died, in walks this absolutely gorgeous chick with old Wag in tow. She asks me if I take dogs, can you believe it? 'Honey,' I said, 'we're a law-abiding pawnshop, not a puppy mill.' Then she tells me that Wag belonged to her boyfriend, a doctor, who had just been killed in a car crash. Apparently the car exploded in a great big ball of fire and he was burned to a cinder. But old Wag had somehow gotten out unharmed, and now she was looking for a good home for him. Man, I have to tell you, she was impossible to resist. The sort of chick most men would die for just to have one kiss. So, of course, I took the dog and …" he smirked from ear to ear "she gave me a little thank-you kiss when she left. She told me that the doctor called him Wagner. I call him Wag for short."

I left the shop strangely elated and completely entranced by the shop owner who defied all my assumptions about pawnbrokers, and in an unsettling way, seemed able to read my mind. I was still sore at his criticism of the passage about the young couple, but as I drove home I realized that he was right. I had had in mind a deeply depressed narrator on a lonely walk through the night toward suicide. But introducing the young woman into the narrative was a brilliant idea. She could be an equally tormented soul, they could have desperate sex in a dark alley in the hope of finding that one spark of human warmth that might save them ... it could go a number of ways and maybe I could end with a double suicide. I looked forward to substantially reworking the story.

I had a good week. I made my deadline, managed to be civil to my agent, made up with my girlfriend, and blew far too much money on a romantic evening at an expensive restaurant. At the end of the five-day loan period, I went back to the pawnshop to repay my loan and reclaim my work.

"Sorry, old buddy, you're just too late. The guy you passed on your way in just bought your piece."

I did not recall passing anybody on my way in. "How do you mean you just sold it? I'm only minutes past the five-day holding period we agreed on. I didn't see anybody on my way in. Who was he? What did he look like?"

The pawnbroker, sensing an imminent explosion, took control of me. "Whoa, whoa, whoa, old buddy. Easy now, you know the rules. You were past the deadline, and your friend came in and bought it ..."

"How do you mean 'my friend'?" I demanded.

"Well, he was obviously a writer. In fact he even looks a bit like you, and he's always in here. Quite a good-looking type of guy—in a smug sort of way—and he's always dressed in black. Said his name was Lucas."

My God, Lucas! Every time I hear his name or see his photograph in a literary review I am reminded of all the reasons why I hate him. Let me count the ways. First, there's the way he dresses: he always wears black. It makes him look suave and sophisticated. When I wear black, I'm the waiter with whom earnest diners discuss the carbon footprint of their kale and fava bean risotto. Second, there are the chicks: when we're at literary functions, the editors—you know, the ones who hide the hunger in their eyes behind smart bookish glasses—slip him their business cards with *that* look. And the literary groupies who decorate the parties we go to are always taking him into the cloakroom for a quick blow-job. When I say hello to any of them, they just laugh and ask me if I've had anything published recently. Third, there are his narrative voices. When his first-person narrator says "fuck," the reviewers say "raw and uncompromising." When I say "fuck," they say "crass and gratuitous." When his third-person narrator ponders the hand of fate, the reviewers say "profound insights into the human condition." When I invoke Tolstoyan forces of destiny, they say "pretentious and derivative." And so it goes on, a thousand ways. And then there's his name: Lucas Garcia-Brown. When I first met him at a writing workshop about ten years ago he was plain old Lucas Brown. Since then he became Lucas Garcia-Brown, with a carefully honed narrative about his culturally diverse heritage with hints of a disadvantaged and painful childhood. As far as I could tell it was all a fabrication: one of his grandmothers (or was it a great-grandmother?) had been born in Buenos Aires, and he had grown up in a well-to-do WASPy Long Island family. I've always known that the guy was a fraud. A fashionably correct scribbler devoid of original ideas who uses his slick narrative technique—and, I hate to admit it, he does have good technique—to conceal his lack of originality. But why doesn't anybody else see it the way I do? Was it because I once told a well-connected editor who had rejected my searing existential epic that he was a moron? But what on earth was wonder-boy Lucas, "… one of America's most talented young writers …" doing in this pawnshop?

A perverse sense of vindication overcame my anger. Suddenly, a lot of things made sense. No wonder his writing, to me at least, seemed so derivative: he was buying his narrative voices and plot lines from the pawnshop. And now he even had the temerity to buy one of my ideas that he would soon be using to earn the plaudits of the literary reviewers. While all these thoughts were cascading through my head, I was aware that the pawnbroker was watching me with an amused grin.

"Never mind, old buddy, it could be worse. I'm sure you've got plenty of good stuff in you, and if you get stuck

I can you give a sweet deal on the story-writing program I showed you when you were in here last week."

This was really insulting: "No way! If you honestly think that I need help with my creative processes …."

The pawnbroker seemed to find my self-righteous pomposity even more amusing and artfully deflected the conversation. "Look, we like to develop long-term relationships with our customers and you're always welcome back. It's time to shut up shop now. Have yourself a real good day," and he waved me on my way.

That night I was alone with my dark and angry thoughts. As writers, we so crave recognition and so few of us get it. Yet there are some writers who, for whatever reasons, maybe real talent, maybe sleeping with the right person, maybe dumb luck, are recognized and lionized by the literary crowd. It's like a snowball effect: once one critic anoints a writer, especially a young and photogenic one, the rest of the literary crowd, or so it sometimes seems, fall over each other to burnish the image of the next "exciting new voice on the literary scene." But who's going to listen to me? And then I hit on my brilliant idea. It isn't always clear what the chattering classes enjoy more: building people up or tearing them down. If the critics could praise Lucas today, they could trash him tomorrow. Now that I knew he was a regular customer at the pawnbroker, and with enough good taste to buy up my work, I could leave him a trail of poisoned bait to lead him to his literary doom. The pawnbroker's suggestion of introducing the female character into my story could be used, but quite differently from the way I would have used it myself. Now, instead of her joining the narrator on a doomed descent into madness, she would be his lifeline to happiness. If Lucas took the bait, and it would require some of my best work to make it irresistible, I could lead him into a mood construction that would take the reader to a vapid denouement. Wonder-boy was now so full of himself that he would probably think he was delivering a prize-winning climax of existential angst and redemption while, in fact, it would be a feeble tale of petit bourgeois self-pity and trite emotions—something the critics would be sure to pounce on. I could already see the reviews: "A disappointing sequel to his previous work," "Clearly unable to live up to his earlier promise," "A conclusion as flat-chested as the self-absorbed heroine of this pathetic tale." I worked hard, very hard, on my new project. It required all my literary skills to develop the false trail of tone and mood that would lead Lucas down the fatal path. There were moments when I almost regretted that I would be pawning it off. In its own way, it was rather good. I had the sense that if, with some subtle changes, I kept it for myself I had a winner in the making. So much for making sacrifices for one's art: I was sacrificing the muse for good old-fashioned revenge with the delicious goal of seeing my nemesis fall.

A week later, I was back at the pawnbroker's. It was as though he was expecting me and greeted me very warmly. Even

Wag came out from behind the counter and did a friendly little stretch and yawn for me.

"Good to see you again, old buddy. Always pleased to see a valued customer back. What can I do for you today?"

I handed him my poisoned portfolio. He looked through it quickly with a thoughtful air. "Hmm ... very nice, very nice indeed. I can see that you've been hard at work. Do I take it you want to pawn the whole manuscript?"

Before I could even answer, he was offering me ideal terms that I quickly agreed to. The selling price was such that a potential buyer, namely Lucas, would be easily tempted. It was all over very quickly: a little paperwork, a wad of cash in my pocket, and a handshake. There was a bottle of Scotch on the counter. The pawnbroker poured out two shots and toasted me. "Here's to you, old buddy."

Just as I was about to leave, the shop door opened and in walked Lucas! For a moment his usual self-satisfied smirk deserted him, and I thought I detected a look of embarrassed guilt. But he quickly adjusted to his usual self-assured form. "Well, well, well, Sam, writers of the world unite."

He laughed, and I could hear the pawnbroker chuckling behind me. Then, I have to tell you, things got very strange. As Lucas continued to laugh, his face—which according to many of my friends was not dissimilar in appearance to mine—started to look more and more like me. The pawnbroker was also laughing loudly, and when I turned to look at him I found that he too had changed in appearance. Suddenly he was inches taller and slimmer, the goatee beard and tinted glasses were gone and, incredibly, he was also starting to look like me as well. I felt as though I were looking in a tailor's three-way mirror at three different versions of myself. To my left, my Lucas self: the writer that I resented, yet secretly felt I needed to be more like—a writer willing to compromise principle for the fashionable literary formulae of the moment that would make me successful in today's ephemeral market. To my right, my pawnbroker self: that persona who could probe deep into my mind, find all my creative weaknesses, and mock my efforts. And in the middle mirror, my own self: the struggling writer who so wanted to produce great work and was still struggling to find a unique voice of his own. Reflected in the background I thought I could even see the shadow of a fourth figure: the master tailor himself, with the eternal measure around his neck and a piece of chalk in his hand, ready to size me up and mark me down. It was all too much. Feeling dizzy and short of breath I ran out of the shop.

Outside the shop it seemed much darker and later in the day than it was when I had arrived—which I thought had been only a few minutes earlier. As I tried to catch my breath, there was a loud roar as a big black pickup truck drove out from behind the store. The cabin light was on and I could see, at the steering wheel, the pawnbroker I knew with his goatee beard, baseball cap, and tinted glasses. He gave me a wave and a sarcastic little grin. It was now clear to me that I was the victim of a very elaborate practical joke being played on me by Lucas and some of his friends. The scene in the shop that had just played out was so bizarre that I suspected the pawnbroker—whoever he really was—had slipped some LSD into the shot of whiskey he had given me. As much as I wanted to go back into the shop and confront whoever was orchestrating this extraordinary performance, my overriding feelings were of fear and flight, and I jumped into my truck and raced home.

When I woke up the next morning my head was clear, and I carefully replayed the previous day's events in my mind. If I thought I could now see how they—whoever they were—had stage-managed their incredible trick, I was in for a further shock. The latest edition of one of the literary journals I subscribed to had just arrived in the mail. On opening it, I found, to my utter astonishment, a short story titled *Last Night*, written by Lucas Garcia-Brown. Furthermore, it had won first prize in a prestigious short-story competition—being praised for its "brilliant modernist take on a Prufrockian walk down the half-deserted streets of despair," and its "profound psychological insights into the redemptive relationship that develops between the narrator and a troubled young woman with whom he has a chance encounter." This was all absolutely impossible: Lucas's story was the one I had just pawned the day before and there was no way it could have appeared in print, let alone won a competition, in one day. My feelings of fear and flight the day before now turned into pure rage. Rehearsing in my head a blistering accusation of fraud and deceit, I drove back to the pawn-broker's at high speed.

When I got to the small strip mall where the pawnshop was located, I found that the shop's windows were dark, and when I pulled on the door it appeared to be locked. I peered through the door. The shop was empty: gone were the displays of electronics, musical instruments, and guns. All I could see were a couple of broken chairs and a pile of crumpled-up paper lying on a dusty floor. I tried the door again. It was well and truly locked. Then I noticed a sign in the shop window: Space Available for Rent. None of this made any sense at all, and I ran into the small convenience store next door. It was deserted save for a middle-aged man of Middle-Eastern appearance on duty behind the counter and talking on his cellphone.

"What happened to the pawnshop next door?"

The shop assistant gave me a very strange look. "They've been closed for almost a year. The management company is still trying to rent the space."

"That's not possible. I've been doing business there for the past couple of weeks. You probably saw my truck parked outside," and I pointed through the window to my dark green pickup. The assistant looked at me nervously and edged toward the till. He put his right hand behind his back—probably reaching for a gun tucked in his waistband.

"You must be mistaken. As I just told you, they've been closed for almost a year. The management company is still trying to rent the space. I can give you the company's phone number if you like."

I didn't know whether I was having an acid flashback or had just lost my mind. I was overcome by a sense of panic. I ran out of the store, jumped into my truck and drove home as fast as I could, running God-knows how many red lights on the way. I agonized for days. What had really happened, how could it have happened, and what had happened to me? Of course, nobody would believe me if I told them. The proverbial men in white coats would take me away. To this day, I'm still not sure what really happened. But then again, as you know, I'm a writer. There is no sharp dividing line between historical truth and narrative truth, and over time that line becomes ever blurrier until it doesn't really matter which truth I've told you. The one thing I do know for sure is that I've never been to a pawnbroker's again.

SECRET AGENT

Jed rolled off her, turned his back, and promptly fell asleep. Linda looked up at the ceiling and, yet again, asked herself why she had married him. She had thought about it too many times, uselessly revisiting the same old ground: a junkyard of memories and disappointments where even the junkyard dog of self-reproach had given up barking at her.

She thought back to their first encounter when Jed, five years slimmer, had walked into Big J's Diner, where she was working as a waitress. He had driven up in a shiny blue Ram pickup truck and came in wearing pressed jeans that were a little too tight for his solid waistline. The buckle on his belt matched the ram on his truck. Under his arm he held a cowboy hat that he placed with elaborate care on the counter. He quickly introduced himself. "Hi, I'm Jed … but you can call me Big J," and had looked at her with an expectant grin to make sure that she had understood his little joke and clearly would have enjoyed the opportunity to explain it to her. Her quick, "Well, you've sure come to the right place, Big J," and the flirtatious smile that the manager had instructed all the waitresses to give their customers was enough to capture his attention. Without looking at the menu he ordered, with a casual man-of-the-world certainty, corned beef hash with three over-easy eggs. "And tell chef to make sure the hash is real crispy." The thought that their short-tempered, short-order cook, who had learned his trade while serving time for aggravated assault, was being referred to as "chef," like a celebrity chef on a TV cooking show had made Linda smile—a reaction that Jed interpreted as approval for his good taste. Yes, the guy was a jerk, but he did leave her a generous tip.

Jed became a regular at Big J's and always made a point of trying to sit at the same place at the counter where she had first served him. If her first reaction to him had been that he was just another jerk, this softened over time. Maybe it was because her situation at home with her endlessly complaining mama was wearing her down, or maybe it was because he wasn't such a bad guy after all when compared to all the other jerks who ate there, and some of them were truly something else. There was Luke, "Call me Dr. Luke," the skinny patient-care technician with greasy black hair and a wispy goatee beard, who worked at a nearby clinic. He always showed up for lunch wearing scrubs in the hope that his fellow diners would think he had just come from performing lifesaving surgery, and he would try to impress her with tales—she suspected they were made up most of the time—of medical dramas at the clinic, embellished with gross anatomical details. And then there was Warren who worked at the post office. At first, she thought he was quite a sweet guy, but there was something creepy about his over-earnest talk of personal happiness through personal relationships while his gooey brown eyes fixated on her breasts. Then there were Clint and Brad. Clint was a construction worker and Brad was a motorcycle cop. They would roar up for lunch on their big motorbikes and strut into the diner wearing big black sunglasses and baseball caps: Oakland Raiders for Clint, and police-department issue for Brad. Clint had his bad boy on a big bike routine, and Brad had his good guy on a big bike routine. What was it with guys? Put a motorbike between their legs and they all expected you to hop on for a ride. But the promise of the open road of love and adventure nearly always ended up at the dead-end of disappointment, sometimes as soon as the first pit stop. She and her friends had all been there.

Apart from his attempts to look like a country-and-western cowboy, Jed seemed to have less of an act. He had a sort of wheedling charm about him and often had funny little stories to tell her. He was the warehouse manager at the local Walmart and would sometimes come to the diner for his lunch break. Even when he came in looking stressed out, which was not uncommon, he always made the effort to be cheerful and polite with her—even when she could sometimes overhear him being a bit snappy with some of the other staff. And unlike Luke and Warren and Clint and Brad and the other jerks who would hit on her, he didn't pressure her into going out on a date with him. At times, he almost seemed like a gentleman.

Jed definitely liked crispy: crispy hash, crispy bacon, crispy fries, crispy toast, and she soon found herself saying, without any thought or prompting from him, "And I'll make sure chef cooks them up nice and crispy for you." Jed told her after they were married that when she started saying that he knew she was going to be his girl. During the early days of their romance, or whatever it was she thought they had at the time, they had some fun times together. They went dancing at country-and-western bars, where she wore tight jeans and thin blouses, and Jed would show her off to his friends. She liked that. He fancied himself as a bit of a pool shark (which he wasn't), and he taught her to play pool, which she became quite good at, sometimes beating him when she felt like it. There were barbecues and softball games with his buddies and their families—activities that continued to be enjoyable after they were married. And, like so many young couples, it seemed easy to turn going steady into the convenience and social status of marriage. Marrying Jed—"Yes, mama, he's a good man who'll take care of me"—was the one way she could leave home with her mama's approval, albeit accompanied by a torrent of self-pitying tears about being "left on her lonesome." Did Linda ever really love Jed? She never really knew. Even if she hadn't seen him as her life's perfect soul mate, she thought he at least offered the hope of building a family life of her own, and an escape from the stifling loneliness she felt living at home with her mama. What she got instead ended up feeling like being in prison, but she was determined not to let it be a life sentence.

Almost as soon as they were married she realized that there were sides to Jed's personality, and intimate details, that she hadn't really appreciated. Some emerged almost immediately, while others took time to surface. Maybe if she hadn't been living at home with her mama she could have spent more time with him and got to know him better. Perhaps she could have moved in with him before they got married, and maybe she would have discovered those hidden emotional potholes of his that kept tripping her up and for which there was no helping hand to get her back on her feet. Maybe. Perhaps. What if? It was now all useless speculation that she had wasted too many sleepless nights fretting about.

In some ways, being married to Jed felt like being back at school where all sorts of lessons she hadn't known about up until then had to be learned. But this time, it was a school she couldn't leave at the end of the day. In fact, the first lesson she learned was on their honeymoon. They had gone to Las Vegas. It was the first time she had stayed at a real hotel. On their first morning, she discovered one of Jed's major obsessions: his bowels. She had woken up and saw Jed standing by the coffee maker. She felt so happy. Ever since she could remember she had always been the first one up: to make breakfast for herself and brew the coffee for her mama—and her daddy when he was around. Now she was waking up in a hotel with her very own husband who was going to bring her coffee in bed. For a few moments her mind wandered in a blissful reverie: coffee brought to her in bed every morning, breakfast in bed on Sundays, a new color scheme and furniture for their bedroom … Then she noticed that, as the coffee was brewing, Jed took a packet of cigarettes out of his suitcase and lit one. This was very strange: she never knew that he smoked and, furthermore, she thought that smoking wasn't allowed in the hotel bedrooms. When the coffee finished gurgling into the pot he poured a cup—just one cup—tucked a copy of *Sports Illustrated* under his arm, took the coffee and the cigarettes into the bathroom, and slammed the door shut behind him. After about fifteen minutes she heard some grunting followed by the toilet flushing, and Jed re-emerged with a self-satisfied grin on his face. "Come on, honey, let's go and find some breakfast." When she went into the bathroom to get herself ready, she was overpowered by the smell of Old Spice that he had obviously sprayed everywhere to cover up the smell of the cigarette smoke. And so she learned that coffee in bed, let alone breakfast in bed on Sundays, would have to wait for another day, and as she would eventually realize, it would probably have to wait for another husband.

In fact, bowels were about the only intimate topic that Jed could talk about. Being regular was a matter of great importance to him; a topic worthy of frequent conversation. A buddy had told him that a cigarette and a cup of strong coffee first thing in the morning was guaranteed to do the trick. And while Jed was generally dismissive of such things as Recommended Daily Allowances—nobody was going to tell him what he could and could not eat—he did take fiber content seriously and conveniently found it in many of his favorite menu items including the bacon-cheeseburgers at Big J's. Overall, life wasn't worth living until Jed had relieved himself, and however long it took, he would take ownership of the bathroom in the mornings until he was done.

And then there was the sex; or rather, the lack of it. Jed's lovemaking that night had been perfunctory, if not typical of the past few years. A few nibbles at her breasts and neck, a few quick thrusts, and that was it. They hadn't actually had a lot of sex before they married, and she had attributed his lack of insistence to him wanting to play the gentleman. When they had made love it had been cozy rather than passionate, and she told herself that once they got married they would let rip every night of the week the way her friend Lisa claimed it was with her husband. But nothing really changed. Jed quickly picked up on her apparent lack of appreciation of his manhood and implied—he was very good at implying things—that it was her responsibility to make her man feel good. She read articles about sex in the women's magazines that her friend Lisa was always lending her. For once all those stupid but tantalizing titles on the cover like: "Ten Ways to a Better Sex Life," "How to Make Your Man Go Crazy for You," and "Love Secrets of the Stars" promised to be useful. There was lots of talk about caring and sharing, and how important it was to tell your partner how attractive you found them. Before long, Linda was persuading Jed that he was the last of the red-hot lovers, a line he readily bought into. While he grunted his way through his quickies, she would sigh and groan and wonder what it would be like to have somebody make love to her the way it was described in those *other* magazines that Lisa would sometimes show her.

So what would it be like? At the supermarket where she now worked as an assistant manager, there was a customer who had caught her eye. He came in once a week, usually with his wife and a young daughter. Sometimes he came in by himself. Linda liked that: a man who could be trusted to do the weekly grocery shopping by himself. She had stopped asking Jed to help with the shopping two years ago after he had come home with half a dozen cans of barbecue baked beans and none of the fruit and salad items she had asked for. Despite his protestations that he had lost the shopping list, she suspected this had been deliberate. Linda found the customer very attractive. He had a slim and athletic build; Jed was stocky and now on the verge of flabbiness. He had thick and curly dark hair; Jed's hair was pale blond and starting to thin. His brown eyes were warm and friendly; Jed's were nervous and pale gray. But the most contact Linda could have with her shopper was when she was on checkout. All she knew about him was his name, Robert Gomez, because it was on his credit card. The most intimate thing she could ever say to him was, "Thank you for shopping with us, Mr. Gomez," and "Have a nice day,

Mr. Gomez." She felt it would be unprofessional to address him as "Robert." But she wasn't the only one in the store who had noticed him. Her coworker, Lilli, had also picked him out. Lilli was plump and promiscuous, and enjoyed speaking her mind. The guy was a dish and had a cute butt. Didn't Linda notice how well hung he was? And that she, Lilli, would happily fuck his brains out if given half a chance. The fact that he was married wasn't a problem. She often did it with married men. Linda felt all this crude talk about her special customer was inappropriate, and exploiting her rank as assistant manager, said as much to Lilli. But secretly she found it rather exciting. Lilli's attitude toward the handsome shopper also gave her food for thought. Linda thought of herself as sensible and smart—qualities that Lilli had little of—yet here she was having fantasies about a guy because he could do the family shopping by himself at a supermarket, while Lilli was admiring his butt and sizing up his thing. Maybe when it came to sex, it was Lilli who was the smart one.

Linda started to have intense sexual fantasies about the shopper, and now that he was in her imagination and not in the supermarket she could call him "Robert." She was sure that he was hardly aware of her existence, but having fantasies that had no chance of becoming reality were, to her mind, the sort of fantasies that were safe to have. Robert would undress her slowly, perhaps as they sipped a glass of wine. Jed's thick, stubby fingers were always hopeless with buttons and hooks, and he thought bringing a six-pack to bed was romantic. They would have long hot showers together when Robert would gently soap her all over. Jed wasn't at all interested in showering with her. "Privates is private". They would have long and luxurious foreplay in which Robert would explore every inch of her body making her tingle all over. Jed's brief foreplay mainly involved mauling her breasts, and after a while she realized that Jed was not only rather ignorant of the female anatomy but also rather intimidated by it. And then there was the actual lovemaking itself in which she and Robert would pound each other for what seemed like hours on end. Him on top of her, her on top of him, every conceivable angle and position until her head exploded with fireworks like a Fourth of July spectacular. And then she would open her eyes and there would be Jed snoring beside her.

Linda looked at the clock on her bedside table. The digital display showed ten minutes past midnight. So many nights watching the minutes tick by. But tonight those red minutes were like the page numbers, and the red hours like the chapter numbers, of a mental marriage album of memories and resentments that she was leafing through from beginning to end. Tomorrow she would start a new album.

Another early lesson in the school of being married to Jed was food. If sex didn't seem that important to Jed, food certainly was. He was very fussy about his breakfasts, and with all those years of making breakfast for herself at home she was almost an instant winner. Well, almost. On Tuesdays and Saturdays, Jed had corned beef hash for breakfast. As she had learned at the diner, he was very particular about just how crispy it should be. She vividly remembered the first time she had cooked it for him when they came back from their honeymoon. She had plated the hash in the shape of a heart and laid out two fried eggs and a link on top of the hash to make a smiley face. Jed took a couple of bites of the hash, grimaced, and handed the plate back to her with, "Please remind chef that Big J. likes his hash *real* crispy."

She soon learned that if Jed could relieve himself in the mornings and then have a good breakfast, he would go off to work in a good mood, which usually improved the chances of him coming home in one. But coming home in a good mood and staying in a good mood would often depend a lot on dinner. On that score, things didn't start too well. Linda had never worried that much about cooking apart from breakfast. Before they married she would usually just have soup or a salad for dinner. Salads to Jed were "rabbit food." He demanded "real food." The only way she could solve the problem other than serving him steaks, which was far too expensive, was to learn how to be a better cook herself. She watched some cookery shows on television, read recipes in magazines, and persuaded her friend Cissy, who worked in a bakery, to show her how to make pies. She didn't know about finding the way to a man's heart through his stomach, but it sure could buy you a lot of peace. Jed was a happy man after a good meal, especially when she served up a blueberry-and-apple pie that was made according to her own recipe. Linda knew Jed was happy with her cooking: not so much because he told her so himself but because he was always bragging about it to his friends. He and his sports-fanatic buddy, Scott, would often talk on the phone after watching a game on television. More often than not, Jed would at some point in the conversation tell Scott, in some detail, about the dinner "the little lady" had served up for him.

In fact, that was the strange thing about life with Jed. When they were alone together at home he hardly seemed to notice her—less and less as time went by—but when they were out together, or when his friends came over to watch football on their big screen TV, Jed would put on a great show of affection. He would always introduce her to his friends with great pride, possessively putting his arm around her waist. After she had made sure everybody was set up with beer and popcorn, chips and salsa, and other snacks, he would always want her to sit next to him on the sofa and put his arm around her shoulder. To begin with, she liked the show of affection even if she wasn't that interested in the football. Jed may have been president of the local chapter of the Couch Potatoes, but she didn't want to waste her time being an honorary member. Using some excuse like fixing more food in the kitchen she would sneak out and read a magazine or get on with her dressmaking. She soon realized that once out of the room she was quickly forgotten.

It was another hot and humid night. The swamp cooler was on and the windows were open. They had had a long-running argument about just how open the windows should be when the swamp cooler was running. Linda knew that the experts said they should be open just a crack, but Jed insisted that they should be open wide—which only made things worse. They had both dug their heels in on that topic, Jed only more so. He took pleasure in telling her, "You're not always right about everything, you know." In the end, she realized that it just wasn't worth arguing about anymore. She was successful in convincing him to let her put a ceiling fan above the bed, but when she tried to persuade him to buy a proper air conditioning unit for their bedroom he refused, saying they were too expensive to run. After all, "A little sweat never did hurt anybody." But the drop of sweat starting to trickle down between her breasts only reminded her of that one-sided debate. She tried to lie as still as she could and stared at the ceiling fan. It almost seemed to be whispering little taunts at her: "Are you feeling hot, Linda? Are you feeling sweaty, Linda? Have you had enough, Linda?"

The cost of running an air conditioner was just one example of Jed's obsession with household expenses and he had become quite mean with his money after they were married. It was going to be their fourth wedding anniversary tomorrow. He had forgotten their last one, and she certainly remembered how cheap he had been for their first. He had asked her what she wanted as a first anniversary present. She told him that she would like to go to Yellowstone National Park and see the bears and other animals. Jed had laughed and told her it was all far too expensive. If Linda wanted to look at animals she would get a much better view on television, and as far as he was concerned, there wasn't much point in looking at a wild animal if you couldn't shoot it. In fact, he seemed to find the whole thing enormously amusing and spent the next few days going around the house and their yard pointing an imaginary rifle at anything that moved, going "Bang, bang," and chuckling. However, he did remember their anniversary day and came home with a rose, a balloon, a bottle of sparkling wine, and a large, flat package. When Linda opened it she found a calendar of "Wild Animals of America." Each month had a lovely glossy photograph of an animal: bears, eagles, deer, bison, and so on. However, closer inspection revealed that the calendar was last year's and had been used. Jed explained that he had seen it hanging on the wall at a friend's gas station and had bought it for two dollars knowing that she would like the pictures. "You see, honey, this way you get to see the animals and I get to save hundreds of bucks, so we're both winners." To Jed it was all a big joke, but it made Linda feel like a loser. As tears welled up in her eyes, Jed started to scowl with the implication that she would ruin their anniversary. In the end, she made the best of it and drew up new calendar pages for the current year and stuck them over the used ones. In fact, she did that every year and kept the calendar in the kitchen. Jed seemed to like that and would often point to it and quip, "There's our two-buck trip to Yellowstone."

Linda looked again at the bedside clock. It was now a quarter of one. Jed was in a deep sleep, and that was the good thing about him: once he was out, he was out, and oblivious as to whether she was in the bed or not. She was restless and needed to do something rather than stew in bed. She tiptoed out of the bedroom, carefully closing the door behind her, and went into the kitchen where she had set up a sewing corner. She took the dress she had been working on off its hanger. One last hem, maybe twenty minutes work, and she would be seventy-five dollars richer. She had always liked having pretty outfits, and when she was living at home she would usually spend what was left of her earnings on clothes. Married to Jed, she quickly found that so much of her money went on "sharing" household expenses that there wasn't much left for anything else. Her friend Maureen had trained as a dressmaker and gave her some lessons. Within a few months, Linda had been able to make herself the prettiest little summer dress. She also made a second one, although not so little, for Maureen as a thank-you present for helping her get started. At first, she just made a few things for herself, but after she had helped a friend with her wedding wardrobe, more and more people started to ask Linda if she could do alterations for them.

Within a year, she had a nice little business of her own on the side and did a quite of lot of work for one of the bridal shops in town. Jed didn't seem to mind her spending a lot of her time at home in the evenings sewing and didn't realize, thank goodness, how much extra money she made for herself doing it. In his usual way he would never tell her directly if he liked one of her dresses, but if they were out and somebody commented on her outfit, he would put his arm around her and quickly boast that she was the best little dress-maker in the state—as though he was somehow responsible for her success.

After Linda had slipped back into bed a little later she continued to recall how money had been such a problem when they first got married. By the time they had met, both of Jed's parents had died, and he had inherited their house with just ten years of mortgage to pay off. It made good sense for his parents' house to become their home. He had explained how important it was that they were "partners" in marriage. He would be responsible for the house payments and utilities, and she would be responsible for food and "other stuff." "Other stuff" turned out to be just about everything else. There were some terrible scenes over who was responsible for paying for things like the plumber and getting the TV fixed. If it were her fault—which, apparently, it nearly always was—she would be responsible for paying.

God, when it came to blame, Jed was a professional. Yes, bowels and blame: that was Jed all over and was probably why he and her mama got on so well. Within a few weeks of their first date, he was calling her "Mama" and buying her chocolates. They quickly became soul mates as they discovered that all their common ills from constipation to parking tickets could be blamed on somebody else. Even now, memories of Jed's blame game and their first big row over money would get Linda upset. The first time the toilet backed up, she called a plumber who had to clear the blockage with one of those long snake things. With the call-out charge, an hour's labor and tax, it was ninety-three dollars. Jed went hysterical. "Didn't she know that plumbers were the biggest rip-off merchants on God's earth," and if she couldn't learn to flush the john properly she was going to have to learn pretty damn quick because he wasn't going to pay for any more plumbers. His outburst left her stunned and when she relived the scene, which she did many times, she wished she could have been strong enough to have stood her ground and challenged him as to who was responsible for the blockage in the first place. How she would have loved to tell him that it was his great big stinking turds that did it. But that was only in her dreams. However, when Jed came home that night he looked anxious and had bought a bottle of sparkling wine that he knew she liked. He didn't actually say he was sorry for being so mean, but he was very complimentary about the casserole. After dinner, he had put on some country-and-western music and insisted that she dance with him.

The plumber episode really shook her up, and when the washing machine broke down soon afterward she got quite scared at the thought of the scene that might follow if she called in a service agent. The only way she could think of solving the problem was to keep quiet about it and simply pay for the repair herself—even though that meant taking some money out of her small savings account. She knew she couldn't continue solving their domestic problems like that, and decided that she had to learn to fix things herself. Her summer jobs at her daddy's garage had taught her not to be scared of mechanical things. She took a few classes at the local community college and found that simple plumbing problems and basic home repairs could usually be taken care of quite easily. When the kitchen sink sprang a leak, she fixed it herself. When she proudly showed Jed her handiwork, he said "I'm proud of you honey, real proud," followed by a rather plaintive, "So how come you're always so good at everything?" He then went outside and sat by himself with a couple of beers. However, a few nights later, when they were out at a bar with some friends he was calling her the best little plumber in the state, and when he thought she was out of earshot he was making crude remarks to his buddies about what she could do with a plumber's snake.

Those early plumbing episodes marked the beginning of one of Linda's most important marriage lessons: learning how to handle Jed's moods. He could sometimes be a real jerk, and when he felt that he was losing an argument he would scowl and raise his voice. He wasn't actually that loud but he could be very sarcastic. The good thing, though, was that he wasn't violent. After they had been married about seven months there was one terrible scene. She couldn't even remember what it was about, probably nothing in particular. He had gone off to work in a bad mood because he hadn't had a bowel movement in two days, had had a row with his boss, and came home in a foul mood. Something over dinner triggered him off and he raised his hand as though to hit her. Somehow she had kept her cool and stared him long and hard in the eye. He suddenly dropped his hand, stormed out into the backyard, and sat sullenly on the rocker for about an hour before returning indoors. She left a portion of pie for him on the living-room table and went into the kitchen to work on one of her earlier sewing projects. Neither of them said a word to each other for the rest of the evening, and when Jed went to bed she slept on the sofa. So that night she learned that Jed was a bit of a coward and could be stared down. And that wasn't all bad either. Some of her friends had husbands who were really mean and would slap them around quite badly at times. She would sometimes see nasty bruises on Maureen's arms, and last year a woman living just a few blocks away had been battered to death by her husband. Jed may have been a temperamental jerk at times, but at least he wasn't a violent one.

It was now almost 3:00 a.m. Linda had, yet again, worn the night out revisiting and reviewing her marriage. It was easy to be angry with Jed. He could be a jerk, mean with his money, a disappointment in bed, and he seemed to feel threatened by her domestic talents despite all his public bragging about them. But just as Jed and her mama enjoyed blaming their ills on somebody else, she had come to realize that as easy as it was to blame him for their unfulfilling marriage, a lot of her anger was with herself. It was her mistake to have married him in the first place when she hadn't really known him that well. It was all quite simple and, in retrospect, painfully obvious: they just weren't a good match for each other. It had all come home to her over the past year when Maureen's cousin, Molly, became a regular at the softball games and picnics. These were the times when Jed was at his best. In a crowd, he could be friendly and funny and, at a distance, his solid build could look more reassuring than overweight. Watching him, beer in hand, socializing and joking around the grill, reminded Linda of why she had been attracted to him originally. Molly was slightly older, divorced, and had two small boys, aged five and six. Everybody said how nice Molly was. Linda had to agree publicly but privately thought Molly was rather plain and boring, and tended to overplay the helpless divorcee. Yet Molly was very cheerful and always brought lots of comfort food to the picnics, like macaroni salad and meatballs on toothpicks. Jed declared them to be "Real good." Linda thought otherwise. Jed was a great favorite with Molly's two boys. Like so many guys Jed seemed terrified of babies—maybe it was the poop thing—yet give him a ready-made little man he could teach to swing a baseball bat, or throw a football, and impress in other ways, he seemed much more relaxed and at ease with himself. Linda was struck by just how well Jed and Molly got on, often spending a lot of time talking to each other at the picnic table, even if it wasn't clear what they really had to talk about. Linda was absolutely sure that there wasn't anything going on between them since Molly was seriously dating Cissy's brother, no doubt with an eye to snagging him as a new father for her boys. Yet watching Jed with Molly and her boys made Linda think that if Jed had married an easygoing and helpless Molly, rather than a Miss Fix-It-All like herself, he would have felt more in charge and become a different and more self-confident person; perhaps even self-confident enough to want to start a family of his own. With that last difficult thought on her mind she finally fell asleep.

Linda woke up as usual at 5 a.m. She slipped out of the bedroom and into the bathroom, quickly showered, and did her hair. Although she waited until just before leaving the house to do her makeup, she always put on a little lipstick first thing. A bright smile in the morning, even if it was just for herself, always helped to get the day started. By 5:20 a.m., she was ready to begin the morning routine. Her first task was to start the coffee maker so that by the time Jed got up for his mission to the bathroom, fresh strong coffee would be ready to help him on his way. The previous evening, she had assembled all the ingredients for a pie for dinner that night. She quickly rolled out the pastry, filled the baking dish, and popped it into the oven. By six o'clock the house would be full of the warm, soothing aromas of baking pie. Baking pies first thing in the morning was often part of her routine. Jed said that he found the smells very relaxing and that they helped him get on with the job, "If you know what I mean, honey." Wednesday morning breakfasts were blueberry pancakes, bacon, toast, and jelly. Once Jed disappeared into the bathroom she would have about twenty to twenty-five minutes to have his breakfast prepared. By six thirty, bowels permitting, Jed would be happily working on his meal while she put on her makeup and got ready to leave the house, either for work or to run errands. On Mondays, Tuesdays and Fridays, her shift at the supermarket started at 7:00 a.m. and would run till 3:00 p.m. On Wednesdays and Thursdays, she would work from 9:00 a.m. to 5:00 p.m. This past year, she also worked part-time at Xanadu's salon as a manicurist: just 4:00 p.m. to 7:00 p.m. on Mondays and Tuesdays. It was a piece of cake. The owner paid her in cash, and the customers liked talking to her and gave her nice tips. Her friendly face was the key to their innermost secrets.

Jed was in a good mood over breakfast: the pancakes were "real good," his team had won their game last night, and his bowels seemed to be in good working order. By seven o'clock, he was out the door with an unusually warm kiss, and she started to wonder if he had actually remembered that it was their anniversary. As soon as he was gone, she loaded up the dishwasher and began her day.

Having checked the driveway to make sure that Jed's truck had left, Linda locked the front and back doors and sat down by her sewing machine. She turned it on its side, and using a small screwdriver she kept in the sewing table drawer, undid the bottom plate and took out a thick envelope that she kept hidden in the base. From the envelope, she counted out $1,400 in one hundred dollar bills and then secured the envelope back in its hiding place. Normally she would change out of the jeans she wore around the house in the mornings and into a skirt or slacks before going to work. This morning, she didn't. She put on a denim jacket that went with her jeans, a baseball hat with her hair tucked inside, and her extra-dark sunglasses. She checked her appearance in the hallway mirror: she liked what she saw. Collecting her purse and the dress she had finished working on that night, she left the house and got into her vehicle—an old Chevy Malibu that was still going strong with more than ninety-seven thousand miles on the clock. She first stopped by the bridal shop and took off her jacket, baseball hat, and sunglasses before going inside to drop off the dress and collect the seventy-five dollars that was waiting for her in an envelope. She then drove to the Greyhound bus station on the far side of town, parked her car around the back, put her jacket, cap, and sunglasses back on, walked through the building to the front entrance and went over to a bank of pay phones. Dialing an out-of-town number and affecting a slightly southern drawl, "Hi, Mr. Svensen. This is Karen Jones. I'm just calling to check if everything is ready today. It is? Great. I'll be over in a few hours with the cash." She went to the ticket window and bought a one-way ticket to a town just across the state line about one hundred miles away.

Sitting in the bus, tucked away in a back seat, she leaned back and closed her eyes. To her friends, she was "Linda." To the older folks she was friendly with, she was "Honey." To Jed, she was, in public at least, his "little lady." But to herself she was now Karen Jones, Secret Agent. It was a really neat name. She often felt that Linda, her grandma's name, was kind of boring. Karen had a sexy ring to it. People could change their names. Brad had told her that he had seen Clint's driver's license and that his real name was Clarence. Being a Clarence didn't really go with playing the badass, so Clarence called himself Clint. When you were a Clint, you could be a badass. Nobody knew of her identity as Karen Jones except Mr. Svensen. Linda liked having a secret identity and she liked having secrets. A secret was all yours and nobody, not Jed or anyone else, could take it away from you. Everybody had secrets but the funny thing was, in her experience, that most people didn't seem to enjoy their secrets unless they could share them with somebody else. Her friends knew that she could be trusted absolutely and would tell her all sorts of things. Whether it was Cissy telling her about the time she'd had sex with her boyfriend's best buddy in the back of his pickup truck, or Maureen's suspicions that her husband was having an affair with their neighbor, or Jeannine having the hots for Lisa's husband, or Lisa telling her about the kinky things that she and her husband did in bed, and so on. They all knew that Linda would take their secrets with her to her grave. What they never realized was that Linda would take her own with her too. Linda, a.k.a. Karen Jones, kept her secrets strictly to herself.

As the bus sped along the country roads past farmland, trailer parks, gas stations, billboards, and exit signs to places unknown, Linda's memory raced back in time to her childhood. When she was a little girl she thought her daddy was the most handsome man in the world. He had warm brown eyes—perhaps Robert's eyes reminded her of him—an irresistible smile, and a movie star's square jaw. He was the co-owner of a successful auto-repair shop. He would often take her there, and she would sit on the counter in the front office charming the customers, especially the many female customers who liked taking their cars to his garage. Her mama was less enthusiastic about the amount of time Linda spent there. "If Linda spends too much time hanging around your garage she'll become a tomboy, and we all know what tomboys turn into." Her daddy laughed. He had a restless energy about him. Although he came home almost every evening for dinner and made a fuss of his little girl, he would often go out afterward by himself to meet with friends—he made friends easily—to drink and play cards. He would come home late and Linda would hear her mama shouting at him in their bedroom. Mama would call him a drunk, which Linda knew was a bad thing. Mama would also call him a tomcat, but Linda liked cats and didn't know whether being a tomcat was a good thing or a bad thing. After the shouting, things would go quiet and then they would get noisy again; but it was a different kind of noise that would often go on for hours, and the next morning her mama would usually get up late and wander around the house in her nightgown looking rather pleased with herself. It was a pattern that kept on repeating itself and, of course, when she was older Linda understood what it was all about. She smiled to herself when she recalled her first childish attempts to make sense of it. "Daddy, if I become a tomboy will I also be a tomcat like you?" She still recalled her father's initial look of amazement and then his roar of laughter, and how he had hugged her. "Kitten, I can promise you that you will never become a tomcat, but you'll always be your daddy's top cat." She liked that: she liked the idea of being the top cat of the most handsome man in the world.

In her early teens, Linda had spent a few summers working at the garage helping out in the front office, but she often sneaked into the back to watch Kenny, the mechanic, and his assistant at work. Kenny was a grandfatherly type with whom Linda was a great favorite. When things were not too busy he would show her what he was doing. Sometimes he would let her operate the hydraulic rack. She liked the sense of power of being able to lift a big truck up into the air. Kenny showed her how he inspected the underside of a truck and told her about the tricks used-car dealerships used to hide leaks and rust. On a few occasions Kenny took her out on his test-drives. If her mama asked her at dinner about her "day at the office," Linda would wink at her daddy and come up with little tales about how she had been tidying up the filing system and price-lists, or running errands for waiting customers.

One night, her daddy didn't come home at all, and then another night, and another. One afternoon, Linda came home from school and found her mama lying on the sofa, her eyes swollen red with tears, and a table lamp lying broken on the floor. There was no need to say anything: her daddy had gone. After that, Linda would often find her mama sitting on the sofa in the evenings staring blankly into space as though she was waiting for him to return. She sat as still as a stone statue. It almost seemed as if she were turning into stone herself as her once soft and pretty face become hardened and chipped with bitterness. Her mama became needy and tearful, and said horrible things about her husband that she knew would upset Linda. On the one hand, her mama would make her feel obligated to stay at home and support her; on the other, she would always be chiding Linda to find a "good man" who would marry her and take care of her. A remark that would almost always be followed by tears over that "son-of-a-bitch daddy of yours who didn't look after me." Somehow it was always *her* daddy who was at fault, never her mama's husband. The atmosphere at home became evermore stifling and leaving home to marry Jed became an attractive idea. Yet in a strange way, Linda saw that her marriage to Jed was a mirror image of her parents': she had some of her daddy's restless energy while Jed had some of her mama's negativity and lethargy. What they didn't have was her parents' raw physical attraction for each other. But maybe there were other things that could have made up for that. She could cook. She could make pretty dresses. She could do household repairs. She could even change the oil of her vehicle. Her mama couldn't do any of those things. Their house was always a mess. Maybe if mama had been a better homemaker, daddy would have stayed. What more could a man like Jed want in a wife? But that was the problem: Jed didn't want more, what he really wanted was less. He wanted a wife who was pretty, who could cook him nice meals, and maybe sew. But deep down, he wanted to be the one who could repair the plumbing and fix their cars. The trouble was that he just wasn't any good at those kinds of things, and he was too lazy to learn. Over time, her need to be the perfect homemaker made Jed feel inferior and resentful while he had to pretend in public how proud he was of her.

Looking out of the bus window, Linda read the passing billboards—a roadmap of her American life. Motel 6: perhaps that was where Lilli met with her married boyfriends to have sex. Denny's: perhaps that would be where Jed would go to drown his sorrows in cheeseburgers and fries. Miller Time: Clint and Brad at their favorite bar, striking manly poses with a beer in one hand and a pool cue in the other. Christian Singles: she could easily imagine Warren signing up, if he hadn't done so already, looking for easy prey. Big Sky Bar and Grill: perhaps if she went in there she would find her daddy sitting at the bar befriending a pretty bartender. Maybe she would pass a billboard saying, "Small Town USA Welcomes Karen Jones." She started to wonder where that small town would be and what it would be like, and how she would fit in. Maybe every small town had its Big J's and she would have to start her new life working there with a new cast of Lukes, Warrens, Clints, and Brads. But this time, if another Jed showed up at the counter he wouldn't have a chance. Reality returned when the bus passed a billboard proclaiming "Svensen's Square Deals Dealership, Exit 263B."

The last phase of Linda's plan needed a used but reliable pickup truck that would be difficult to trace. A few months earlier she had come across an advertisement for Svensen's dealership specializing in secondhand trucks and jeeps. It was in a town about a hundred miles away with the added advantage of also being out of state. When she had first gone to visit Svensen's garage, he oozed a certain, Jed-like, charm. That was a big mark against him. Svensen showed her a short-bed GM truck with 110,000 miles on the clock that was on "special offer" for $3,200. He had made a big deal of showing her Svensen's Quality Guarantee Check List: a list of basic functions that were all ticked off as having been checked. Linda took the truck for a test drive. Svensen had recommended driving it around the block. Instead, Linda accelerated out of the garage, raced it to the edge of town, and put it through its paces for more than ten minutes. As she suspected, it was no bargain: the ride felt uneven, the braking was weak, and the exhaust was noisy. The Quality Guarantee Check List was clearly a total rip-off. When she got back to the garage, Svensen was clearly irritated but still turned on the charm.

"Just runs smooth as butter, don't it, honey."

"Just fine, Mr. Svensen, but I'd like to put it up on the rack to look underneath."

"Hey, Lester," Svensen shouted out to the young mechanic in the workshop, "the little lady wants to put it on the rack." Calling her "little lady" was a big mistake.

"Sorry boss, there's a pressure leak. It ain't working right now."

Linda walked into the workshop and gave Lester a sweet smile. She went to the rack, pulled the control lever, and raised and lowered it.

Svensen coughed awkwardly. "Well, I'll be darned. It must be working after all."

Linda turned to Lester, "OK, Lester. On the rack, NOW."

"Yes, ma'am!"

Before Svensen could stop him, Lester drove the truck onto the rack. Svensen hovered around nervously as Linda inspected the chassis using a flashlight and big screwdriver from Lester's toolbox. It was just as she suspected. The exhaust pipe was rusty and had been disguised with paint, a rear shock absorber was leaking, and although the tires had been painted up shiny black the inner tread of two them were at the legal limit. She came out from under the truck, folded her arms, and looked Svensen squarely in the face.

"You know there's a law in this state about selling lemons."

"Now, looky here little lady … ."

"No, you look here, Mr. Svensen." Pointing to his Quality Guarantee Check List, Linda proceeded to reel off the precise faults with the truck and his illegal attempts to disguise them. Kenny would have been proud of her. Lester's eyes were as round as saucers. Mr. Svensen looked pale and his tone was now very different.

"You're not one of them inspectors are you, Miss Jones?"

"No, but my daddy owned a service station and taught me all there is to know about trucks, and …" after Svensen's "little lady" she had to slip in, "I'm a real good friend of the secretary of the local Chamber of Commerce."

She had no idea if there even was a Chamber of Commerce in this town, but it was worth a try. Svensen then launched into a long story about his long-time buddy Joe Watkins who often supplied him with used trucks, including this one, for resale. He had always trusted Joe, and all the trucks were real good deals. He couldn't believe that after all these years old Joe would try to cheat him, and Lester should have done a better job of checking it out. Lester, who had been grinning from ear to ear while this was going on, looked mad when he heard Svensen's attempt to pin the blame on him.

"Well, Mr. Svensen, I don't know about your Joe Watkins but I do know that I want a square deal on this truck. This is what I propose," and Linda listed all the repairs that were needed. If he did them she would pay him $2,800 for the truck in cash: $1,400 up front and the remaining $1,400 when the repairs were completed. If everything was done satisfactorily she wouldn't report him. Kenny had taught her well. She smiled sweetly at Lester, who was now in awe and in love.

"Lester here will do a real good job, won't you Lester?"

"Yes, ma'am."

By now Svensen was putty in Linda's hands. They went into his office and drew up the contract. Svensen was the sort of dealer who understood that an all-cash transaction meant no questions asked. He was now respectful and seemed eager to please. Linda had stood her ground and she had won.

As the bus approached the township where Svensen's dealership was located, Linda savored the memories of that earlier trip to his garage. Cutting that deal on the truck had been one of the most enjoyable days of her life. In some ways, it made up for many of the times she had backed down in her arguments with Jed. When the bus finally came to a halt at the depot, she put on her best game face and walked the few blocks to the dealership. A very polite Svensen greeted her and proudly showed her all the work Lester had done, under his close supervision, of course. The cash and paperwork were exchanged and the truck was hers. It was all over in a few minutes.

Linda drove the truck home, taking back roads when possible, and as she reached the outskirts of town she drove it through a big puddle—splashing the truck all over with dirt and obscuring the registration plate. She drove in through the little alley at the back of their house, improving the chances that nobody would see her. She went in through the kitchen door, sat down at her sewing corner, and took long, deep breaths to steady her pounding heart. The moment had come. She reopened the base of the sewing machine and checked the contents of the envelope. Even allowing for the money she had just used to buy the truck, there was still more than $5,000 in cash. When she had first thought up her plan over two years ago she knew that it would succeed only if she had a lot of cash in hand. Through saving and economizing, her supermarket job, and other part-time jobs, she had gradually built up her savings. It was also important that they were undetected by Jed. They had their checking accounts, but never a joint one, at the same bank. Other banks were always advertising special deals for new customers, and Linda opened another account at a local Savings and Loan. For a mailing address for the statements she got herself a post office box on the other side of town. Setting up that secret bank account had been her first act of deception. At first, she was nervous about doing this, but once done, the other small acts of deception followed easily. During the past few months, she had run down all her accounts and assembled her hoard of cash in a way that wouldn't arouse suspicion.

The next step was one Linda had gone over in her mind many times. She ran into the bedroom and, in ten minutes, had packed two suitcases with all her clothes and shoes, makeup, hair dryer, and other toiletries. She put the cases in the truck along with her sewing machine and other sewing equipment, her tools, an album of photographs, and an old footstool that had belonged to her grandma. All told, she had the truck packed with most of her worldly possessions in fifteen minutes. She then sat down at the kitchen table with a Coke, a pen and a sheet of paper, and prepared to write her farewell letter to Jed.

As Linda sipped her Coke, she looked around the kitchen. The set of shelves she had put up—her first DIY project—for their coffee mugs and glasses, her sewing corner where she had spent many satisfying hours in a space of her own, and that wretched anniversary calendar hanging on the wall. She recalled how, early in her marriage, she would sit at the kitchen table daydreaming about the happiness she thought lay ahead of her. Later, she would think about how those daydreams had turned into reflections about why things weren't working out as she had hoped. Ultimately, those introspections had turned into moments of bitterness as she realized that her marriage had failed. So much for her mama's advice of finding a good man who would look after her: it had turned out to be the other way around, and in looking after Jed she had learned how to look after herself. But she so didn't want to end up like her mama, whining and bitter. Rather, she realized, it was time to be like her daddy—wherever he was now—and just get up and walk away. Would Jed end up calling her "That bitch who didn't take care of me"? She didn't know, but she hoped he wouldn't. She tried to imagine what would happen when Jed came home that evening. Perhaps he had remembered their anniversary and would be anticipating a nice anniversary dinner. All he would find would be her letter and the pie she had baked that morning. She was sure her sudden departure would be a huge shock to him and that he wouldn't know how to react or what to do. Maybe he would throw a table lamp on the floor, but most likely he would end up on the sofa in a daze, watching ESPN and mindlessly eating his way through the entire pie. Linda felt a little bit sorry for him. Just a little bit. She wasn't sure how things would play out for him down the road. She entertained herself for a moment with the thought that, if things didn't work out with Cissy's brother, Molly would show up offering sympathy and comfort in the form of meatballs and macaroni salad. These would then be followed by other, carefully rationed, comforts until she got what she wanted.

For one last time Linda went over her plan. The truck was loaded up and ready to go. Her bank accounts had been closed, and she had handed in her notice at the supermarket a few days earlier. Her only regret was not being able to sell her Malibu. She reckoned she could have made a cash sale of at least $900. But selling it locally could have blown her secret, and driving away in it would have made her easier to trace. Still, there was a sort of drama about leaving it abandoned at the bus station, and at some point this would probably result in the police (perhaps it would be Brad) coming by to talk to Jed. She could imagine Jed trying to pretend that everything was under control, explaining that Linda had had to leave town suddenly on a family emergency and that he'd been too busy to pick it up.

It was time to go. She wrote the letter that had already been written and rewritten in her head many times. She wrote it neatly and deliberately. It was as though the period at the end of each sentence marked the end of a chapter in her now-closed marriage album. She sealed the letter in an envelope and propped it up against the pie dish that she had carefully centered on the kitchen table. She locked the kitchen door behind her, dropped the house keys in the mailbox, and drove away.

KOANIM

When they returned to the house after the funeral there was a small group of family friends and congregation members waiting to greet the mourners and serve them refreshments. Elliot instantly recognized some of them as old friends of his parents or the mothers of his childhood companions. And some he needed to look at again to draw back the veil of accumulated lines and disappointments to reveal a more familiar face underneath. His uncle Max, who had scarcely acknowledged his presence at the funeral, insisted that they observe tradition and cover the mirror in the hallway, and that the immediate family sit together as the mourners offered condolences. Some of the visitors shook Elliot's hand, wished him long life, and spoke the usual platitudes about love and loss and what a great man his father had been. He nodded politely thinking that they, in their narrow lives, didn't grasp that there was no love, no loss, no life. There was only the eternal cycle of Samsara in which they were unwittingly trapped, and from which he was learning to be free. There were other visitors whom he did not recognize, and he could see them look in his direction and whisper among themselves.

A cluster of well-wishers formed a cocoon around his mother and older sister, Annie, who were sitting together on the sofa. Annie's arm was around her mother's shoulders. Other mourners sat around the large living room, drinking tea and talking in low, respectful voices, mixing reminiscences of his father with inoffensive small talk. Elliot separated himself from the family group and sat quietly in a corner, sipping a cup of herbal tea, and observed the gathering. He was struck by the way his immediate family, sitting with their friends and relatives, seemed enveloped by a warm cloud of affection that he felt no part of. He got up to go outside to sit on the patio and finish his tea. Just as he was about to step through the French windows his Uncle Max came up to him, his portly body projecting strong vibrations of anger, and looked accusingly at him.

"So, Elliot, the wandering Jew returns. Your poor father had to wait for his own funeral before his son returned to the family home. How can you stand there looking so calm, so detached?"

Max's wife, Sonia, sensing that an explosion was imminent, glided over from the other side of the room, pulled Elliot into a gentle hug, and turned to her husband. "Max, Max, leave the poor boy alone. This isn't the time," and she led her husband away.

Elliot was relieved to be by himself as he sat on the patio and looked out over the back garden of his childhood. The simple layout had not changed: a rectangular, neatly mowed lawn fenced in by large lilac bushes. Along both sides of the lawn ran colorful flowerbeds with gladioli, daffodils, and roses, and next to the patio there was a small herb garden. Halfway down the lawn, on either side, were two weeping willows, still magnificent, like giant half-drawn curtains revealing the garden's backstage of apple trees and dogwoods. Tucked away in one corner of the garden had been a swing that he and Annie used to play on. It had now been replaced by a newer, double swing—no doubt in anticipation of additional grandchildren who had never come. His mother tended the herb garden. His father had no interest in gardening other than to profess delight with the fresh-cut flowers that his mother always put on the dining room table on Friday nights.

They had had a gardener called Ken Reiner, and Elliot wondered if he still worked for the family. Elliot remembered him as a tall, bearded man with a small ponytail. Ken had a dagger tattooed on each bicep, some Chinese symbols tattooed on the left side of his neck, and he always wore a Vietnam Veterans baseball cap. He was a man of few words with a strange, faraway look in his eyes. The only time Elliot ever saw Ken smile was when he smiled to himself as he mowed the lawn. Perhaps the simple steady rhythm of the mowing was Ken's way of meditating. Elliot had been intrigued by, and slightly scared of, Ken and had wondered how many men he had killed in Vietnam. But now he understood that it was really Ken who had been killed, and killed many times over. On his travels, Elliot had met a number of vets. Many of them had that same faraway look in their eyes that reminded him of Ken. He had come to appreciate that the two of them probably had much more in common than he had recognized back then. It would be interesting to talk to Ken now, to ask him about his journey, and to tell him about his own. He would ask his mother if Ken was still around.

Mourners drifted in and out during the afternoon and their number gradually dwindled until, at sundown, there was another influx. This time they were mainly men. Some had been at the funeral and others, not all of whom Elliot recognized, turning up to help form the *minyan* of ten males required for a full evening service. *Minyan* men, Elliot thought derisively: men who made an identity for themselves by being useful on solemn occasions. Uncle Max, scowling but somehow not projecting quite as much hostility as before, propelled Elliot to the front of the assembled group and silently handed him a yarmulke to put on his head. Mr. Reif, a long-time friend and business associate of his father, led the service, running through it quickly to reach the recitation of the *Kaddish*. Elliot joined his uncle in the prayer, reciting the ancient Aramaic words clearly. He hadn't been to a synagogue service for more than ten years, but his natural gift with languages and perhaps, above all, some deep-seated memory of the words his father had taught him, enabled him to recite them fluently—just as he had done at the funeral earlier that day. He could sense the relief in his uncle and the look of appreciation on his mother's face that he, despite his terrible transgression, did not embarrass the family by bungling the recitation of the ancient prayer in front of so many of their friends. Elliot was able to handle it all with great calmness: as the prayer began he started his own private meditation. As he recited the opening words "*Yitkadal, Ve Yitkadash, Shemay, Rabo …*" his mind clicked on the mantra: *Rabo, Rabo, Rabo …* He allowed the word to echo through his mind as he outwardly completed the rest of the prayer. As the service drew to its conclusion, Elliot thought about his journey and how he had learned to meditate: first from a master in India and then at the Theravadan monastery in New Mexico. It had been more than three years of hard work to gradually learn how to empty his mind and take himself out of a state of being and into the state of not being.

On the second evening of the seven-day mourning period, many of the family friends who had visited the previous day returned. His mother again sat on the sofa as friends took turns to sit with her and Annie, while Aunt Sonia bustled around offering the guests tea and cookies. Mr. Reif again ran the evening service. When they got to the *Kaddish*, Elliot again fluently intoned the words: "*Yitkadal, Ve Yitkadash, Shemay, Rabo. Beulmya, Di-vraoo, Chiroosey, Veyamlich …*" For an instant, he had an image of his father, maybe twenty years before, teaching him the prayer and how he had always stumbled over the word *Veyamlich*. His mind locked in on the new mantra: *lich, lich, lich …* The journey had been hard, most of all at the beginning with the rupture from his family and, especially, the arguments with his father that were usually followed by long silences that were even more painful than the arguments. His parents could not understand Elliot's need to break away from what had seemed like a preordained path leading to medical school and a prestigious profession, if not a brilliant career. That a successful young doctor would have no problem in meeting the proverbial nice Jewish girl from a good family all seemed to be part of their well-meaning family calculus. They could only think that his sudden announcement that he would quit his residency at Columbia Presbyterian meant that he must somehow be sick. Maybe he had been working too hard and needed a holiday. His father would send him on a luxury cruise. Maybe he had got involved with a bad woman. He should have married a good girl like Betty Reif. Maybe, God forbid, it was drugs. They had read about overworked doctors getting involved with drugs. When he tried to explain to them about his spiritual state they looked at him blankly. The more he tried to explain the worse it got, and in the end he knew he had to leave.

After the service, some of the older family friends stayed on for a while. Elliot politely listened to Mrs. Reif tell him about her son-in-law's growing dental practice and the new grandchild, her third, on the way. Perhaps she was also trying to tell him how much he had missed out by not marrying her wonderful Betty—a childhood friend in whom he never had the slightest romantic interest. For sure, if he had married her she would have bolted him down to the hardwood floor of conformity, and there would have been no messing around—which is how Betty would have seen it—with Eastern mysticism. And by now he would have been the successful, but soulless, young neurosurgeon, or cardiologist, or internist, or whatever career it was that Jewish in-laws wanted for bragging rights.

By the time Elliot went to bed that night he already felt he was suffocating under the weight of the memories stirred up by his family and their friends. As much as it would hurt his mother and sister, he was sure that it would hurt his inner being even more if he didn't leave within the next few days. After breakfast the next morning he started to broach the subject. It was as though his mother already knew what was coming, and she started to cry before he had barely begun to explain that he was planning to leave. Annie got up from the breakfast table, firmly took his hand, and pulled him out of his chair and onto the patio outside the breakfast room. She looked at him straight in the eyes, the way she used to when they had their staring competitions—which she always won. But now there was anger in her eyes.

"Elliot, you shit, you absolute shit. What do you think you are doing? You're breaking Mama's heart. You know that you have to stay with us for the full seven days of the *Shiva*. You can't leave now and embarrass the family. It would be an insult to Papa's memory and to all his friends."

If Elliot was honest with himself he had never really felt that close to his parents. He knew that they were the most decent and dutiful parents a child could want, and duty and decency were their way of showing their love for him. But it was Annie, with her curly brown hair and warm brown eyes, whom he truly loved. He could always turn to her with confessions of his silly schoolboy anxieties or his conflicts with their parents, and she would always listen and straighten him out. He knew that she had felt deeply betrayed when he left the family. On his return, he had felt a strange mixture of strong hostility from her combined, still, with that love of their childhood.

"Look, Annie, it's difficult to explain. I haven't really come home, I'm just passing through home …"

"Elliot, I can't believe you've just said that." Annie's eyes blazed. "This is your home. We are your family. Everybody here still loves you. I'm not going to pull the usual crap on you about staying for Papa's sake or for Mama's, or for mine. For God's sake, Elliot, stay for yourself." Then she suddenly smiled. "Take it from a little suburban housewife. We've learned stuff on our journey too."

He was too tired to resist his sister and he agreed to stay. It was his Karma. His mother fussed over him at lunch, and for the first time since he had been home he helped her around the kitchen. They made a little small talk about the pecan cookies, his favorite, which she used to bake for him when he was a boy.

By that evening they were down to the hard core of mourners: just the handful of immediate family and close friends, and those forever-reliable *minyan* men. Maybe, Elliot wondered, they were actually being more than just useful. When they got to the third sentence of the *Kaddish*: "*Yehey, Sh'mey …*" his mind locked in on the *Sh'mey*, and he allowed this new mantra to reverberate in his mind. Somehow, he couldn't concentrate as well as he had done on the first two evenings. As he glanced around the room he could see his Uncle Max deeply engrossed in the prayer as though trying to communicate directly with his departed brother. Elliot recalled that his father and Max had had their ups and downs over business matters and that voices would sometimes be raised, but his Aunt Sonia and his mother were always quick to patch up any family quarrels. Sonia would always say, in her simplistic way, "What's a family without quarrels? But it's always family first and quarrels second."

Elliot liked his Aunt Sonia. She had quit high school at seventeen to marry Max, borne him five children, and spent her whole life immersed in the joys and sorrows of being a full-time mother and grandmother. She was poorly read, and her only expressions of spirituality seemed to consist of singing Passover and Hanukah songs (usually out of tune). But when he left, she was the only one who didn't reproach him. Indeed, she went out of her way to wish him well. He often thought about that. She had rarely stepped outside her native Cleveland, let alone trekked through the Far East, yet she exhibited more warmth and human intuition than many of those whom he had met on his way. But, in truth, it made him uneasy to think there might be self-realization within a bourgeois heart like hers, without meditation, without exploration, without pain. He had sometimes wondered if he could ask her how she had achieved her state of self but felt that the conversation would be fruitless. In all likelihood, she would not even understand the question.

After the service, as those who remained drank tea with the family, Aunt Sonia sat next to him and, in her usual open way, started talking about her oldest grandson's Bar Mitzvah earlier that year. How wonderful it was that Elliot's father had got to see at least one of the next generation pass that great step, how beautifully Benjamin had sung his prayers, the wonderful food at the smart hotel where they had held the reception, all the presents Benjamin had received, and so on. There was a simplicity and enthusiasm to his aunt's narrative that made it difficult for him not to smile and nod attentively—even if, to him, Bar Mitzvahs now seemed like crass extravaganzas symbolizing much of what he saw as the materialism and social snobbery of the religion he had rejected. After she had finished her reminiscences she said, "Elliot, go and talk to your Uncle Max."

"Come on, Auntie, he hates me. He's barely spoken to me since I've been back."

"Don't be silly, Elliot. Of course he doesn't hate you. You're his only nephew. He'd love to talk to you. Have you forgotten what family means? Go on, talk to him. Look, he's sitting outside on the patio with Mr. Reif. Go on, go!"

Awkwardly, but somehow propelled by some mysterious force, he went outside. As he stepped onto the patio Mr. Reif got up, nodded coldly in his direction, and went back inside leaving Elliot alone with his uncle.

"So, Elliot," his uncle looked at him with sad, rather than angry, eyes. Elliot felt very uncomfortable.

"Well, Uncle Max ..."

"Well ... ?"

"Auntie Sonia told me about little Benjamin's Bar Mitzvah"

"So now you want to talk about my grandson's Bar Mitzvah?" His uncle's tone was still hostile.

"She said he did really well and sang beautifully."

His uncle softened. "Yes, he did very well. We were all so proud of him, and so grateful to your dear father for helping him learn his piece."

Elliot suddenly felt a strong pang as he remembered his own Bar Mitzvah lessons, how he had struggled under the tough old rabbi's tutelage, and how his father would always help him practice after the lessons. Elliot quickly changed the subject. "So how's cousin Simon? He left straight after the funeral and I didn't get to talk to him."

Simon, Max's only son, had been one of Elliot's best childhood friends, and their relationship alternated between closeness and fights, just like the two fathers. Simon had not gone to college after high school. He went straight into the family business and married fat Miriam Hirsch, whom he had dated since he was sixteen. They promptly produced a string of children, or more importantly, as it sometimes seemed, a string of grandchildren for Max and Sonia to boast about. Elliot still recalled his last meeting with Simon just before he had left for India. By then they had absolutely nothing in common.

The conversation with his uncle proceeded, maybe a little awkwardly, but a conversation it was. They reminisced about this and that and about a particular fishing trip that Max had taken the two cousins on. How Simon had fallen into the water, claiming, as usual, that it was Elliot's fault. The small fish Elliot had caught (his first) and how he had made his uncle unhook it and throw it back into the water. He remembered how he had watched the fish swim away to its regained freedom.

Max got up to go back inside and patted Elliot on the shoulder. "We're glad you're back, Elliot; back at last."

When Elliot went to bed that night, he thought about his conversations with his uncle and aunt and how those little acts of family closeness had brought approving smiles from his mother and sister. But his uncle's "… back at last …" made him nervous. It somehow implied that they thought he was back to stay. He immediately rebelled at the thought and turned his mind to his brothers and sisters in Oregon and how much he missed their group meditations. Elliot did not sleep well that night. He kept on thinking about his interactions with his aunt and uncle, and about his father rehearsing his Bar Mitzvah tunes with him. It was all rather disturbing. On the one hand, he had to admit to himself that he was pleased, in some strange way, to have reconnected with his family. On the other hand, he felt trapped inside the old family home and desperately wanted to leave. But he had promised Annie he would stay, and stay he would.

The next day, his brother-in-law, Barry, came by the house. He had been at the funeral but had left after the first evening service. Annie was sleeping over at the family home to be with their mother while her husband stayed at their house on the other side of the city. Now Barry was bringing over their only son, Jonathan, to stay for a few days. The little boy was just six. He had been born after Elliot had left home and, until the funeral, Elliot had only seen photos of him that Annie had sent in her occasional letters. Barry was a stockbroker, smug and successful. He regarded his errant brother-in-law with amused contempt. The feeling was mutual. Barry didn't stay long. Elliot observed Barry and Annie talking and gesticulating at the front door, and the dutiful kiss Barry planted on Annie's turned cheek when he left.

Jonathan was clearly fascinated by his mysterious uncle and followed him around the house at a respectful distance. At one point in the afternoon he summoned up his courage and climbed onto Elliot's knee.

"Mommy told me you've been on a long journey. Did you go in a big boat? Did you have to fight with pirates?"

Elliot thought that his Zen master would have enjoyed the nature of these questions. "Which boat? Who were the pirates?" Instead, Elliot told his nephew—and it was strange to think that to someone he was an uncle and presumably, by definition, an object of respect and love—about a trek he had taken to the top of the world. About the snow-covered mountains that reached up to the stars, and the magicians who could lift themselves off the ground by just thinking about it. For the most part, he felt awkward around children but found himself enjoying the little boy's round eyes of amazement and requests for more and more details about this wonderful land his uncle had been to, and that his uncle should drive him there tomorrow as long as they could stop off at the donut shop on the way.

At sundown, the evening service began again. Elliot did not feel like finding a mantra hidden within the *Kaddish*, but as the service progressed he surreptitiously did some of the simple breathing exercises he had learned during his earliest meditation lessons. That night, as he lay awake, he thought about little Jonathan's questions about his journey. Memories came flooding back of similar questions he had once asked his grandfather. He remembered his late grandfather as a rotund little man with a bald head and an apparent obsession with food. Of that Elliot was the happy beneficiary. The old man was always slipping him cookies and candies. When his mother would protest, his grandfather would always say, "Let the boy eat. May he never know hunger."

When Elliot had asked his mother where Grandpa had come from, she said something about him coming a long way on a boat. Now that Elliot thought about it, he had asked his grandfather almost the same questions that Jonathan had asked him that afternoon.

"Grandpa, Mama said you went on a long journey on a boat. Where did you come from? Did you meet any pirates?"

But his grandfather's reply had been very different. He looked very sad, ruffled Elliot's hair, and just said, "It was such a long journey. A very long journey."

At the time, Elliot didn't understand this. But later he wondered what his grandfather's journey had been like. The old man had died when Elliot was ten and there was never the chance to ask him. Maybe it was his Karma that, just as his grandfather had undertaken a long and dangerous journey to escape from persecution and find a new world of freedom and prosperity, he too had embarked on a long journey to find a spiritual freedom and well-being of his own.

Elliot could not get to sleep. He found himself thinking again about his nephew and the way the child had trusted him and climbed on his knee. Elliot had mixed feelings about children. At most of the communes he had lived in, there were nearly always a few single women with young children in tow. At first he had found the mother-child image rather appealing, but as he got to know the women more closely he started to question just how committed they were to the quest. They were always worrying, often over simple material matters, about their child. They rarely stayed the course and at some point would usually leave the commune.

For three years Elliot had travelled with Shastri. She was an Australian girl from a wealthy family. Her real name was Rose Holmes. He had met her at a Sufi community near Santa Fe. They said that they had felt an instant connection to each other and had become soul mates and body mates. They had traveled to India together: his second trip and her first. They stayed in ashrams, studied Sanskrit together, explored the Kama Sutra together, and trekked to Tibet together. When they returned to the States and moved to a commune in northwest Washington, she suddenly announced that she wanted to have a baby. This came as a bombshell. He tried to dissuade her—reminding her of the Buddha's teachings and the sacrifices one needed to make to achieve the anatman. It all became very emotional. She said she was tired of all the traveling, that she loved him, and that all she wanted was to have a child by him. In the end she had a complete breakdown, and he put her on a plane back to her family in Australia. In retrospect he realized that he should have seen the warning signs right from the beginning of their relationship. The very fact that she called herself Shastri in order to belong should have alerted him to the fact that she didn't.

He always traveled under his own name, Elliot Stone. He rather liked his name. It defied obvious labels, and he enjoyed making up little koans with his last name. But he did have another name, the Hebrew name by which he was summoned in synagogue: Eliyahu ben Shimon. It might have been a high honor for some but that summons always filled him with dread. He kept that other name from that other life strictly to himself. After Shastri, he always traveled by himself. It had been a close call. He laughed to himself. It could have been worse: it could have been Betty Reif in Cleveland.

Elliot's lack of sleep showed the next day, and his mother fussed around him in a well-intentioned way that he found slightly annoying. But he didn't have the strength to throw her off and instead found himself spending a lot of time with her. He helped her prepare the tea for the visitors, and he sat next to her on the sofa while she talked to their guests. That evening during the service, when they got to the *Kaddish*, he decided that this time he would just say the prayer without looking for mantras or breathing rhythms. He found himself caught up in the ancient emotive words, and as they finished the service he caught Max looking at him rather strangely. Later, he volunteered to put Jonathan to bed and read the child a bedtime story.

Elliot went to bed feeling tired and disturbed. He found himself thinking more and more about his family, and more and more memories of his father came back to him. He felt he was becoming less able to maintain the calm, almost out-of-body, state he had worked so hard to achieve. He had a ridiculous urge to smoke a joint to calm his nerves. Smoking pot was one of the first things he had given up as he started his long process of physical and spiritual purification. He decided that he must regroup his thoughts. Strange things had been happening to him since he had come home, and he analyzed the thoughts and feelings that had come to the surface. He felt threatened by his own feelings: they were somehow trying to take away all he had struggled for. But as he wrestled with this conflict, he realized that he could resolve it all by being more objective and simply treating his coming home as yet another part of his journey. It was not a threat: it was just another strand of experience that could be woven into the fiber of his being. He could think freely about his late father. He could recite the *Kaddish* without looking for some hidden mantra or koan. He could hug his mother. This intense introspection made him feel much more relaxed and, at last, he was able to sleep quite soundly.

The next morning, Elliot overheard Annie and his mother talking in the kitchen. Annie was saying that Stephanie Klein was in town visiting her mother, and they were both going to come over to pay their respects. A piece of news that resulted in a snort of derision from his mother, followed by a giggle from Annie. Elliot hadn't thought about the Kleins for many years. There was little of significance to remember except for one memorable incident. He and Stephanie were in the same grade at high school. She was quite pretty, but not quite as pretty as she would have liked, and she was blond. She was very proud of being a Jewish blonde, and not in that order. She was also very spoiled and in her senior year at high school was driving the new BMW her parents had given her for her eighteenth birthday. Stephanie was haughty and manipulative, and despite their parents' wish for them to be friends, perhaps with a longer-term agenda in mind, Elliot didn't like her. She sensed this and deliberately flirted with him just to annoy him. Her father was the senior partner in a successful medical practice, and if Dr. Klein was mild-mannered his wife was most definitely not. She reveled in her husband's wealth and status, and enjoyed lording it over gentler souls like Elliot's mother. Stephanie was definitely a chip off her mother's block, and a big chip at that. However, it was a conversation between his parents about Mrs. Klein that Elliot always remembered. Apparently she had said something that had really upset his mother. His father was trying to console her.

"Look, Ruth, the only thing that woman has on you is that her lot came over on an earlier boat than your lot, and I'm sure their boat stank just as much as the one your family came on … if not more so."

At that point his mother, who had virtually no sense of humor, shrieked with laughter. And from that day on the evil spell of Mrs. Klein and her obnoxious daughter was broken. Dear old papa, in his own way he could sometimes nail it perfectly. Elliot always remembered that piece of wisdom. In some of the communes he had visited he found an implicit social hierarchy, and if he felt annoyed by those who tried to assert superiority over him, albeit in a subtle way, he would ask himself just how much their boat stank.

That afternoon Elliot sat on the patio contemplating the back garden while a mockingbird perched in one of the willow trees was running through its seemingly infinite repertoire of song. Elliot's mind wandered over all the family currents and fables that, over the past few days, had rolled out in front of him like a map charting old territories and the occasional minefield.

Elliot thought more about Stephanie. Like him, she had had her fall from grace. During her senior year at Brandeis she had married, right on script, a law student and they moved to Chicago where he worked in his father's law firm. Mrs. Klein was soon bragging about her daughter's luxurious lakefront apartment and her son-in-law's family with their holiday homes in Aspen and the Bahamas. And then, rather suddenly, the noise stopped and Mrs. Klein began evading questions about Stephanie and her husband. Eventually there were mumblings about a separation and a divorce, and although there were implications that the son-in-law was to blame, they didn't ring true. If he had been at fault, Mrs. Klein would have unleashed a never-ending torrent of invective against him. This all happened around the time that Elliot had quit his residency and although, by then, he had little interest in the social politics of his parents' circle of friends, he could not help but get a little malicious glee at Stephanie's fall and her mother's discomfort. Knowing Stephanie as he did, Elliot was pretty sure that she had been the cause of the divorce. The spoiled princess had probably wanted, and possibly taken, one thing too many and had met her match in her young husband and his family.

Elliot also recalled that in one of Annie's letters she had mentioned that Dr. Klein had dropped dead of a massive heart attack. That must have been at least three years ago now. Dr. Klein had taken a paternal interest in Elliot, had encouraged him to go to medical school and, Elliot suspected, had used his connections to ensure Elliot's admission to Columbia. And this morning, Annie had made some comments to the effect that with Stephanie's divorce, Dr. Klein's death, and some subsequent financial difficulties, Mrs. Klein had become a much-reduced figure now in need of the friends she had so happily put down during her glory days. Annie also mentioned that Stephanie had not remarried.

"Hi, Elliot."

Stephanie's still familiar voice roused him from his reminiscences. Physically, she did not appear to have changed that much. Perhaps her face looked a little narrower and her nose a little sharper, but she was still the quite pretty Jewish blonde—but maybe now more Jewish than blonde. She said the usual things: how much she had liked his father, how much her parents had admired and respected him, and so on, and "I know mom will be there for your mother."

"So, Elliot, do you think you might go back to medical school? Daddy always said you would make a wonderful doctor and …" with a flirtatious smile of old, "you know, I think he had plans for you and me. Funny, isn't it?"

He wasn't sure what was funnier: the idea that he might consider going back to medical school or that she was still playing her old tricks.

"Yes, that's very funny. But I really did like your father, and I was very sorry to learn that he had died so suddenly."

If Elliot was now at a loss for anything else to say, Stephanie was not. He got to hear her life story since her divorce. It was like listening to a résumé: her move to Scottsdale, the real estate company she worked for, the country club she had joined where she played tennis at least twice a week. And, can you believe, one can play on an outdoor grass court practically every day of the year? How the Phoenix area had a much better cultural scene than one might have imagined. Elliot pretended to listen attentively. Stephanie hadn't changed a bit and he still didn't like her. As her monologue wound down he was relieved to see Annie motioning to them through the window that the service was about to start, and they went inside. Stephanie gave Elliot a little kiss on the cheek. He and Annie exchanged a wink.

The next day Elliot helped his mother with various household chores, discussed her future with Annie, and played for a long time with little Jonathan. He enjoyed the service that evening and somehow felt refreshed by the prayers and the sense of community with the others present.

They had reached the seventh and last day of the mourning period. That evening, as they cleared away the last teacup and said goodbye to the last well-wishers, the house felt very empty. Annie put Jonathan to bed. Their mother confessed to being very tired and excused herself early. By nine o'clock, Annie and Elliot were alone together in the family room.

"I'm glad you stayed, Elliot."

"Yes. I'm glad I stayed too, Annie. I'm glad I stayed."

"You seemed different these last couple of days. You became part of the family again. You made Mama very happy."

Elliot proudly explained to her his thought processes of the last few days and how he had realized that his return home was all part of his continuing journey. His sister did not seem at all impressed. In fact, she seemed downright angry.

"You just don't get it, do you, Elliot? Your family isn't just something you pass through on the way to wherever it is you're going to, looking for whatever it is you're looking for. You may rationalize the experience," and she said the word "experience" very sarcastically, "of returning home any way you like. What you don't seem to understand is that your family is, Mama is, the *Shiva* is, the *Kaddish* is. None of them are little existential exercises to help you purify your soul. They are the real world. Part of what really counts."

She could see that he was stung and surprised by her outburst, and she tried to lower the tension with her little quip of several days ago. "As I told you, Elliot, we little suburban housewives know it all."

Elliot was very confused. He had always known his sister had anything but the mind of a little suburban housewife, and he remembered how dismayed he was when she had thrown in her doctoral studies at NYU to marry that schmuck David. In a different sort of way, she was like his Auntie Sonia. Somehow those two women always seemed in tune with people's feelings and, as a result, people would be drawn to them and feel their intrinsic warmth. Annie's emphasis on the "is" while driving home her point about their family showed an innate understanding of profound concepts. Somehow she seemed to understand the notion of "is" and "is not" quite naturally, while he had struggled so hard and so long to grasp it.

"Look, Annie, it isn't that simple. I really have suffered and have tried to understand things better. It's been such a long journey, a very long journey."

"So tell me, Elliot, why did you leave?"

Perhaps for the first time, he started to tell her, to tell anyone, how he felt he had been trapped on a fast track, trapped by his family, by his high school, by his university. All he had really wanted was just a little time to stop and look around. He probably would have been quite happy being a doctor or a surgeon, but there was never any time to do anything but work, work, work. At the hospital he became overwhelmed. Everybody had such high expectations of him. He was always made to feel special and destined for great things, yet he was forever frightened that he wouldn't be able to realize those expectations, and then nobody would love him anymore. The doctors around him all worked incredibly hard. He admired them for their dedication but he couldn't understand how they would often allow themselves to be party to billing practices that to him looked like robbery. In the end, it all became too much. When he tried to explain his torment to his family and friends, and when it seemed that nobody would listen to him, let alone understand him, he decided to quit.

"So tell me, Elliot," she said gently, encouraging him to continue talking, "where did you go?"

He had gone everywhere. He had gone to India. He had been terribly ill with dysentery and returned to the States. He had stayed briefly with a Nichiren community in upstate New York. He had learned to meditate at the Theravadan monastery in New Mexico and told of the countless hours he had spent in the shrine-room. He had gone to Santa Fe and stayed with the Sufis and learned their dances. How he had met Shastri there and how they had traveled to India together. How they had trekked to Tibet where they had been harassed by the Chinese authorities. How they had traveled back to the States and stayed in a commune in upstate Washington started by a Scottish Taoist they had met on their travels in northern India. Why Shastri had gone back to Australia and how he had then always traveled alone.

He told Annie about what happened in a town in northern California when he had walked into a small bookstore. From the outside, it just looked like another touristy New Age shop. However, as he started to talk to the owner she seemed to instantly recognize him as a fellow spiritual traveler and she invited him to stay for a while. This made him realize that he was now projecting an aura that must have developed as a result of his years of travel and self-denial, and his long program of spiritual study. Just briefly, he had felt a great sense of self-esteem and, strangely, it crossed his mind that in this new state of self he could have gone back to medical school and resumed his studies without feeling stress. But he knew the dangers of too much sense of self and quickly worked hard to liberate himself from any feelings of achievement that he might have felt. He stayed and worked at the store for three months. He and the woman were never intimate, but they often held each other during their joint meditations. One day, however, she broke away from their silent embrace and started to kiss him on the mouth and unbutton his shirt. In the past, especially before he had met Shastri, such events were not uncommon. Perhaps driven by the excitement and sensuality of a tantric ritual or, as then, stirred by the sense of closeness in a spiritual moment, women would offer their bodies to him. He would take them and feel, through the sense of energy being both released and gained, that this intimacy advanced his understanding of self. Sometimes the women would want to become attached to him, but he would always evade their wish for a deeper companionship. He would explain to them—sometimes in quite tearful scenes—that they were both merely travelers and to loiter together would impede their progress toward enlightenment. But this woman's expression of desire had caused him deep anxiety. He felt very threatened by the fact that she might arouse his physical self, and he left the next day. He traveled further north to Oregon where he found a small community practicing a synthesis of Mahayana Buddhism and Jungian analysis that appealed to him. However, he had to confess to his sister that he had started to find within the serene atmosphere of that group a hint of smugness—an intimation of a journey well-traveled and a goal that had actually been realized. This had disturbed his fundamental principle of continuous spiritual renewal and he was starting to wonder where he should go to next when news of their father's death had arrived.

He reassured his sister that he had never been a free-loader. He had drawn sparingly on his savings and the small bequest from their grandfather, and he would always take part-time jobs in bookstores, or community centers, or small cafes. To hide himself from the world he disguised himself by always presenting a clean-shaven face and dressing conservatively. He did wear a tantric neck charm that Shastri had given him, but he always made sure that it was concealed under a shirt. His nonthreatening appearance seemed to hold up a mirror to the outside world that showed them a reflection of what they wanted to see. In this way he never had any difficulty getting a job, and was never harassed by small-town police. To the outside world he was just a loner, not a drifter, passing through.

"So tell me, Elliot, what did you learn?" Annie was now like his guru, coaxing out of him his innermost thoughts and secrets.

He had learned so much, or so it seemed. He had learned about all the great Eastern religions, about the atman and the anatman, about being and not-being. He had struggled with ancient koans. He had meditated in front of a blank wall for two weeks. He had learned about Karma, Samsara, Nivarana, and had wrestled with the elusive mysteries and complexities of the Dharma. He had learned about Tao. He had studied Sanskrit. He had learned a little Chinese medicine. And all the time he was seeking his true state of self and not-self.

Elliot had been talking for hours. The antique clock on the mantelpiece showed that it was already past midnight, and although he was starting to feel physically tired he was also feeling a sense of lightness, and certain stresses in his neck and shoulders seemed to have been released.

"Did you ever find your state of self, Elliot?"

"No. One never can."

Those simple words seemed to tumble out of his mouth without thought. He was amazed at the artlessness of his statement. In the past, he would have said that it was the journey and not the destination that mattered. But now he saw the emptiness of that overworked mantra. At that instant, he had simply, if not unthinkingly, stated what he always knew he must ultimately face up to and declare explicitly—not to himself, not to a remote master in a far-off land, but to somebody who loved him unconditionally. He found it almost frightening, yet it was also an immense relief. For a moment, he saw himself as a fisherman caught and wriggling on his own hook of self-realization. And then the fisherman became the fish, and the fish was put back in the water and swam free.

Annie put her hands on his shoulders and looked at him. "If you could ever find this 'self' that you have been looking for, what would you do with it if you found it?"

Elliot stared back at her. It was as though her question had completely broken the long spell he had cast over himself. He knew with an extraordinary sense of clarity that he couldn't answer her. It was as simple as that. He just didn't know. Maybe his whole long journey and absence from his family, his Dharma, was just to tell him that. And now he had to tell her this fundamental truth.

"I just don't know, sis. I just don't know."

She gave him a little hug and then pulled away and changed the subject. "What are your plans now, Elliot?"

He looked at his sister. He looked around the family room: the fireplace in which they had toasted marshmallows as children, the old clock on the mantelpiece that as a boy he had enjoyed winding under his father's supervision, the framed photograph of his grandfather, the little display of other family photographs, and the antique menorah that had belonged to their great-grandparents. All families have their legends and the menorah was one of theirs. Their great-grandparents had died in the Holocaust, but the menorah, repeatedly lost and found with each retelling of the story, had somehow survived and ended up on the mantelpiece in his parents' home.

"I'm not sure right now, Annie, but I think I'd like to stay around for a few more days."

MEMORY LANE

"Excuse me, sir, aren't you Dave McMillen. Dave McMillen the …"

David McMillen looked up from his armchair in the airline business lounge and maintained a cool, impassive look. He knew what was coming. It was nearly always "David McMillen, the writer," or "David McMillen, the author of …" It happened all the time. He didn't know what irritated him most at that instant: being interrupted while he was checking messages on his phone or being addressed as "Dave." Despite his many years in the public eye as a successful writer he did not enjoy these types of ambush, however well-intentioned and flattering they might be. When he was by himself he liked to be left alone with his thoughts. But he also knew the importance of maintaining his cool and being polite when he was recognized. He completed the sentence. "Yes, I am David McMillen, the writer."

The man addressing him blushed with pleasure. He looked to be in his late twenties and had, to David's eye, the universal MBA look. Clean-shaven, with a fresh-faced arrogance, neatly groomed in a dark business suit, albeit slightly rumpled from travel, and a red power tie—the signature stripe on the plumage of a cocky young bird. No doubt he made sure that all his coworkers knew he got up at five o'clock every morning to go for a five-mile run and always tried to be the first in his office in the mornings. David sometimes wondered if they were actually breeding such young men in the airport business lounges in those locked rooms marked Staff Only.

"Wow, I thought it was you. I just wanted to tell you that I'm a great fan. Actually, both my wife and I are great fans. You know …"

David maintained his impassive look, now decorated with a tight-lipped smile, but inwardly he shuddered. He knew that he would now have to listen to yet another earnest tale of how his books had impacted other peoples' lives.

The MBA clone continued. "I always remember when my wife and I met on our first date. The conversation seemed to run dry pretty quick, and then she asked me if I was reading anything, and it turned out that we were both reading your wonderful novel, *Promise Me*. Suddenly, we found that we had a whole lot to talk about after all, and I think we both knew there and then that this was it. Every time you publish a new book we buy each other a copy so that when I'm away on a business trip we can both be reading it at the same time. It helps us keep connected when I'm traveling."

David tuned him out as his mind wandered. God, trite but cute, I suppose. At least you actually read something other than the *Wall Street Journal* and *Forbes*. My goodness, my novels helping you stay connected to your wife when you travel. For me, travel was a way to get disconnected from mine.

"Well, sir, I won't disturb you any longer. I must run to catch my flight. It's been a thrill to meet you in person. I can't wait to tell my wife when I get home that I've met the great Dave McMillen." The man laughed like an excited schoolboy at the thought and walked away to the lounge exit with a brisk, self-confident stride.

Well, David thought, at least the kid didn't ask me to sign a copy of one of my books. He looked around the business lounge. It was about to close and the few remaining travelers were scattered about like pieces from an abandoned chess match: the pawns and knights of that great American game of business and travel. Custodial staff were quietly collecting the debris of coffee cups, half-finished drinks, and snack plates. Today's road warriors' office party was winding down and it was time to go to the boarding gate.

The cabin attendant smiled sweetly at David and addressed him as "Mr. McMillen" when she asked if he wanted to eat dinner. He was relieved to hear her call all the other business-class passengers by their last names as well, and nobody seemed to recognize him. He felt tired. He declined the meal, asked for a couple of whiskey miniatures and a tumbler of ice, closed his eyes, and tried to relax. It had been a typical road trip. When he had been a young writer they all seemed so exciting and important. Now they were just another day at the office. There had been a long and tedious book signing session at a major bookstore—one of the few that had managed to survive the age of Internet book sales and e-books.

"In such a fan of yours, Mr. McMillen."

"I've read every one of your books and can't wait to read this one."

"Could I ask you to sign a second copy? It's a present for my sister."

"You've been such an inspiration to me, Mr. McMillen. Reading your books made me want to go back to school."

"I'll always remember the wonderful reading you gave at UCLA two years ago. It was the last outing I had with my wife before she died."

And so on, and on, and on. David's publisher had organized a by-invitation-only reception afterward, of which he could remember nothing. In fact, the only thing he could remember about that part of the trip was that he didn't like his hotel room and the frustrating hour it took to have it changed. His agent's assistant was meant to have booked him his usual preference of a room on a higher floor with a good view but, for some reason, either the hotel or the assistant had bungled it.

The campus visit had been much more enjoyable. An old college classmate, Mike Koslov, had had little success as a writer but considerable success as a teacher and now directed a highly regarded writing program. Mike was a close friend, and one of the few friends from his college days that David hadn't shed as his own career had taken off, and he would periodically accept Mike's invitations to visit. There was a short reading to a packed lecture theater followed by a Q&A session. These sessions also had a predictable sameness to them.

"Where do your characters come from?"

"How many hours a day do you write?"

"I wanted you to know that your books inspired me to become a writer, and I wanted to ask, who inspired you?"

"What do you think it takes to become a successful writer?"

Students always laughed when he said, "Dumb luck" in answer to that question, but little did they know how true that really was. Nonetheless, he generally liked being around students and now preferred their company to that of his fellow writers whose conversations had become all too predictable. It was nearly always gossip about the latest publishing-house intrigues, complaints about their agents or the morons who reviewed their books, and when they struck gold they couldn't stop talking about it.

Mike's students had organized a party for David. They swirled their wine in rented long-stemmed glasses and sipped it with an air of studied sophistication when, like him at their age, they would have probably preferred to chug it down straight out of the bottle. Some of the young women, in what looked like a coordinated effort, had shown up in little black cocktail dresses. Some of them looked absolutely gorgeous and a couple irresistibly so, and that was most likely intentional. He had the strong feeling that if he had invited one, or maybe even two, back to his hotel for a nightcap, they would have happily accepted. But he had learned his lesson. Entanglements with students were invariably messy, and he certainly wasn't going to make that mistake again; at least not for now, and certainly not with any of Mike's students.

He had hoped to sleep on the flight, but he could not stop thinking about something that had been on his mind recently. Memories and how people recounted, and accounted for, the past—not only to others but also to themselves—were important themes in his writing. But recently, he had become very conscious of what seemed like a sort of asymmetry in his relationship with his readers. They remembered his books in detail and sought information about his personal life, while he knew nothing about them. There was, he felt, a certain lack of reciprocity in the interactions between author and reader. His book signings, public readings, book-fair panels, and the like often acquired a special time-stamped significance for those who attended them. Things that he said or did at those events became, for a variety of reasons, memorable moments in the lives of others. Yet he had no reciprocal memories of these people and what they told him. They quickly became a blur, rather like the passing scenery on a high-speed train journey. He might remember if his seat was comfortable or if the train was late, but he would have little or no memory of the actual scenery racing by. By now, he should have forgotten every exchange at last week's book-signing, but that infinitely sad "I'll always remember the wonderful reading you gave at UCLA two years ago. It was the last outing I had with my wife before she died," kept on coming back to him. Something he had done several years ago—just a routine book reading of little importance to himself—had created a powerful and poignant memory of loss for a man he would never know. It felt like a burden. And then there was that kid at the airport lounge just a few hours earlier, telling him that his books helped him and his wife stay connected when he was away on business trips. What would happen if they stopped liking his novels? Would he be responsible for the breakdown of their marriage? He had come to dislike the past—it was too intrusive. He tried to avoid personal memories—they got in the way of his writing. They cluttered up his interior world where his characters roamed free. When a narrative element tripped over a memory of an event from his own life, it distorted the storyline and broke his concentration.

David sat up to pour himself another shot of whiskey. Observing this, the man sitting next to him leaned toward him. He was a plump, older man with thinning blond-gray hair and round rosy cheeks and, or so it seemed in the dim cabin light, little round eyes and a little round mouth. He spoke to David with a quiet confidential air. "I heard the young lady address you as 'Mr. McMillen,' and I was wondering if you were …"

Oh God, here we go, and I'm trapped in the window seat by Mr. Porky Pig here who will, no doubt, want to chew my ear off for the rest of the flight.

"If you were any relation of Warren and Bobbi-Jo McMillen who live in Omaha?"

David could have almost kissed his neighbor in relief. What a welcome change: to be a nobody instead of a well-known writer. The wheels of his writer's imagination spun at lightning speed. Why not say "Yes"? He could be Dave from Duluth and, yes, he was distantly related to Warren and Bobbi-Jo, although he hadn't seen them for quite some time now. And how were old Warren and Bobbi-Jo doing, and did Bobbi-Jo still bake the best cornbread in Nebraska? And then there was the whole narrative about the Duluth branch of the McMillen family. Why not talk about cousin Jeb? What a character he was to be sure. And then there was Jeb Junior who had got to play a few minutes as a back-up offensive lineman for the Iowa State Cyclones and is now working at Jeb Senior's dealership. And then there was Great-Aunt Martha who had just turned ninety-nine. Never knew a day's illness in her whole life. Said it was her daily shot of moonshine that kept her going. And then there was Uncle Billy's pig farm … but there he'd better be careful because he was sure his neighbor knew a lot more about pigs than he did. It could all be such fun, but he just felt too tired to pull it off. David smiled and shook his head, "No, I'm afraid not."

"Oh well, sorry to have disturbed you. But I have to say, though, you look the spitting image of old Warren." Mr. Porky Pig held out a plump little trotter. "I'm Pete, by the way. Pleased to meet you"

"And I'm Dave. Very pleased to meet you too."

The problem was that there was still at least an hour to go before they landed. David pretended to suppress a small yawn. "These late-night flights home sure are tiring aren't they, Pete?"

Whoever he was, Pete was a true gentleman. "They sure are, Dave. I reckon we both need a little shut-eye before this baby lands," and Pete leaned back in his seat and closed his eyes.

David did the same and now dozed in peace for the rest of the flight. In his head he wrote a children's story about Petee the Pig, the friendly little porker who traveled the friendly skies, making friends wherever he went.

When David finally got home and went to bed, it was with the contented thought that he had actually had an encounter with an ordinary person that he would want to remember. But just as he was about to fall asleep, he suddenly wondered if this memory would be reciprocated. Would Pete also remember sitting next to him on that flight? It was impossible to resist one last spin of the story wheel. Maybe on his next trip to Omaha, Pete would visit with Warren and Bobbi-Jo and tell them about the time he was on a flight to New York and sat next to a fellow who looked just like Warren, and how he had asked him if he was any relation, but he wasn't. "But would you believe …" and here Pete would pause for dramatic effect, "when I was in the luggage hall, waiting to pick up my suitcase, a woman standing next to me by the carousel said, 'I saw you on the plane sitting next to a guy who looked just like David McMillen. You know, David McMillen, the famous writer.'" And Bobbi-Jo would say, "Oh my, oh my, and what did you say, Pete?" and Pete would proudly report his reply, "Dave McMillen? Never heard of him." And they would all roar with laughter. Now that, thought David, would be perfect.

Over the next few weeks David exchanged some e-mails with Mike Koslov who was organizing a summer writing workshop at which David would make a guest appearance. Mike's e-mails were always business-like, but his last one had ended with "Call me at home this evening, there is something I need to talk to you about." Their phone conversation was brief.

"David, I had a call from Katie this morning."

"And what did my beautiful daughter have to say?"

"She just wanted me to tell you that the arrangements for Clare's memorial service have been finalized. It will be held at Barnard College on October 31 at 7:00 p.m."

"Am I being asked to say something?"

"Apparently not."

"Did Katie say if she would like me to be there?"

"No."

"Did Katie say if she *didn't* want me to be there?

"No."

"God, she's so like her mother."

There was an awkward silence. Mike and his wife had been true friends to David and Clare during their divorce and like second parents to Katie, but David's long estrangement—that puzzled his friends and sometimes himself—from both mother and daughter was a topic they avoided. There was little left to say and they soon hung up.

It was dusk, his favorite time of day, and David stood for a long time at his living-room window with its wonderful view of the New York City skyline. As the sky started to darken, the window became a partial mirror in which he could see a faint reflection of himself—a reflection that highlighted the streaks of gray in his hair—and, at the same time, he could see through himself into the early evening sky. He never tired of watching the city as evening fell. When he and Clare were first married they had a tiny apartment in Brooklyn. They sometimes went onto their apartment-building roof with a bottle of whatever they could afford to drink that week and spend hours staring at Manhattan as evening fell. Clare, with her poet's eye, was always captivated by the colors of twilight and, in particular, that band of turquoise sky bridging the fading hues of sunset to the darkening curtain of night. With Clare it was always about the light. He recalled some lines from a poem, one of her first to be published, that she had written during those early and happy days of their marriage—that movable feast he had squandered.

I walk the streets at the still point of the turning
    day when
Twilight colors like spectral bands of ever-
    darkening blues
Ascend as a staircase to the moon,
Uncertain of its time and place in the early
    evening sky.
The clouds as brush strokes upon a distant beach
Where memories, like driftwood, lie.

And now, here he was, alone, watching the twilight sky from the vantage point of his luxury high-rise apartment in midtown Manhattan—but the turquoise band of sky was still the same.

Another road trip, another book signing. David was signing a book for a young woman who looked rather like Katie. She was performing that incredible juggling feat that only young mothers seem able to pull off: a baby on one hip, a big purse, a stroller, a shopping bag or two, a teddy bear—all miraculously secured with just two hands. He suddenly wanted to tell the young woman about the time when Clare had been overloaded carrying Katie, too many shopping bags, and a backpack containing her dissertation. Clare had pulled her back, and to entertain her while she was bedridden for the next few days, David had quickly run off a story about a magical planet where new mothers miraculously sprouted a third arm that enabled them to perform amazing feats of domesticity; and even more amazing feats to please their husbands. David recalled how Clare had promised to emulate those feats when her back was better. But, of course, he didn't tell his fan any of this. Instead, and somewhat uncharacteristically, he engaged her in a relatively long conversation about what she had studied at college, about her baby, and what she liked about his novel. His agent's assistant, who was accompanying him that day, had to whisper in his ear that he was holding the line up.

At a reception a few days later he found himself talking to a complete stranger: a petite woman, probably in her early seventies, with snow-white hair and intelligent eyes that held his attention. She told him how his books had been a great source of comfort and, in the best sense of the word, a distraction while she had undergone a long course of chemotherapy. She was now enjoying her third year of remission. As she talked, David recalled when Clare had been diagnosed with pancreatic cancer, and his visit to her in the hospital just before he had left for a lecture tour in Europe. They had not spoken for a long time and he did not know what to say to her, but he did know that he absolutely needed to see her. Clare was sitting up in the bed. Her face was white: a flat white, tinged with gray. It was a face in which the sun had gone out. David already knew that look from when his father had died of cancer years before. He still didn't know what to say: it would either be too little or too much. But Clare could read him like a book—she always could—and she kept up a light-hearted conversation for a few minutes. She then took his hand and said, "It's OK, David: you can go now." Clare died two weeks later while he was away. By the time Mike had been able to track him down with the news she had already been buried. David didn't tell any of this to the white-haired woman. He talked to her about his latest novel and then found himself telling her that his own father had died of colon cancer before the drugs that could have saved him were available, and that he was so very pleased that her treatment had been successful.

He had a call from his agent. "Fantastic news, David. NPR is going to do a series on contemporary American authors. Live interviews, with a studio audience, by the senior editor of the *Book Review,* and they want you to be the first interview. I needn't tell you what an incredible opportunity this is. Actually I've been working with them on this for quite a while now, but I didn't want to tell you any of this until it had all been arranged."

"When exactly is this going to be?"

"The first broadcast will be on October 31 at 7:00 p.m."

"But that's exactly when Clare's memorial service is being held."

"I'm sorry, David, I really didn't know. Look …" his agent paused for a moment, "… if you *really* feel that you have to be there, I'm sure they'll understand, and they can probably rearrange the schedule to make you the second or third interview. Just let me know what you decide … but I will need to know by tomorrow morning at the latest."

"No. That's OK. I'll do it."

"I knew you would."

The studio audience was in place, and last-minute adjustments to the lighting and sound were being made. It was to be a free-ranging discussion about writing and writers. No prearranged questions, but each author would first be asked to talk for a few minutes about the most importance influences on their writing careers. After an effusive introduction it was now David's turn to speak. He made the usual statements of appreciation for this wonderful opportunity, and then turned to the topic of influences on his career.

"As far as major influences are concerned, the great masters of the past: Chekov, Dostoyevsky, Henry James, Hemingway, have all played their part. But I have to say that the single greatest influence on my writing life, and my life as a whole, was my first wife, the poet Clare Barnsley who died a year ago today after a brief battle with pancreatic cancer. More than anybody else, she opened my heart to the world around me and helped me turn my natural shyness into that interior world that defines my writing today."

The interviewer's initial look of surprise at these unexpected personal revelations quickly turned into a self-satisfied little smile as he realized that a writer well-known for protecting his private space was now opening up on his show. This was quite a coup.

David smiled into the camera and continued. "Like all the best love stories, ours began with a chance encounter when we were both students at Berkeley …"

THE SHOW NEVER STOPS

The bartender poured two glasses of overpriced white wine and slid them across the bar with an obsequious smile. Of course I recognize you, you smug bastard, he thought. We all know who you are: the god-almighty theatre critic preening yourself on public display in the interval and trying to impress the chick hanging on your arm. She's doing a good job of stroking your ego, and no doubt she'll be stroking something else before the night is done.

"Thanks, old chap, keep the change," said the critic as he casually tossed a twenty-pound note on the bar. God, he thought, I'm really not sure what to make of this play. The *London Review* has already anointed the director as a rising star of contemporary British theatre, so I'd better find something complimentary, but not too complimentary, to say. Got to keep up my reputation as a trenchant and independently minded critic; but whatever I say I need to praise the leading lady. Hmm … I can write something about her raw sexuality. She'll like that and then maybe she'll like me in return. OK, here's the plan: I'll take Samantha—I think that's her name—backstage at the end. That'll impress her and should get me a blowjob tonight. While she's thinking that she's all grown-up talking to the director and the cast, I'll make a date with the leading lady—to discuss her interpretation of her part, of course. He took a surreptitious look at himself in the mirror behind the bar and straightened his expensive silk tie.

Samantha also took a quick look at herself in the mirror and adjusted her designer blouse to reveal a little more cleavage. God, what a prick this guy is. Those who can, act; those who can't, direct; and those who can't direct become theatre critics. In a moment, he's going pat my thigh and tell me that we'll be going backstage at the end of the play to meet the director and the cast. And he thinks I'll be so impressed that I'll give him a blowjob tonight. She gave him a moist, sexy smile and briefly brushed his hand. He'll be in for a big surprise. If I play my cards right it'll be the director getting laid tonight.

The thing about being the mirror at the theatre bar is that you get to see everything. I've been watching this human circus for decades now. The posing and the preening, the backslapping and the laughing, the sulking and the scowling, young lovers and old farts, rich snobs and earnest intellectuals, and tonight it's that self-important critic and the groupie who's always hanging around here. Of course, most of the time I have to look at the back of the bartender and his bald spot that he's always trying to hide—especially when he's flirting with the young woman who sells ice cream in the intervals. I really don't like him. He doesn't clean me properly: just the occasional grudging wipe with a dirty rag that leaves streaks on my face. I have feelings too, and I take pride in my appearance.

I've been here a long time, but the mirror before me was here even longer, and he had some amazing stories to tell. When I was replacing him—which was almost fifty years ago—we had a couple of days together side by side as he was being taken down and I was being put up. He told me that when a man or a woman looks in a mirror we often see a side to their characters that nobody else can. He also told me that, back in the good old days, *you-know-who* would sometimes come to the bar to mingle with his fans. All very charming and suave, but when he would sneak a look at himself in the mirror to straighten his hair or adjust his tie, one could see a self-satisfied little smirk on his face that gave away the nasty, narcissistic side to his character that his adoring fans didn't know. He also told me, at least a dozen times, about the famous incident that marked the end of his days as the bar mirror. Our theatre was one of the first to stage plays by Mr. Osborne, and he recalled a premiere when a very nasty argument broke out in the interval between two well-known critics of the day. There was a lot of shouting, things got out of control, and a whiskey glass was thrown across the bar. It cracked his face, and it was soon after that that the management decided to replace him with me.

We mirrors have seen a lot and know a lot about human nature, but I don't think anybody really sees me for whom I truly am. However, a few years ago, there used to be a man who would sit by himself at the end of the bar and stare at me for the whole interval. At first I thought he was just fixated with himself, but then I realized that he was watching the world through my eyes. Sometimes at the end of the interval, when he got up to return to his seat, he would give me a conspiratorial wink. I don't see him here anymore. I wish I had got to know him better. Maybe he was a playwright. Maybe he was working on a play about us. Yes, if I hadn't been a mirror I would have been a playwright. I can see it now: the main character is a struggling author, rejected by the critics, who forms a relationship with a bar-room mirror, just like me. By observing the world through the mirror, the emotional states of the characters in his play—which is a play within a play—are reversed and they have to resolve their internal conflicts by a process of reflection, or something like that. But I digress. I must get back to my job of enabling the world to admire itself.

The second act was about to begin and the audience started to drift back to their seats. The bartender looked longingly at Samantha's magnificent backside, highlighted by her tight-fitting skirt, as she walked out of the bar with the critic. A woman like that would never give me a second look, let alone a first one, he thought; but why that plain-looking ice cream girl is always giving me the cold shoulder, I just don't know. Man, I'm really fed-up with being the bartender here. Yesterday, the assistant manager complained that I wasn't cleaning the mirror behind the bar properly. Asked me why I wasn't using a glass-cleaning spray. Told me he wanted to see the mirror sparkle. I had a good mind to tell him to put his glass-cleaner up his sparkle and clean the mirror himself, but of course I didn't. God, the guy's such a creep. Always insists on mixing the leading lady's two martinis and delivering them to her in person in the interval. Claims she always asks for two. I wouldn't mind betting he knocks back one of them himself.

Some people think it's cool to be a bartender, mixing exotic cocktails for chic customers and all that. But I have to tell you at a theatre bar it's bloody hard work. It's such a rush in the interval: juggling all those orders at once and having to be polite to a bunch of wankers who think you are some sort of robot to be bossed around. Sometimes I think that the scene at the bar could be a scene in a play—not that I could write a play if I tried. But I'm really good at spotting the customers: which ones will be rude, which ones will be polite, and which ones are going to show off to their girlfriends. Some of the customers call me by my first name and some of them do it because they actually want to be friendly, but most of them do it to show off. You know, to give the impression that by being a regular here they are somehow important and get special service. Ha!

I'd really like to try my hand at something else, but if I had to work in the theatre I'd like to be the lighting operator. You can be powerful but anonymous: making the theatre go dark and then suddenly putting a spotlight on the actors caught in some scandalous act in a way that makes the audience gasp. Of course, what I'd really like to do is swing the spotlight onto the audience and pick out that rude bugger who tried to short-change me, or the snot who complained that his glass of white wine was lukewarm. They'd know why they got picked out and would have to put up with everybody staring at them. Now that would be power.

They say that all the world's a stage but, as a stage, I have to tell you that we are all the world to the people who come through our theatre: audiences, actors, playwrights, directors, critics; all of them thinking that they are so important in their day. But compared to me—who has been here forever—their days are practically nothing. There is nothing I haven't heard or seen.

Take this evening's ridiculous play, for example. During the rehearsals last week the director told the cast that the play, *his play*, was breaking new ground: a raw, existential masterpiece that would challenge the norms of postmodernist theatre, whatever that means. But it was a phrase he was so enamored with that he repeated it at least ten times at the first rehearsal. As far as I can tell, "challenging the norms," just means a lot of shouting and stamping, which gives me a headache, and involves a revolting scene in which condoms are thrown all over me. I feel sorry for the stagehand. He has to sweep them up every night and then—and this is the disgusting part—they use them all over again the next night.

The director is such a poseur: prancing around in black jeans and steel-tipped boots that scratch my face, and always hurling obscenities at the cast. Much to his chagrin, the one person who doesn't seem to be the least bit impressed is the leading lady. I don't understand why she would want to work with him, although there's a rumor that she needs the money to cover her legal fees in a high-profile libel suit—something to do with a tabloid claiming that she's having an affair with a Russian mobster.

And tonight, when this farce of a play is being acted out to an audience that doesn't really have a clue what it's about, I can see that obnoxious theatre critic sitting in the front row with his groupie girlfriend, ostentatiously taking notes and making sure that everybody sitting near him can see that he's a VIP. Maybe, in his heart, he knows what is obvious to me: in twenty years time nobody will know who he was or care what he wrote about. In twenty years time I'll still be here and audiences will still be flocking to see me.

I have to say that times have changed a lot. I remember when Mr. Coward directed and acted in plays here before the war. He always treated me very nicely, walking on me in soft, patent-leather shoes. A real gentleman. Another change, and I don't think anybody in the audience realizes this, is that a lot of the actresses these days don't wear undies. The things I have seen as an old stage are beyond imagination!

Talking of old stages, one of the boards in my left wing claims that he is one of the originals and that none other than the divine Ellen Terry used to walk on him. He likes to go on about how he is probably the last board left to have seen up Ellen Terry's skirts, and how she had red ribbons on her corsets. I'm not sure if I believe him. You know how it is with old boards: they groan a lot and their memories tend to be a bit creaky. The other day I overheard the stage manager tell his assistant that they were thinking of pulling the old boy up and putting him in a glass case in the lobby. I almost envy him—I've still got to get through the second act of this piece of theatrical drivel.

Thank God the interval is almost over, she thought as she sold her last ice cream. I'm not sure who I dislike the most: those snotty old bastards in their fancy striped shirts pretending to be so polite with their "thank you so very much" when I know that I hardly exist at all in their upstairs-downstairs world; or those loud American tourists who show up in shorts, T-shirts, and flip-flops and chew gum through the entire play. Still, if I had to choose, I'd take the Yanks. My sister married one and now lives in New Mexico. She says I should join her and leave England, Bloody England, behind. Maybe I will. Still, working in the theatre can be fun. I'm allowed to watch the plays, and the actors—a right randy bunch—sometimes flirt with me. Take this play. The guy who plays the spoilt, sex-crazed son always winks at me during the curtain calls. Yesterday, he had a note sent to me inviting me backstage. But I'm not falling for that one. The girl who works here on matinees told me that he played the same game with her and as soon as they got to the dressing room, he wanted to fuck—and they did. What a slut. Still, the idea of it is more exciting than doing it with that dreary bartender who's always following me around like a puppy dog with his tongue hanging out and always trying to hide his bald-spot.

I haven't a clue what this play's about, but I like the set: a sort of open-plan living room. But I think the zebra-striped sofa where the son spends most of his time trying to screw his aunt doesn't match the rest of the decor. If I were designing the set, I'd use one of those stylish Italian sofas in black leather. While all my girlfriends like reading *Cosmopolitan* or *Closer*, I really like looking at interior-design magazines, even though I could never in a million years afford to buy a single thing in them. Not even a lousy ashtray. Yes, if I wasn't selling ice creams, I'd like to be a set designer. Maybe if I moved to America I could get a job working on sets in Hollywood, and I'd be close to my sister. New Mexico can't be that far from Hollywood, can it?

My friends think I'm weird wanting to be a set designer when they all want to be actresses. Doesn't appeal to me one little bit: having to take off one's clothes and doing pretend sex scenes on stage like they do in this play. God, the way they go at it, one might think they were actually doing it for real. I don't know how the leading lady can bear to be pawed all over by that randy little bugger who plays her nephew. Although, come to think of it, she has a bit of a reputation herself; and with women too, or so I heard the assistant manager tell the usher. When she took a curtain call at last night's performance she suddenly looked right at me and gave me a big smile. I'm sure it was me she was smiling at. Maybe she was giving me a come-on. Or maybe she thought she was doing me a big favour by smiling at me. You know, thinking that I would be absolutely thrilled and run home and tell my friends that the great Miss La Di Da had smiled at me. Ha! Oh well, the lights are dimming— time for the second act. I better go and sit in my corner. If I watch this play enough times maybe I'll understand it.

Thank God for the interval. I don't know how much more of this crap I can take, she thought as she threw herself onto the sofa in her dressing room. But sometimes one has to sacrifice one's art for the money, especially with all my legal fees mounting up. I'm sure my solicitor is spinning things out, but my agent assures me he's the best in the business. God, I feel as though I'm surrounded by pricks. They must be breeding them now. The solicitor's a prick. The theatre critic's a prick. The director's a prick. And as for that randy little bugger I have to act with—"exploring" our ridiculous pseudo-incestuous relationship because I'm his mother's identical twin—he's the biggest prick of the lot. He actually suggested that we do it for real on stage in the interests of artistic authenticity. Claimed that the lighting is so dim for the scene nobody in the audience would be able to tell. I told him that if he so much as got hard, I'd have him *so* castrated professionally that he'd be lucky to get a small part in a pantomime at an old peoples' home in Coventry; and maybe I'd even have him castrated for real. It was that last threat that really scared him. He saw that wretched tabloid picture of me in a nightclub with that Russian mobster who's set up shop in London, and he'd read that castration is one of the Russian mob's calling cards. Ha!

And tonight, that imbecile of a theatre critic is here, sitting in the front row and making sure we can all see him. He's with that theatre groupie I keep on running into. She's always showing up backstage at all the plays I've been in recently, and always sticking her tits in the face of whoever the director is. I'm sure this play's idiot director will fall for her little tricks. It's all so predictable. Tonight the theatre critic will come backstage with the groupie—hoping she'll be so impressed that she'll give him a blowjob—and then start chatting me up, saying nice things about my performance with the unspoken hint that I'll get a better review in return for me giving him a hand-job. He wouldn't dare ask me for anything more. I've dealt with self-important little morons like him a million times, and I know just how to play him along.

Sometimes I think I'd like to chuck it all in. A simple uncomplicated life: maybe like that Miss Nobody who sells ice creams in the interval and watches the play every night. She probably doesn't have a thought in her head or anything to worry about. At last night's curtain call I looked directly at her and gave her a big smile. I'm sure she ran home and told everybody that the famous Miss S—— had smiled at her.

The only person I like in this theatre is the assistant manager, and maybe that's because he's drunk half the time. But he does mix a great martini—far better than the bartender's—and he always brings it to me in the interval. God, I always need at least two of them to get through the second act. Time to go back on stage.

Well, I suppose someone has to do the dirty work, but I often wonder why the Fates chose me to be the Gents. I know we are the one room in the house that is indispensable, along with the Ladies next door, of course. But knowing one is essential doesn't compensate for what we have to put up with. It doesn't matter who they are: rich or poor, tall or short, fat or thin, they all have a willy—well nearly all of them, but that's another story. And they all have to pee in the interval. Oh my, I've seen, heard, and smelt it all: everything from the deep sighs of satisfaction as they relieve themselves with a foaming torrent to the groans of agony as they struggle to dribble out a single drop. They say you can tell a man by the way he dresses, but I tell you that you can really tell a man by the way he pees. I've no idea what goes on with the old girl next door, but I imagine the things she has to put up with in the stalls on the other side of my wall must be just as bad. But there are compensations: one does overhear some interesting things, although some of the old lines like, "To pee, or not to pee, that is the question," get pretty stale after a while. It's a favorite with the old dribblers. You know, the ones who go to the theatre wearing blazers and cravats and try to make friends with the man standing next to them at the urinal. The other day there were a couple of American gents in here standing next to each other, and they had a good laugh when one of them said, "In the long run, men hit only what they aim at." Apparently that was a quote from a famous American philosopher. But I have to tell you, whoever he was, he was dead wrong: the aim in here is absolutely terrible. And then there are the emergencies. There's always some idiot who can't hold it till the interval and rushes in looking deadly pale, ripping open his trousers and throwing himself onto a toilet. Whew ... what a stink. More often than not, it's the curry they wolfed down just before the play at that Indian restaurant next door. Still, at the end of the evening I usually get a nice clean. I certainly need it. I was sorry that old Tom retired last year. Took pride in his job. Always mopped my floors thoroughly, wiped out my sinks nicely, and cleaned my mirrors very carefully. He'd started to mumble to himself rather a lot this past year. Maybe that's why he retired. The new man isn't as careful but he cheers me up. He's always singing calypso songs as he cleans, and sometimes he does a little dance routine for himself in front of the mirror.

In the end, I think it's the smells that are grinding me down. We Gents have a very refined sense of smell and no amount of lemon-scented toilet cleaner at the end of the day can make up for what we have to put up with. I know a job's a job and it could have been a lot worse: I could have been a public lavatory at a bus station in the old Soviet Union. But what I would really like to be is the leading lady's dressing room. Don't get me wrong. I'm no Peeping Tom who wants to pry on naked ladies. It's the scents that I crave, the perfumes they wear, the smell of the makeup and the cleansing creams. I think I could be a wonderful dressing room: warm and welcoming, somewhere they would look forward to retiring to after a rehearsal or in the interval. I can see it now: beautiful actresses—not that I ever see any in here, well that's not quite true—slipping into a silk dressing gown and reclining on a sofa while a dresser fusses around them and somebody brings them a drink. Oh my, that would be nice.

Back in the day, being an usher meant you were somebody. I had a big bell that I would ring and call out, "Ladies and gentlemen, time to return to your seats, please." But now it's some stupid electronic pinger and a recorded message in English and French with a snotty bitch accent. Still, I was able to persuade the management to let me use a small bell to round up the smokers who stand on the street outside the theatre. Nothing wrong with the occasional ciggy, I say. But rules is rules: absolutely no smoking on the premises, and I'm the enforcer. "No smoking in the lobby, madam," and "I must ask you to extinguish your cigarette, sir." That's what I love about the English language: you can use it in ways that lets you be really rude while pretending to be really polite. Makes me proud to be British. I can turn practically any phrase into an insult. "This way, sir" really means, "Fuck you, you toffee-nosed old bastard," without them realizing it. It's all about the body language and how you roll the words off your tongue with a touch of irony. A crisp "sir" doesn't do it, but if you accentuate the "s" and draw out the "ir" into an "err," you can get just the right effect. I've lost count of the number of people I've told to fuck off while politely answering their stupid questions with a deferential tilt of the head. Yes, if I hadn't been an usher, I would have been an actor. I can see it now: the leading role in a play about life in a theatre. I'd play the usher, but an usher with a difference. He'd really be a playwright pretending to be an usher. I'd finally be able to say it how it really is and make big statements about the human condition. I'd have great lines like: "Sod off, you old bastard, you can't see my play"; or "I don't care who you are, you stupid old wanker, there's no smoking in my theatre"; or "If you don't like it you can shove it up your fat arse." The audience would absolutely love it because I know, deep down, that's really what they all want to say to each other.

Bugger, there're a couple of wankers still smoking outside. Look like foreigners to me—South Americans, I think—and the second act is just about to start. I'll give them the polite treatment, just for a change: "OK gents, the second act is about to start."

That went quite well, thought the director as the last guest left the backstage reception he had arranged for the theatre critic. That guy is such a prick, but I have to say, for a change, I rather enjoyed talking to him this evening. When I told him my interpretation of the play, he seemed to like it. In the original version, the spoilt son's affair with the neighbour's wife was a way of getting back at his father. The playwright had been much praised for using this as a vehicle for a scathing indictment of petit bourgeois morality. But, as I explained to the critic, the playwright had got it all wrong. The affair was a substitute Oedipal thing, and my brilliant—although I say it myself—idea was to turn the aunt, a rather minor character in the original play, into the boy's mother's identical twin for whom he develops an unbridled sexual obsession. When I told the playwright what my plans were he got downright nasty. Called me a second-rate mediocrity. Reminded me that I hadn't been to Oxford and made sarcastic remarks to the effect that he wouldn't have expected anything less from someone who'd got their degree from the University of East Anglia, or wherever it was I'd been to. Told me he'd make sure that I'd never direct in the London theatre again if I attempted the slightest change to his play. Well, as luck would have it, the stupid old bugger dropped dead of a massive heart attack the next week and there were no more barriers to implementing my version. Drunk or sober, he was a miserable sod and, in my estimation, grossly overrated. I believe the theatre critic agreed with me about that. Well, maybe the critic has his moments.

After all he did bring Samantha with him tonight hoping that she'd be so star-struck that she'd give him a blowjob. Little did he know that she'd leave the party early pleading a headache, and then slip back in after everybody had left. I noticed that the critic left with our famous, or should I say, infamous, leading lady. I'm sure she'll eat him for breakfast.

I think I'll pay a quick visit to the Gents before Samantha shows up. Of course, I've got my own private director's loo, but I might just catch the cleaner on his way out and wish him good night. It's a good idea to occasionally show the other half that one knows of their existence, not that I envy him his job. It must absolutely stink in there by the end of the day. Still, the last time I went in there I had this great idea for a play set in a theatre Gents. A sort of seven stages of man drama exploring man's losing battle with time as experienced through the evermore-painful process of urination—an uncompromising examination of the human condition, and all that.

I have to say that I love being a director. Acting was never my thing. Not intellectually challenging enough. But I sometimes wonder if it might not be fun to be a theatre critic instead: all that power without responsibility. I could make absolute mincemeat out of my fellow directors, and what a bunch of Oxbridge pricks most of them are. Still, there are perks that go with being a director, not least of which are the Samanthas of this world and, talk of the devil, that must be her I hear coming up the backstairs. Time for her audition.

The evening was finally drawing to a close. The play was over, and the audience and cast had all gone home. The critic had already left the reception with the leading lady, the cleaner was now with his mates at the pub next door, and the assistant manager was passed out in his office. The theatre was now almost empty save for the last two actors on our eternal merry-go-round. The director walked onto the stage with Samantha on his arm. There was no doubt in his mind that his title of Director was the world's strongest aphrodisiac. He could now show Samantha that he was master of the universe as he waved his hand around the theatre and described the way in which he had staged all the scenes and changed the playwright's plot line and dialogue. All in the interest of artistic truth, of course. She was clearly very impressed, gazing into his eyes with rapt attention and moist lips. He stroked her backside and, with a flirtatious smile, motioned her to follow him to the director's office. As they walked off stage, Samantha smiled to herself. An audition would soon be in the offing.

Eventually all was quiet, and the theatre breathed a sigh of relief as she had done almost every night for the past two hundred years. The director, Samantha, and the assistant manager, whose job it was to secure the building, had all left. The assistant manager, who was drinking too much again, had for the second time that month forgotten to lower the fire-curtain and close the door that led to the bar. A safety light twinkled over the bar mirror and flashed messages to his old friend the stage. For a moment, it felt a bit like the good old days—before all those tiresome safety regulations—when we, the stage, the bar, the Gents, the Ladies, the spotlights, and everything else that makes us the great theatre that we are, could all be together at the end of the day and talk about the play, the cast, and the audience. To us, the actors and the audience are all the same: just another group of players in their own little plays. However big or small their parts, we see the same old story decade after decade. It's just the costumes that change while we, the theatre, never changes—however much they repaint and remodel us. We are here forever and the show never stops.

HOME AGAIN

Jean Jones is a full-time professional house sitter, if there is such a profession, who works in the Scottsdale area. She has an excellent reputation: so much so that she's booked up pretty much the whole year round and isn't always available when you want her. She also takes a couple of weeks off in the spring and fall to visit family in Idaho. If you ask her clients what she looks like, they'll probably pause for a moment because, in truth, her appearance isn't something they've given a lot of thought to. Is she old, is she young, is she fat, is she thin? In fact, she is none of the above. On reflection, her clients will tell you that Jean is a middle-aged woman, probably somewhere in her forties. If pressed for more details, her clients will most likely tell you that Jean is, well, nice looking. If her clients looked a little closer they would see that Jean has high cheekbones and that her lightly tanned face is almost wrinkle free. But Jean doesn't wear makeup, and when she's making notes of her clients' instructions she puts on a pair of rather old-fashioned gold-framed glasses that she wears on a chain around her neck. The rest of the time, she's usually wearing large sunglasses—like every other sensible person who lives in Arizona—so you never really get a good look at her face. And what's the color of her hair? Well, she always has her hair in a tight bun and usually wears a white golfing visor or, in the hotter months, a floppy hat—like every other sensible person who lives in Arizona—so it is difficult to say too much about her hair color other than it looks brownish, maybe a hint of red. But come to think of it, there doesn't seem to be any gray in it. But is she fat, or is she thin? Most of her clients will tell you that she is, well, medium height and medium build. If they thought about it a bit more they might say that she's a bit above medium height and definitely not overweight. "Trim" might be a good way to describe her. But then, who really cares about the shape of their house sitter? And, anyway, it's difficult to tell much else because she always wears slightly baggy, but well-pressed, black pants and loose-fitting long-sleeved sweaters; light cotton knit in summer and heavy cotton or wool in the winter. But you certainly couldn't call her dowdy. Indeed, you could say that she's well groomed in a modest sort of way. And Jean doesn't wear any jewelry: just a small gold crucifix on a gold chain around her neck and a simple gold wedding band. If you were to ask her about her husband, which you probably would when you first interviewed her, she would sigh and twist her ring and tell you that her Larry had been struck down in his prime. Although quite how he was struck down was never revealed and, anyway, who would be callous enough to ask? She had never wanted to

marry again. It was after Larry had died that she decided
to leave her native North Dakota to make a fresh start in
Arizona where the sun always shines—such a welcome
change from those long Dakota winters. Jean might also
tell you that she had grown up in a small town that nobody
has ever heard of, and you would probably laugh—in all
likelihood because you didn't know anybody else who had
grown up in North Dakota. And then there was her name:
Jean Jones. Such a straightforward name and an Anglo one
too, but you'd never want to admit that that was a consid-
eration. But her unpretentious background and name, like
her unobtrusive appearance, was one that instilled confi-
dence in those looking for a reliable house sitter; a house
sitter you could always count on. Her reputation was truly
excellent. When you came back from your trip everything
was in perfect order. The mail was carefully sorted and the
phone messages written up in neat handwriting. Although
the house cleaner would still come once a week, the house
would somehow look that bit cleaner and tidier, and the
houseplants perkier, when Jean had been there. And then
there were the family pets. Did I forget to tell you that Jean
loved, simply loved, animals? When you returned from your
trip your skittish dog would be less skittish and his coat
would be shinier. Your aloof Siamese cat would be more
affectionate, at least for a while until she got used to you
being back in the house again. And, of course, Jean was
one hundred percent honest. The quarter or twenty-dollar
bill you had accidentally, or not accidentally, left lying by

the telephone was still there, exactly in the same place. At some point, you would probably ask Jean how she spent her time when she was house-sitting for you. Jean was, of course, always busy: bible study twice a week, a yoga class three times a week, and the time would just fly by when she was making quilts for various charities.

Her regular clients had further reports of Jean's outstanding qualities. When they were away, Jean didn't mind if household repairs were made. Her Larry had been in construction and she knew how to keep an eye on the workmen and they, in turn, always said that it was a pleasure working with Mrs. Jones. And most impressive of all was how Jean had recently helped out Mr. and Mrs. Kowalski. Mrs. Kowalski's elderly father lived with them and, until recently, would accompany them on their vacations, but this past year he had been too frail to travel. When Jean learned this she revealed that she had once worked as a nurse in a geriatric ward and would be happy to take care of the old gentleman while Mr. and Mrs. Kowalski went on their vacation. The whole venture was a great success. Mrs. Kowalski's grown-up daughter, Anne, who lived nearby, would stop by regularly to check up on her grandpa and was able to report that he was being very well taken care of, and seemed far more cheerful than he had been for quite some time. Anne told her mother that, on one occasion, she and Jean had had quite an intimate little chat over coffee. Jean had told her that she really loved being with old people, that some of her happiest memories were the summers she had spent on her grandparents' farm, and that her grandpa, just like Anne's, had also enlisted near the end of World War II. Jean was so proud of her grandfather's service to his country and how honored she was to help take care of another old hero like Anne's grandpa. In short, Jean Jones was an absolute treasure and the circle of Scottsdale citizens who used her services felt themselves very lucky, if not blessed, to have her as their house sitter.

Now almost everything I've just told you about Jean is true, and her reputation as the World's Best House Sitter was well deserved, but there are a few things that need to be corrected. It is true that Jean had once worked in a geriatric ward, but it was as a Nursing Assistant, not as a Registered Nurse. She had probably told Mrs. Kowalski this fact, but for Mrs. Kowalski the narrative was more impressive when she could report that Jean was a former RN. If you ever bothered to look at a map of North Dakota you would have the greatest difficulty finding that small town where she had grown up; and, come to think of it, Jean had never actually told you its name. And, I'm afraid to say, Jean didn't know if her grandpa had served in World War II for the simple reason that she didn't even know who her own parents were, let alone anything about her grandparents. And there never was a Mr. Jones, and there is no family to visit in Idaho. How do I know all of this? It's because I'm Jean. So it's time for me to tell you more about Jean, and also about Jeannie and Sister Jean. Let's start with Jeannie.

The first thing you need to do to become acquainted with Jeannie is to ask Jean to let her hair down—literally. When she unties her tight bun and brushes out her hair you see that it is a rich and wavy chestnut brown that comes down to her shoulders. She already looks different, and when she puts on a touch of lipstick, a little eyeliner, and a hint of bronzer on her cheekbones, the transformation is quite remarkable. That somewhat nondescript middle-aged house sitter is, in fact, a rather beautiful woman. If she told you that she was thirty-five, you would probably believe her. But that's only part of the story.

To get to know the whole Jeannie, as it were, you need to ask Jean to take her clothes off—well, at least down to her underwear. Jean pulls off her loose-fitting sweater and pants. She's wearing tiny, black-lace Victoria's Secret panties and, if you're an expert on the matter, you would notice that her bra is a little on the loose side. That's because it helps make her breasts less prominent in keeping with her profile as the respectable Jean Jones of indeterminate shape. So to complete the transformation, Jean/Jeannie turns her back to you and puts on a different bra, a 34C balconette, and now she's the full-fledged Jeannie. If you're a guy your eyes are going to pop out of your head, and if you are a woman you're going to be jealous. Jeannie has a beautiful figure, with well-turned legs and hips, and smooth, round buttocks that are surprisingly firm for a woman of her age—whatever that really is. Her stomach is flat, there isn't an ounce of flab, and her breasts are practically perfect. If you saw a picture of Jeannie in a little black bikini you simply wouldn't believe that she was also Jean Jones. How does Jean/Jeannie keep in such good shape? Although Jean tells her clients about her yoga classes she doesn't tell them that they are actually advanced Zumba classes. Yoga classes sound sensible for an apparently middle-aged house sitter, while Zumba classes might suggest a wild side, and some of Jean's older and more conservative clients might worry that this could mean raucous parties with Brazilians at their homes while they were away. In fact, Jean/Jeannie has been doing vigorous dance workouts for a very long time. It all started when the owner of the strip joint she started working at as a pole dancer when she was fifteen told her that if she wanted to keep her job she needed to keep in shape, real good shape. But that's another story for another time and Jeannie has to change back into her Jean Jones persona and go to her next house-sitting job.

The McGregors are new clients. Mr. McGregor is a retired Lutheran minister and Mrs. McGregor is a part-time charity worker. They have a large house in one of Scottsdale's better neighborhoods, and one would have to suspect that there was some money in the family for them to be able to afford a home that looks beyond the means of a typical minister. Mr. McGregor is tall, thin, and grim-looking, and Jean can imagine that the wrath of God featured prominently in his sermons. Mr. McGregor greets Jean at the front door with a brief handshake—his hands are cold—and a tight-lipped smile that is really a scowl masquerading as a smile. However, Jean detects a flicker of approval in his eyes when he sees the little gold cross around her neck. Then it's over to Mrs. McGregor, who is also tall and thin, and only a little less grim-looking than her husband. But she's quick to heap compliments on Jean's record as a house-sitter for their friends, the Larsens and the Blackmoors. It's very much a routine assignment. The McGregors will be away for two weeks visiting family in Wisconsin; the maid service comes once a week; the gardener comes once a month and has just been, so Jean won't be seeing him; and there is a weekly pool service. Jean is welcome to use the pool if she wants to. It's not heated, though, because Mr. McGregor likes a cold plunge in the mornings. While they're talking, Jean notices a young man cleaning the pool, and Mrs. McGregor thaws out a little.

"That's our grandson, Joseph. He's working a summer job for a friend of ours who has a pool company. Joseph turned eighteen a few months ago and has just graduated from high school. He'll be starting at Wisconsin in the fall. Mr. McGregor and our son Carlton are Wisconsin alumni, you know, and Mr. McGregor's brother lives in Madison, so he'll be able to keep an eye on Joseph."

"That's wonderful, Mrs. McGregor … oh my, eighteen … how quickly they grow up."

Mrs. McGregor waves to her grandson to come in and a quick introduction is made.

"Joseph, this is Mrs. Jones who will be house-sitting for us. I've already told her that you come on Thursday afternoons and that you are not to disturb her when you're here."

Joseph blushes a little, gives Jean a shy handshake, dutifully kisses Mrs. McGregor on the cheek, and leaves. Jean hears him call out to his grandfather, "Have a great vacation, sir."

By the following weekend, Jean is in the McGregors' house and settling in. Everything is very tidy: the furniture is precisely arranged, there is a large display of official family photos on a side table, and some southwestern-themed historical paintings on the living room and dining-room walls. Mr. McGregor's study has dark paneling. The wall opposite his desk is covered with framed diplomas and there is a big crucifix on the wall behind his desk. Clearly, God watches over Mr. McGregor. There are just a few house-plants in the hallway and living room, and a silk-flower centerpiece on the polished oak dining-room table. The front and back yards are desert landscaped: gravel, assorted rocks, and cacti. To Jean, the best part of the house is the large rectangular pool with bright blue tiling that makes the water look sparkly and inviting. But overall, it's a cold sort of house that makes Jean feel that you would still feel cold in it in the middle of summer with the air-conditioning turned off. Perhaps the best way to actually feel warm is to sit outside by the pool.

On Thursday afternoon, Jean is in the swimming pool when Joseph arrives to clean it. He looks embarrassed when he sees her. "Gosh, I'm so sorry to disturb you, Mrs. Jones. I can come back later when you've finished swimming."

"No, no, Joseph. I've just finished and was about to get out. I seem to be on the opposite side of the pool from the steps. Could you take my hand and help me out."

Joseph takes her hand … but it's Jeannie, not Jean, who slowly emerges from the pool, wearing a little black bikini.

When I'm finally standing up on the edge of the pool I'm only inches away from Joseph. He's mesmerized by my breasts, and his face is beetroot red with embarrassment and excitement. He can't stop staring and, at the same time, he knows that he shouldn't stare, but he can't help himself. I quickly put on the bathrobe I'd taken down to the pool and wrap it tightly around myself. I think he's almost relieved that I'm now covered up.

"Well, thank you for helping me out of the pool, Joseph. I've some fresh-pressed lemonade in the kitchen. Would you like a glass before you leave?"

"No, no, no. Thank you, Mrs. Jones." The poor kid is stammering. "I don't want to be, be late for my next pool, Mrs. Jones."

"I quite understand, and Joseph …"

"Yes, Mrs. Jones."

"There's no need to be so formal. Please call me Jeannie," and with that I walk off into the house. I don't need eyes in the back of my head to know that Joseph has a big grin on his face.

On the next Thursday afternoon, I'm sunbathing by the pool in my bikini when Joseph arrives. He again apologizes for disturbing me. I tell him not to be silly: I won't be in his way while he cleans the pool—which he does rather slowly, sneaking glances at me while he works.

"It's a hot afternoon today, Joseph. Are you sure you don't have time for a lemonade before your next pool?"

"I'd love some lemonade today, Mrs. Jones." He couldn't quite manage to call me Jeannie. "You're my last pool today," he explains with a pleased look on his face. I put on my bathrobe and we go indoors.

We're standing in the kitchen and Joseph is sipping his lemonade and trying hard not to stare at my cleavage.

"Your grandma told me that you've just had your eighteenth birthday and will be starting at the University of Wisconsin in the fall."

"Oh, my birthday was ages ago. I'm really excited about going to college but …"

Something is bothering him. I give him an encouraging smile and he suddenly opens up.

"I sometimes think that I only got in because grandpa and my dad are Wisconsin alums."

"I'm absolutely sure that's not the case, Joseph. You got in on merit."

"Thank you, Mrs. Jones."

"Jeannie, please."

"Thank you … Jeannie." He giggles. "Gosh, grandpa would be really mad if he heard me being so, like, so familiar with you."

"Well, your grandpa isn't here, and you're certainly not being familiar with me, not at all." My bathrobe has slipped open a little and Joseph can't stop staring at my breasts.

"Do you have a girlfriend, Joseph?"

He blushes deep red. "Yes, I mean no, I mean …"

"I'll take that as a no, Joseph."

I step forward, put my hand around the back of his head, and gently pull his face into my chest. He trembles, and I can feel that he's about to burst out of his jeans. I unzip them. He's rock hard and as soon as I start to stroke him he comes in my hand. He looks deeply embarrassed and doesn't know what to say or do. I quickly wipe him up with a paper towel—that's one use for them they never tell you about in the TV commercials—and whisper in his ear, "Don't give it a second thought, Joseph. There's plenty more where that came from."

And so there was: we spent the rest of the afternoon making love in his grandparents' bedroom. It was time that frigid icebox of a house felt some warmth.

So, what do you think of Jeannie now? If you're a mom with a teenage son you're probably thinking that I'm an evil predator who should be put away for life. But before you get too judgmental, take a look at yourself in the mirror. Didn't you read *Fifty Shades of Grey* on the sly on your

Kindle? And when your son's best buddy was frolicking in your backyard pool, didn't you admire the young man's smooth, firm limbs, notice the bulge in his Speedos, and think some impure thoughts? But, of course, you say to yourself, you're not doing anything wrong because they're just thoughts, thoughts that you would never act on. And quite rightly too: you're a married woman and a mother, and you would never dream of doing anything to disgrace your family. And, of course, you love your husband. He still satisfies you in bed when you have sex once a week although he isn't telling you that he's now popping Viagra from a stash he keeps hidden in his den. Although he's started to get up in the middle of the night to pee, a spluttering pee you can't help overhearing, and you can see a few wrinkles on his butt, he's still your guy, the father of your son. But what about your teenage son? Is he really an innocent boy? He's a teenager: he thinks about sex all the time. How do you know he's not having sex at this very minute with an underage high school girl—some promiscuous kid who might get pregnant and/ or give him a nasty infection? Yes, in many ways, Joseph is an innocent boy, but he's also eighteen. I made damn sure of that. Legally, he's a man. Think of all the things he can do independent of your parental consent: he can drive a car, fight for his country, get married. All those things that are likely to be far more dangerous for him than having legal sex with an older woman who won't get pregnant. Think about it.

So why do I do it? I don't do it for the pleasure. I do it for the feeling of affection, the warmth that the physical contact, the closeness, brings. But why with such young men rather than with men whom you would say are of a more "suitable" age for me? It's nothing to do with the youthful bodies. It's because with the Josephs of this world, those innocent boy-men, I'm the one in control. And if you think I enjoy being Jeannie, you'd be wrong. I'd much prefer to be Jean all the time. Well, that's enough for now. By next week, Jean Jones will be house-sitting for the Taylors.

Mrs. Taylor, cocktail in hand, comes out onto the driveway to greet Jean. Mrs. Taylor is probably in her mid fifties. She's wearing shorts and a pink tank top that are far too tight for her plump, tanned body, and her plastic flip-flops reveal blue-painted toenails. No doubt the Mrs. McGregors of this world would be very critical of the way Mrs. Taylor dresses, but Jean knows better than to judge people by the clothes they wear. They go into the living room to discuss the house-sitting arrangements for the coming week. Jean declines the offer of a cocktail, explaining that she doesn't drink. They don't have a gardener because Steve, who's currently in the Jacuzzi, likes to do the yard work himself. The pool guy, Craig, who Mrs. Taylor thinks is rather cute, comes early Tuesday mornings. Their little Yorkie, Peppers, who has already jumped onto Jean's lap and is licking her face, likes to go out for a daily walk around the block where he can meet all his little friends. Peppers is an absolute sweetheart and Mrs. Taylor knows that Jean will absolutely fall in love with him. Jean should make herself completely at home, help herself to anything she wants, and definitely take advantage of the Jacuzzi that has extra powerful jets. Mrs. Taylor and Steve love to soak in the tub every night with a bottle of wine. There's a splashing sound outside and Mr. Taylor emerges from the Jacuzzi, wraps a towel around his middle, and pads into the living room through the open French windows. He, too, is plump and tanned, and has a thick gold chain around his neck. He scratches his belly, says "Hi" to Jean, and then goes back outside and flops into a deckchair by the pool. After a brief tour of the house Jean leaves with a set of house keys, and Mrs. Taylor joins her husband by the pool.

The Taylors' house couldn't be more different from the McGregors'. Their living room is scattered with soft easy chairs and there is an enormous white leather sofa-ottoman combination. The big screen TV is wall mounted. The dining room set is all glass and chrome with red-leather-backed dining chairs. On one of the living room walls is a very large semiabstract painting of two nudes. In the master bedroom, whose king-sized bed is piled high with brightly colored pillows, there is a less abstract version of the same painting. When Jean checks Mr. Taylor's den to make sure that everything is turned off, she notices some girlie magazines in a rack under his desk. A few days later, when

Jean is forced to rummage in the Taylors' master bathroom to find some toilet tissue, she comes across a box of dildos and vibrators. Now, at this point, you might be thinking that this is just the sort of house where Jeannie would feel right at home. You couldn't be more wrong: she detests the loose familiarity of the Taylors and people like them. Both Jeannie and Jean find the whole atmosphere of the house to be rather sleazy. They feel very uncomfortable there. It's a good thing that Sister Jean is available to help.

It's early Tuesday morning, only a little past six, and I'm sitting on the Taylors' patio with my morning cup of coffee. I'm watching Craig clean the pool, although he hasn't noticed me yet. When I see that he's finished, I wave to attract his attention and beckon him to the patio. He's a bit unsteady on his feet.

"You must be Craig. I'm sure the Taylors told you that I would be house-sitting for them this week."

"Yeah, that's me. How ya doing today, ma'am?" He wipes his hand on the back of his shorts and holds it out.

"You look as though you could do with a cup of coffee, Craig. Would you like some?"

This was an unexpected and welcome invitation. Craig had woken up with a splitting headache from a night of heavy drinking and neither the early-morning joint or slice of leftover pizza for breakfast, washed down with a couple of beers, had helped. He had planned on picking up a coffee at the McDonald's drive-through on the way to his next pool, so this offer of free coffee was a godsend.

"Thank you, ma'am. That would be absolutely great."

"Very good, Craig. Just follow me into the kitchen and please take off your shoes before you step inside."

We're standing in the kitchen and Craig is gulping down a big mug of black coffee fortified with three spoons of sugar.

"This is absolutely great, ma'am. I can't tell you how much I needed a coffee this morning."

"I think I can see that Craig, and Craig ..."

"Yes, ma'am?"

"Please stop calling me ma'am. Please call me Sister Jean."

"But you're not my sister. My sister lives in El Paso."

I knew he wouldn't understand. I give him a little smile and explain. "Of course I'm not your sister in *that* sense, Craig, but we are all brothers and sisters in Christ."

Craig recalled that Mrs. Taylor had told him that the house sitter was real nice, but she doesn't look at all nice to him. She's wearing some baggy blue smock thing that makes her look like a sack of potatoes and has a big wooden crucifix hanging around her neck. Her hair is in a tight bun and she's wearing gold-framed glasses. She reminds him of a mean old Sunday school teacher he once had. Craig has the feeling that he's been trapped by some crazy old church lady, and wishes he hadn't accepted the coffee.

"Brothers and sisters in Christ?"

"Yes, Craig. The Good Lord watches over all of us and knows all our sins. I can tell that you've been smoking cannabis and drinking beer this morning, haven't you?"

"Now look …" Craig wants to say, "Mind your own fucking business" but immediately realizes that he's in a tight spot. If this crazy bitch reports him to the pool company, he'll lose his job. He absolutely cannot lose his job. He has a mountain of credit-card debt and is behind on child support. He recalls something about Jesus loving repentant sinners.

"This isn't how it looks. Yes, I did smoke a joint this morning. It's medically permitted in Arizona, you know. But I didn't mean any disrespect to you or to Jesus. I've been having a hard time recently. Personal problems, you know."

"Yes, Craig, the Good Lord is always testing us. Testing us with drugs and alcohol and other abominations. Just look at all the filth around us. That is why we must pray to Jesus to ask for forgiveness, and ask for His help to save us from temptation. Have you been saying your prayers recently?"

"Yes, I mean no, I mean …"

"I'll take that as a no, Craig."

Craig wants to say, "You're one crazy screwed-up bitch," and leave; but he's in his socks, and Sister Jean is standing between him and the kitchen door. He also knows that he cannot risk doing anything that might cost him his job and that he has to play along with whatever's coming.

"You're right, Sister Jean. It's been a long time."

"I'm glad you're being honest with me, Craig. Honesty is the first step toward redemption. You don't want to be a sinner, do you Craig?"

"No ma'am … I mean Sister Jean."

"Good. Now what we're going to do, Craig, as brothers and sisters in Christ, is pray together."

"Pray together?"

"Yes, and on our knees, and then you can leave. Now kneel down next to me, Craig, and repeat after me …"

Five minutes later, Craig is in his truck and racing out of the driveway. He can't believe what has just gone down. What would his buddies think if they knew that he had just been forced to his knees by some whacko old church lady? The only thing he does know is that he now feels stone-cold sober.

Sister Jean suddenly feels very tired. Being Sister Jean is sometimes necessary, but it's also very draining, just as being Jeannie is in a different sort of way. Jean wishes that she didn't have to be either of them. She takes off Sister Jean's blue smock and crucifix, unties her hair, and slips on her black pants and a loose cotton sweater. She goes over to the Taylors' cocktail cabinet and pours herself a large shot of whiskey.

After the McGregors and the Taylors, it is such a relief for Jean to now be house-sitting, for a whole month, for Dr. and Mrs. Simons. They are some of her oldest clients. Their home is warm and friendly, elegant but not fussy. They have a pair of beautiful Maine Coon cats and a lovely garden. Their long-time gardener, Oscar, and Jean get on very well and she practices her very bad Spanish on him. Jean knows better than most how much a house reflects the personality of its owners and she very much likes the Simons' home. A home without demons, a home where Jean can relax and just be Jean. In the early morning she likes to sit on the patio, with one of the cats on her lap, sipping her coffee and watching the early-morning sunlight play on the distant mountains. She feels at peace and sometimes allows herself to wonder what might have been.

Mrs. Kowalski was very pleased to be the one recommending Jean to the Iversons and only too happy to tell Jean all about them. Mr. Iverson's sporting-goods business has stores all over the greater Phoenix area. He's active in local politics, a member of the Scottsdale Chamber of Commerce, and the recipient of a number of awards for his charitable work. And as for Laura Iverson—it was a second marriage for both of them—she's an absolute sweetheart. The Iversons used to go on long and exotic vacations: safaris in Africa, river cruises in Europe, and they often spent a couple of weeks in Paris in the spring. But since Mr. Iverson's accident that left him in need of a wheelchair, the most they can do for a vacation is drive over to La Jolla to stay with Laura's sister. They were planning such a trip next month but needed to find a new house sitter. Jean would be just the person they were looking for.

Jean's meeting with Mrs. Iverson to go over the arrangements was brief but very cordial. She didn't meet Mr. Iverson who was watching a golf tournament on TV in his den, and Mrs. Iverson thought it best not to disturb him.

Jean's week at the Iversons was very quiet. Their house was large and perfectly furnished, but to Jean it felt more like an interior designer's showpiece than a home; so very different from the Simons'. When the pool guy and the gardener came, Jean just waved to them from the kitchen window and didn't go out to talk to them. She spent her time during the day doing a lot of quilting—yes, Jean really did do quilting—and on most afternoons she went to the movies. Quite uncharacteristically, she skipped all her Zumba classes for that week. In the evenings she did more quilting and read her bible—yes, Jean really did do bible study. She also spent a lot of time on the Internet. When the Iversons returned from their vacation they found, of course, their house to be in perfect order, and Jean had even managed to revive two of Mrs. Iverson's favorite houseplants that had appeared to be on their last legs.

A couple of weeks later, Jean receives a phone call from Mrs. Iverson who confides in Jean that she has been feeling rather run down of late. Her doctor recommended that she spend a week at the Miraval spa outside Tucson. The problem is finding someone to take care of Mr. Iverson. The previous home-care services she had tried didn't seem to understand her husband's needs. Mrs. Iverson is at her most charming and persuasive—in the way that people who are used to getting their own way often are. Enid Kowalski had given a glowing report of Jean's care of Enid's father, and Jean, being a former RN, would be the ideal person to take care of Mr. Iverson. Would Jean, just possibly, be interested? Jean agrees. She suggests that before Mrs. Iverson goes away, she spend an afternoon alone with Mr. Iverson so that they can get to know each other better, while Mrs. Iverson goes off to do something nice for herself. Jean also suggests—and this was based on her many years of nursing experience—that it would be a very good idea not to tell Mr. Iverson that Jean would be looking after him until after their afternoon together. Mrs. Iverson is both delighted and impressed. She just knows that she made the right decision in asking for Jean's help. They agree that Jean will visit this coming Friday afternoon.

A very cheerful and smartly dressed Mrs. Iverson takes Jean to meet her husband, who is in his den, and then leaves for an afternoon of shopping with some girlfriends. Jean and a slightly frosty Mr. Iverson exchange pleasantries. Jean tells him that she saw something in the paper about an award he had received recently. Mr. Iverson warms up and happily tells Jean about it and some of the other awards he has received. Mr. Iverson then tells Jean that he would like to go outside onto the patio by the pool to get some fresh air, and asks if she can help him move from his armchair to his wheelchair. As Jean eases him into the wheelchair he suddenly grabs at her breasts. Shocked, Jean steps back and instinctively slaps him across the face. Iverson smiles at her awkwardly.

"Look, I'm terribly sorry. That was an accident, just an accident. I thought I was going to fall as you were moving me. I wasn't trying to grab you, not at all. Look, let's forget this ever happened and I won't tell my wife that you hit me."

Jean looks at him coldly and slaps him again. This time much harder: one-two, forehand, backhand. Iverson is stunned, and before he has time to react, Jean has taken a couple of plastic ties out of her pocket and shackled his wrists to the arms of the wheelchair.

Iverson explodes. "What the hell are you doing, you crazy bitch. Unshackle me immediately. Immediately. Do you know how much trouble you're in? This is aggravated assault of a senior. An assault on a helpless old man in a wheelchair. The DA is a friend of mine. He'll crucify you. Absolutely crucify you. I guarantee it."

"I don't think so, Mr. Iverson," and just as he opens his mouth to shout for help, Jean takes a small revolver out of her purse.

At this point, you must be as shocked as Mr. Iverson at what has just happened. This is not the Jean Jones that you know: the sensible and sober Jean, the Jean who so conscientiously watches over your homes and pets, the one who only a few months before took such loving care of Mrs. Kowalski's elderly father. Nor is this Jeannie or Sister Jean. They would never behave in this way. I realize that their occasional appearances must have made you think that Jean is a bit of a whacko, but you never thought of her as a psycho. However, there is something I now need to tell you. Although I told you about Jeannie and Sister Jean, I never told you that there was also another Jean. I never told you for the simple reason that I never wanted to. That other Jean hides in the shadows, the darkest shadows. In a better world she wouldn't exist at all, but she does. The Jean you thought you knew tries to keep that other Jean hidden away and hopes, and even prays, that one day she'll simply disappear. But she never does, and now I need to let that other Jean speak for herself.

I put the gun down on a small table by the wheelchair. "Don't worry, Mr. Iverson, I'm not going to hurt you. I just want to show you something." I reach into my purse and take out a photograph. It's an old Polaroid photo, slightly faded, but the picture is still clear. In it a naked girl of about eleven is kneeling in front of a man whose hand is gripping the back of her head. There is a distinctive tattoo on the man's forearm, but his head is outside the frame of the photo. Iverson turns his head away in disgust.

"You're crazy, absolutely crazy. This is disgusting. Why are you showing me this revolting picture?"

I point to the girl in the photo. "Look, can you see that s-shaped birthmark on her right hip?" I then roll down the waistband of my pants to reveal the same-shaped birthmark.

"Are you telling me that the girl in this photo is you?"

"Yes, Mr. Iverson."

He quickly gathers his thoughts. "Look, I think I now understand what's going on here. If that's really you in the photo, my accidentally touching you a few minutes ago must have triggered off some horrible childhood memories of yours. That doesn't justify your actions but it helps explain them. I'm a reasonable man: if you unshackle me now, leave the house immediately, and promise never to come here again, I won't report you to the police or say a word to anybody about you abusing me. I can't be fairer than that. What do you say?"

"I don't think so, Mr. Iverson ... or should I call you Papa Bear?"

He goes deathly pale. I show him another photograph. In it the girl is lying on a table and the man with the tattoo is standing over her. Now he's looking straight at the camera. There is no doubt who he is.

"Shall we roll up your shirtsleeve, Papa Bear, and look at the tattoo on your arm—just in case you're wondering if the man in this photo is really you? And if you're still not convinced, we can look at all those nice family photos you have on your desk from when you and Mrs. Iverson were first married. When I was house-sitting here last month I saw those photos and realized who you were. I've spent my whole life trying to forget you, Papa Bear, trying to block you out of my mind. Now here we are. Just you and me, Papa Bear. Just you and me."

He groans and looks at me like a trapped animal.

"If the police saw these photos they would surely want to know who took them, don't you think? Look …" and I show him a third photograph. In this one, the girl has been forced over the back of a sofa and another man, thickset with a military-style crew cut, is standing behind her. "Look at what he's doing to me, Papa Bear. Look at what he's doing." I then point to the shirt. "Look at the shirt, Papa Bear. It's a sheriff's shirt and you can just make out the name badge on it: Parsons. That must be your old buddy, Bill Parsons. Uncle Billy you told me to call him."

Iverson is now deathly pale and sweating profusely.

"Do you stay in touch with your old buddy Bill, good ol' Billy Parsons? No? I didn't think you did. Well, as I understand it, Uncle Billy has made quite a reputation for himself in our old home state as a big law-and-order man. Why, he's running for a fourth consecutive term as sheriff. With all those roughnecks coming from everywhere to work the oilfields, parents worry about the safety of their children. It's a good thing they have Uncle Billy. His election posters say 'Bill Parsons for Sheriff. Your Kids will be Safe'."

"What do you want? Do you want money? I can give you a lot of money."

"No, I don't want your money, Papa Bear. I just want to tell you a story."

I pick up the revolver in my right hand and, squeezing his jaw with my left, push the barrel of the gun into his open mouth. He starts to choke.

"Now take it easy, Papa Bear. You won't choke if you relax and breathe through your nose. I'm sure you remember telling me to do that and a whole lot more, don't you, Papa Bear? Now let's begin at the beginning. Once upon a time there was a little girl called Jean. Let's call her Little Jean. Her mother had given her up at birth, and Little Jean never knew who her father was because her mother didn't know, either. Little Jean was a ward of the state and spent her childhood in the foster-care system. For a few years she lived with a Mr. and Mrs. Olsen, along with two other foster children. Mr. Olsen worked in a bank and was a Methodist lay-preacher. He was a hard, cold man. There was plenty of prayer but no love or affection. No hugging and kissing of the sort that children need. On one occasion there were some workmen at the house for a few days, and one of the older workmen took a liking to Little Jean. He was just a kind, grandfatherly type who liked children. He never behaved in an improper way. He was just a nice man being nice to a little girl looking for some kindness. One day Mr. Olsen came home early and saw Little Jean sitting on the workman's knee while he was having a coffee break. Mr. Olsen took Little Jean into his study, told her that she was a terrible sinner, and beat the hell out of her. He beat her often. But eventually Little Jean's luck changed: the Olsens decided to move out of state. After a few moves through some other homes, Little Jean was taken in by a Mr. and Mrs. Ivers—that was your name back then, wasn't it? He was a young fire captain and she was a nurse, and they were obviously a perfect couple to be foster parents. For a while, Little Jean was very happy. Her foster parents were kind and affectionate—especially Mr. Ivers who told her that he was her Papa Bear, and he taught her to play softball. Mrs. Ivers had a little black cat called Snicky who slept on Little Jean's bed and became her best friend. Little Jean started puberty when she was eleven and Mrs. Ivers, being a nurse, was able to explain it all to her. Then one weekend, when Mrs. Ivers was working at the hospital, a sheriff's deputy came to the house and you introduced him to Little Jean as Uncle Billy. Then they all went down to your den in the basement. Do you want me to tell you what happened in the basement on that day and on many other days, Papa Bear? I can tell you all the details, if you like. No? You don't want to know? I wonder why? You told Little Jean that if she told anyone what happened in the basement you would kill Snicky, which you knew she wouldn't want, and nobody would believe her anyway. Little Jean was terrified and powerless. As much as she had hated Mr. Olsen she remembered how he had often told her that Jesus would save repentant sinners. So every day Little Jean prayed to Jesus to forgive her. Would you like to hear her little prayer? No? I didn't think you would. And then Jesus answered her prayers. It's not clear why it took Mrs. Ivers so long to work out what was going on. Maybe she just didn't want to know. But once she finally realized what a monster you really were, she just upped and left, and took Snicky with her. The good thing was that because of Mrs. Ivers leaving, you could no longer be a foster parent and Little Jean was immediately moved to another home. But you told her that if she ever said a word about you and Uncle Billy you would hunt Snicky down and kill her. But you forgot one thing: you and Uncle Billy had taken so many photographs, and thought that they were so well hidden, that you never bothered to count them. Little Jean found them and something told her that she should take a few, and keep them in a safe place.

Little Jean was a difficult child and quickly ended up in a home for problem children, run by a Catholic charity. She felt safe and secure there: Jesus was there to protect her. She learned to quilt and enjoyed her bible study classes. The school administrator, Miss Hawthorne, was nice to Little Jean, said encouraging things to her, and told her that she would find her a new foster home. Then, one day, Miss Hawthorne told Little Jean, now an attractive young woman of fifteen, that she had some good news to tell her. Jean went to Miss Hawthorne's office. Miss Hawthorne took Little Jean's hand, said strange things to her, and started to touch her. Little Jean ran away the next day."

I paused for a moment. "I could go on for a long time about what happened to that poor girl since then, but I don't think there's really any need. You ruined her life, Papa Bear. That's all you need to know. You ruined her life. Don't you wish that Little Jean had never been born? I often do," and with that, I took the gun out of his mouth.

Iverson spent the next few minutes gasping and heaving. He was soaked in sweat. He was a broken man, terrified and powerless.

"What are you going to do now? Are you sure you don't want money? I can give you anything you want."

"I really don't want your money, Papa Bear. What I want to do is take care of you."

"I don't understand. What do you mean 'take care of me'?"

"Didn't your wife tell you? She's going off to a spa next week for a few days. The poor thing is finding taking care of you very tiring, so I'm going to be moving in to take care of you while she's away. You're going to be calling me Mama Bear, and Mama Bear will be helping you go to the bathroom and giving you baths." I spin the cylinder of my revolver. "You and Mama Bear will have lots of nice little chats like the one we've just had. We'll talk about the past and if it's possible to make things better. Maybe we'll pray to Jesus together. I'm sure that will help us both. Now, now, Papa Bear, cheer up. Your wife will be home soon. When she gets home, I want you to look real happy. If you tell her that you don't want me to look after you, some of these photos might end up in her mail and at the DA's office. You wouldn't want that, would you?"

He weakly nods his head in agreement.

"Good, I knew you'd see it my way. I'm going to unshackle you now and put you on the sofa where you can have a little rest by yourself until your wife comes home. I'll be in the living room until she does. If you need anything, just give me a shout."

Jean—and at this point it doesn't really matter which one—closes the door of Iverson's den behind her and goes into the living room. She curls up on the floor behind an armchair in the corner and sobs uncontrollably for what feels like a lifetime.

Later, when Jean hears Mrs. Iverson's car in the driveway, she puts on her sunglasses and steps outside with her purse over her shoulder and car keys in hand. Jean apologizes for not being able to stay, admires Mrs. Iverson's collection of shopping bags from the Scottsdale Fashion Square, and reassures her that everything has gone very well. Jean and Mr. Iverson are now great friends and understand each other perfectly. He seemed a little tired and is having a rest on the sofa in his den. Jean is looking forward to taking care of him next week.

But that next week never came because, a few days later, Jean reads in the newspaper that Mr. Iverson had died in a tragic home accident. Apparently he had gone outside late at night to get some fresh air, had fallen out of his wheelchair into the swimming pool, and drowned. Mrs. Iverson had woken up the next morning to find his body floating in the pool. A terrible tragedy and a great loss to the community. Jean calls Mrs. Iverson to expresses her condolences, offers to help in any that she can, and asks if she can stop by for a few minutes to pay her respects; but, of course, only when and if Mrs. Iverson feels up to it.

A few days later, Jean pays her visit. She brings Mrs. Iverson some flowers and talks to her in soft, soothing tones. "I was so shocked when I heard the news, Mrs. Iverson. I've been praying for you and Mr. Iverson all this week. I so enjoyed the afternoon I spent with him. He reminded me of the father I never had. Mine died when I was very young, you know." The two women clasp hands.

"What are you going to do now, Mrs. Iverson?"

Mrs. Iverson tells Jean that she is thinking of moving to La Jolla to be near her sister.

"And what about you, Jean? Your house-sitting business here is so successful. I hope you are going to keep it up. All our friends love having you look after their homes when they're away."

Jean looks pensive. "It's so kind of you to say so, Mrs. Iverson, but I've decided to stop house-sitting."

"But why's that, Jean? You've made so many friends doing it. Has something happened?"

"I don't want to burden you, Mrs. Iverson."

"Not at all, Jean … and please call me Laura."

"Well, Laura, just recently somebody I've known since childhood passed away. Although we didn't see each other very often we always kept in touch. She had a very hard life and a very difficult childhood. I often felt that if more could have been done to help her, her life would have been much happier. Her death made me think about that a lot. So I've decided to move to Tampa and enroll in a pediatric nursing program there. I can't think of anything more worthwhile to do at this stage of my life than helping children."

"You're such a good person, Jean. You really are."

"I try my best, Laura, I really do."

SIR GEORGE AND
THE DRAGON

George Tomkins placed his chipped, but much-prized, Silver Jubilee mug of freshly brewed tea on the table by his "comfy" chair. He used the Jubilee mug only when watching special sporting occasions such as the FA Cup Final or Wimbledon. He walked over to the television set to turn up the volume. Remote controls, he felt, made you lazy. He then returned to his chair, adjusted the cushion behind his back, and made himself comfortable. With the reassuring warmth of the mug of tea in one hand and a chocolate digestive biscuit in the other he was ready to enjoy the televised spectacle of the 151st Grand National. He was not a racing man and certainly not a gambling man, but there was something special about the Grand National, and the yearly ritual always brought back memories of his childhood with his Uncle Sidney and Aunt Betty. "There's nothing wrong with a little flutter," his uncle would say. It was, after all, his only bet of the year. But Aunt Betty, who had wanted to join the Salvation Army, would always reply, "Gambling's not right, you know, Sid." The young George never knew if his uncle actually placed a bet, but even if he did, the horse he claimed to have chosen never won. That he was now watching the 151st Grand National also reminded George that it was now 1998. It was difficult to believe that it was already 1998. But, then, it was difficult to believe that he was about to turn 64. The years, like the horses, were racing by.

Sipping his tea, George listened to the commentator read off the list of entries and he chose his horse the way he always did: a horse with a nice name and fairly long odds. Everybody liked the idea of an outsider winning, and even if he or his late uncle had never spotted the winner it was always fun to try. And that, of course, was what it was all about: having a try and doing your best. The vicar, along with every vicar the length and breadth of England, or so George suspected, would nearly always give a sermon the next day about "The Great Race of Life." Even if it wasn't very original, the vicar's intentions, bless him, were always the best. No, it was not the race itself or the glamour of the winner's enclosure full of sharp-suited punters and women in impossible hats that appealed to George. It was that moment as the last horses passed the post. The commentator, usually a little hoarse and breathless, would be rattling off the names of all the horses as they crossed the line: "First, Pink Cypriot, 11-2; second, Gladiators Folly, 5-3: third, Bounty Hunter, evens favorite; fourth, The Jazz. Also ran: Sundance Kid, Royal Knight, Kingway, Sugarbaby, Second Empire." *Also Ran*—that was what mattered. You ran the race, you may not have won or even come second or third, but you got that honourable mention. It was that little bit of respect that made all the difference. He wasn't Sir George Tomkins KBE, MC; or the Right Honourable George Tomkins MP, OBE. He was just, no not *just*, he was: *Mister* George Tomkins AR.

The importance of respect was something that George's uncle had instilled in him from an early age. George's parents had been killed in the Battersea Park train crash when he was only three, and his mother's sister, his Aunt Betty, and her husband, his Uncle Sidney, adopted him. They had no children of their own. His uncle worked for the Post Office. It was, after all, His Majesty's Post Office and his uncle took the responsibilities of being a postman very seriously. George could remember little of his first few years living in their semi-detached in the outskirts of Swindon until one Sunday in September when he was playing in their back garden. Every child in England must have had exactly the same experience that day. The adults listening to the radio and becoming very quiet as Mr. Chamberlain read his fateful speech. Whatever it was, he knew along with all those other children that nothing would ever be the same again.

In fact, truth be known, young George really enjoyed the war. His uncle became a very important person in the neighbourhood: he was the air-raid warden. He took on his new duties with gusto. Not only did he have to ensure that His Majesty's mail got through during the day, but that Hitler's bombs never got through at night. George's uncle never appeared happier than when he went out on his dusk patrols. Young George was allowed to help in the preparations for the night's mission by checking the contents of his uncle's kit bag: the torch, the gas mask, the first-aid kit. His aunt would give his uncle's tunic a thorough brushing, and then General Sidney Tomkins would step out on behalf of King and Country proudly wearing his warden's helmet and armband, and twirling his whistle chain. Although it was against regulations (and his uncle took regulations very seriously) he sometimes allowed the young George to accompany him to the end of their street before sending him back home. But even in those short expeditions the conversations were enthralling. "Fixed those blackout curtains yet, Mrs. Peters? How's the new shelter, Mr. Morris? Terrible raid in London last night, Mr. Cartwright." And back would come the reply: "Yes, Mr. Tomkins." Except Mr. Harris, who lived at the bottom of the street. He would always give a mock salute in an insolent sort of way and say, "Keep up the good work, Sid," or "With a secret weapon like you, Sid, old Hitler hasn't got a chance." Uncle Sidney did not appreciate Mr. Harris calling him "Sid," and would mutter, "No respect, that man, no respect at all." Respect, Uncle Sidney explained to young George, was very important. It didn't matter if you were *Mister* Churchill the Prime Minister or *Mister* Tomkins the air-raid warden; you were *Mister* Somebody doing his job and defending The Realm. For some reason, though, in all other contexts it was quite all right to call Mr. Churchill "Winnie." So, along with the dusk patrols, the interruptions at school for air-raid alerts, and the occasional hunt for German pilots who were rumoured to have been shot down nearby, George and his friends played their way through the war. In fact, it was not so much fun afterwards: there seemed to be even less to eat, and people didn't seem as friendly any more. But ever since those dark but glorious days the words of his uncle resonated in his head: "Never forget, George: hold your head up high and people will call you *Mister* Tomkins."

Maybe it was the daydreaming about his childhood or the soothing effect of the tea that caused George to doze off, but he suddenly woke up with a start realizing that he had slept—not, if he was honest, for the first time—through the entire race. He looked at his watch. It was already past five o'clock and time to go down to the pub and catch up on the latest news from Mr. Jakes. George took his mug and plate into the kitchen and gave them a quick rinse. Attired in his blue windcheater and trusty old tweed cap, he stepped out of his house and set out for the pub. He liked to cut across the village heath to reach the high street. It was a lovely April afternoon. Rays of sun splayed out in ephemeral golden bands over the distant green hills, and as the clouds rolled across the sky a shadowgraph of patterns played out their silent theatre across the secluded fields bordering the village. The yellow flowers of the gorse bushes added to the brightness of his mood, and the brambles held the promise of summer plenty. Maybe Mrs. Winter would make a batch of her delicious wild blackberry jam and give him a pot. "Oh to be in England, Now that April's here." Or was it: "Now that April's there"? Today, George couldn't quite remember the exact line of the poem, but it didn't matter. It was just a glorious April afternoon in the English countryside. Maybe he could hear a chaffinch singing, or maybe it was a thrush. Mary knew all the birdsongs. But now George used to joke, albeit with a twinge of sadness, he couldn't tell the difference between a barn owl and a foghorn. He liked to hum as he walked along. On such a beautiful day as this, as he crossed the village heath, it might be the pastoral theme from Beethoven's Sixth or, if he was in a patriotic mood or had won a game of darts at the pub, it might be Land of Hope and Glory.

As George walked along the village high street he gave a nod and a wave to Mrs. Baxter talking to Mrs. Patel outside the Newsagent's. George also gave a touch of his cap in a mock salute to old Mr. Smythe who, it seemed, would never forgive George for beating him at the village's homegrown tomato competition for three years in a row. Across the street there was Mrs. Arno. Such a nice young woman—a pity about her husband—with her pretty little daughter clutching a teddy bear. "Look," he could hear Mrs. Arno say, "there's Mr. Tomkins. Wave to Mr. Tomkins," and they would exchange exaggerated waves across the street. These walks through the village and all the little social exchanges and polite greetings were very important and life affirming to George. The village was his family. He knew almost everyone and they all knew him. Well, in the old village at least. There was a new development on the south side; mainly a younger crowd that worked at a nearby industrial park, and he rarely ran into them. They had a modern pub. Called itself a gastro pub. Tommy Smithers, landlord of the Golden Crow, kept things simple with a nice Ploughman's and sausage rolls. He explained that gastro pub food was just pub grub tarted up. Bangers and mash were now *artisan* sausages with *horseradish* mashed potatoes. Mr. Jakes had snorted in derision at this information. He was perfectly happy with good old bangers and mash and a little Coleman's mustard with his bangers, thank you very much.

There was certainly a lot of news in the village at the moment. The new resident of the "Big House" was the topic on everybody's lips. The last owner had been some Arab prince, or so Mr. Jakes had claimed. They never saw him, just his Rolls Royce that would occasionally sweep through the village. Then, apparently, his father—an even bigger prince—had been assassinated and suddenly the young prince and his Rolls Royce disappeared. "No great loss," Mr. Jakes had declared. It was rumored that the young prince had wanted to give an enormous sum of money to the church—a matter the vicar had refused to discuss with anyone. Apparently, the new man was a real gentleman: Sir George Stanmark, no less, a former Tory MP. He was reputed to be very rich. But then there was nothing wrong with old money, was there? However, Mr. Jakes, a firm disciple of the "where there's brass there's muck" school of thought, maintained that the money wasn't so old and that Sir George had made his pile in the construction business, and that his father had been a Polish railway worker called Stanimarski. George's opinion was very different: he surmised that the name's origin was from the French Saint-Marc, probably originating with a knight who had come over with William the Conqueror. Then there was Sir George's wife: a general's niece, no less. A real lady. The poor soul was now confined to a wheelchair—something to do with a hip operation that had gone wrong. Or so Mrs. Briggs claimed the vicar's wife had told her. But Sir George absolutely doted on his wife and would always push her wheelchair himself. There was no doubt about it, Sir George and his wife would be a great addition to the village. Mrs. Jakes had heard that he had already invited the vicar and Colonel Potter over for sherry, was absolutely charming, and very keen on gardening.

As George walked home from the pub that evening he thought about the new resident. Definitely the right sort of person to have in the Big House. He looked forward to meeting him, probably after church tomorrow. He knew exactly how to address him: "Sir George, how nice to meet you." One had to get the "Sir George" just right: friendly but respectful, but definitely not obsequious. A man knighted by the Queen certainly commanded respect, but then so did he. They might even start a little conversation. George could talk easily with virtually anyone on all sorts of topics: the weather, the Royal Family, gardening—especially the secret of growing good tomatoes—books, and so on. He was, after all, a popular and respected man in the village and there was no reason why he and Sir George shouldn't hit it off. Perhaps, before long, Sir George would also invite him over for sherry. Why, they both had the same Christian name; they were practically related! Enough of this daydreaming! George turned his mind to tomorrow: not only was there church, but things to do in the garden, and he had promised Mrs. Peterson to fix her drain with the little contraption he had designed to stop it from clogging up with leaves. Very simple really: just a couple of old clothes hangers and some wire mesh. But now "Mr. Tomkins' invention" was becoming quite the rage around the village and the vicar wanted him to fix up all the drains in the churchyard.

It was a lovely Sunday morning: bright but brisk, and it reminded George of all those Sundays, long ago, that he and Mary had walked to church together. Sir George was there, maybe arriving a trifle late, but nobly wheeling his wife's chair. As the service got underway the immutable security of the village church, its cool stone walls and the soft light, pastel shaded by the few remaining stained-glass windows, was often a place of introspection for George—at least in the summer. In the winter it was more a matter of trying to stay warm. Church had been an integral part of George's upbringing. Grace was said before every meal; they went to church every Sunday; his uncle liked saying, "Thou shalt not"; and his aunt would often sing Onward Christian Soldiers to herself when washing up in the kitchen. But there was never any talk about religion itself. And, despite George's inquisitive nature, that didn't really seem to matter. It was that strong sense of order and community he had grown up with that so appealed to him, and it was exactly the way Mary had felt too. They went to church every Sunday, and standing next to each other they would exchange secret little smiles as they sang their favorite hymns like Rock of Ages and Onward Christian Soldiers. After Mary had died George went through a phase of worrying about the meaning of it all and tried to discuss Salvation and the Eucharist with the vicar, who seemed rather uncomfortable and vague when talking theology. That was the old vicar. He was rather stiff, and privately George thought that he was a bit of a snob. But maybe he was just old school. Mr. Hamlin didn't like the old vicar one bit. Thought he was too High Church. But then Mr. Hamlin, who didn't really like anybody, didn't approve of the current vicar either. Thought he was too modern—apparently because he sometimes wore jeans on the weekend. But George liked the new man and particularly liked his wife for whom he was an eager helper in her church and village projects. She well understood that there was little a sociable but lonely widower wouldn't do in exchange for a cup of tea and a few minutes of friendly conversation. It took her more than a year to persuade him to call her Rachel.

At the end of the service, George took up his customary station by the church door to exchange pleasantries with the vicar's wife and shake hands with members of the congregation as they trooped out. Many of them were old friends and long-time residents of the village: Mrs. Peterson, Mr. and Mrs. Briggs, the Baxters, Mrs. Winter, old Mr. Smythe, and Mr. Hamlin who, despite his reservations about the vicar, was a regular. If nothing else the sermons were something for him to complain about when they met at the pub. George was sorry that Mrs. Arno had stopped coming to church, but after her husband had been arrested for drunk and disorderly he could quite understand. Recently George had become more aware that his fellow worshippers were becoming an ever-smaller group. Just one of the many reminders that times were changing and that they were all getting older.

Sir George seemed to be engaged in conversation with Colonel Potter at the back of the church and was one of the last to come out. At a distance, Sir George cut an impressive figure: smartly dressed, tall and tanned with a square jaw, and a full head of carefully groomed grey hair.

"Good morning, Sir George. Good morning, Lady Rowena," enthused the vicar. "So good to see you," and turning towards Mr. Tomkins, "I would like to introduce you to Mr. Tomkins. One of the real stalwarts of our little congregation."

Sir George put out his hand. "Ah, yes, Tomkins. And, Vicar, we'll be seeing you for sherry this evening?"

George's carefully rehearsed, "Sir George, how nice to meet you" disintegrated into a strangled cough as he shook the offered hand. The vicar, sensing something was wrong, quickly ushered Sir George and Lady Rowena down the path towards the gate and called over his shoulder, "Good-bye, Mr. Tomkins. Do drop by soon to discuss the church drains with me."

"Mr. Tomkins did seem strangely put out this morning when I introduced him to Sir George, didn't you think, my dear?" the vicar said to his wife later that day.

"Dear old Mr. Tomkins," came the reply.

"Ah, yes, Tomkins. Ah, yes, Tomkins" reverberated in George's head as he walked home from church. Damn the man. How dare he call him "Tomkins" as though he was the butler? No respect, no respect *what so ever*. It was "*Mister* Tomkins," definitely "*Mister* Tomkins." It all brought back terrible and very private memories of the day his Mary had died. Dear, sweet, Mary. She couldn't have hurt a fly even if she had tried. They had been so perfect together. On Sundays, when they would get ready for church, she would always pick his tie for him, "a nice cheerful one," and straighten the knot after he had tied it. They would walk together to church, arm in arm, and everybody would say to themselves, or so George liked to think, "Such a nice couple." In the privacy of their home, one of their favorite pastimes was to read to each other—especially Dickens, and *David Copperfield* was their special story. Mary would lovingly address George as "Mr. Tomkins," and he in turn would call her "Mrs. Tomkins." Then one day, she suddenly retired to bed with a terrible headache that got worse and worse until she was in such pain that he called an ambulance and she was rushed to hospital. There were X-rays, talk of brain tumors, an emergency operation, and that interminable wait while she was in the operating theatre. Then a tired and grim-faced surgeon came out of the theatre and whispered something to the doctor. The doctor came over to George and said, "I'm sorry, Tomkins. It was too late. There was nothing we could do to save her." His manner was kindly enough, but why didn't he call him "Mr. Tomkins"? After all, he was always "Mr. Tomkins" to Mary. The doctor had a slightly patronizing manner and reddish face. Those were terrible days. George remembered getting ready for the funeral and tying his black tie. It was at that point that he almost collapsed as he realized that she would never be there to straighten the knot for him again. But then, suddenly, it was as if an invisible hand did straighten it for him and a voice seemed to say, "It will be all right, Mr. Tomkins, it really will." And that was how he got through that day and, indeed, on every Sunday she was always there to straighten his tie before church. And now Sir George had to come along and stir up all those memories. The wretched jumped-up Polish construction worker! Mr. Jakes was probably right after all. Now hold your horses, George: you're overreacting. Probably Sir George was concerned about getting Lady Rowena's wheelchair down that awkward step by the church door. Yes, that must have been it. Such a heavy personal burden; how he sympathized. There must have been times during his great loss when he, too, had forgotten the niceties. No, no, Sir George was fully exonerated. Next Sunday he would make sure he helped Sir George with the wheelchair down the church step, and before you could say "Jack Robinson," they would be sipping sherry together.

The rest of the day, after that brief upset, turned out very satisfactorily. Mrs. Peterson was delighted with his invention and gave him tea with his favorite lemon sponge cake, "Baked specially for you, Mr. Tomkins." Bless her. She was one of the older Church Ladies, as he liked to call them— a group with whom he was a great favorite. It would be difficult to think of a Sunday when there wasn't a teatime welcome for him at one of their homes. In the first few years after Mary had died they were a great source of comfort. They missed their departed friend almost as much as he missed his wife. However, there was that awkward time with the widowed Mrs. Henry who became a little overzealous in her acts of consolation. She started to make it clear that her intentions were more than those of a friend. "It's not right that you should spend the rest of your life alone, Mr. Tomkins. An eligible widower like yourself should think about marrying again." It all started to make him feel very uncomfortable. In the end he had to say, and he had thought very carefully about how to say it, "To love once is enough, Mrs. Henry. Let us not discuss these matters any more, if you don't mind." Firm but polite, that was the way to deal with the situation. A little while later she left the village to live nearer her grandchildren. There was, he suspected, a little gossip at the time but that was all long forgotten. If Mary had been his Dora there was never an Agnes to take her place, and he was quite content with his role in the village as an eligible, but unobtainable, widower.

That evening, after a light supper of a ham salad made with his famous homegrown tomatoes, George settled down with the *Time Literary Supplement*. Some of the articles did seem to go on a bit too much about things that didn't really seem to have anything to do with the book under review. Well, that was scholarship for you. Despite almost a lifetime involved with books, he would never claim himself to be a literary man, but thanks to dear old Mr. Lasky he certainly knew a thing or two about books.

My goodness, what a day for reminiscences, he thought as he put the paper aside and started to think back to the beginnings of his career in books. George had finished school at the age of sixteen. The Headmaster's final report described him as "Quite bright but too much of a day-dreamer. Needs to learn not to ask so many questions." His Uncle Sidney insisted that he work at the Post Office. "Keep up the family tradition," he had told George. But George was never happy in his clerical job, and after a few years he left the Post Office and found a job at the local public library. His uncle was unhappy about the move, although since the end of the war there didn't seem to be much that he was happy about. "The Post Office not good enough for you? It's a very respectable job, you know. Why should anyone want to be surrounded by books all day?" But Aunt Betty took George's side, and after a while his uncle seemed to accept the fact that he would be the only Tomkins taking care of Her Majesty's Mail. In fact, he would sometimes drop by the library "just to make sure things are all right." Checking up on things was very important to Uncle Sidney and the little library visits seemed to make him happy—a little bit like the good old days when he was the air-raid warden.

George was very content at the library. He liked the quiet formality of it all. It was so satisfying to help somebody find a book and he would always ask if they enjoyed it when they returned it. He would remember their comments and pass them on to other readers. "A good plot with a dramatic twist," or "A moving story, very sensitive." These useful morsels of advice soon earned him the reputation of being both helpful and well read. Mr. Lasky, the chief librarian, patted him on the shoulder and told him to keep up the good work. George quickly learnt the names of the regulars and would enjoy addressing them personally: "How did you enjoy the Maugham, Mrs. Jenkins?" This personal touch earned him the reputation of being "a most pleasant young man," and Mr. Lasky patted him on the shoulder and told him that he was a credit to the library. At first George was rather intimidated by Mr. Lasky: a short stocky man with a foreign accent who always came to work in a heavy and rather worn three-piece suit and bow tie. Miss Crisp, the assistant librarian—a thin, plain woman who wore her greying hair in a bun and whose tight-lipped little smile spoke of a life unfulfilled—explained to George that Mr. Lasky was a wartime refugee who had lost all his family during the war and, in confidential tones, told George that Mr. Lasky was a Jewish gentleman. George was fascinated by this piece of intelligence since he had never actually met a Jew in person before, and as far as he knew, neither had his aunt and uncle. When he told Aunt Betty and Uncle Sidney this revelation over high tea his aunt looked at him rather blankly, and his uncle simply said, without looking up from his ham salad, "There's nothing wrong with the Jews." However, his uncle did not feel the same way about the Catholics and, while generally not given to merriment, always took great pleasure in Guy Fawkes Night. Every year he would organize a bonfire and a few fireworks for the children in their street and, every year, remind George of the dastardly papal plot to blow up Parliament. It also gave him the opportunity to put on his old air-raid warden's helmet again—for safety reasons, of course.

After he had been at the Library for a few months, Mr. Lasky had asked George a question about his parents. On learning that he had been orphaned at the age of three, Mr. Lasky looked at George with an infinitely sad smile and, just for a moment, his eyes seemed to moisten. After that, Mr. Lasky took a kindly interest in George and would recommend books for him to read, starting with Dickens and Kipling, and then Austen and Eliot, and lots of Shakespeare. George was never happier than in the evenings after tea, sitting in the family living room by the gas fire while his aunt knitted and his uncle snoozed, reading Mr. Lasky's recommendations.

Nonetheless, after a few years George started to feel that something was missing. His more outgoing side started to feel hemmed in by the hushed ambiance of the library. One couldn't really *talk* with the people who came in. One could certainly pass a brief comment on a given book and wish them "Good day," but a library was not the place for a good natter. It was, above all, a place where peoples' quiet was to be respected. Still, he would never complain about his job at the library for a very special reason. Just around the corner from the back entrance was a little tobacconist and sweetshop where he would normally stop off twice a week to buy two tubes of Polo mints. And that was where he had met his beloved Mary who worked behind the counter. She seemed so shy and unaware of his interest in her. After a while, she realized that he couldn't be coming in *every* day just to buy a tube of mints. They used to laugh a lot about that afterwards. Of course she had noticed him too, although at one point she wasn't sure if she wanted to go out with somebody who ate so many mints. She encouraged George to look for another job, and he still remembered the excitement and anxiety he felt when he saw the advertisement by Crumb and McKenzie for a "Bright and presentable young man with interest in books." They were the finest bookshop in town and a job there would be so respectable, as well as offering "good prospects." With a job like that he could hold his head up high and ask a girl to marry him. Mr. Lasky seemed happy that George had found someone and wanted the chance to move on, and he wrote George a strong letter of recommendation.

George had worked at Crumb and McKenzie for almost forty years. He knew it would soon be time to retire, but he liked the idea of waiting until he had completed his forty years—a really good innings. He was, by far, the company's longest-serving employee. It was something to be proud of. A couple of years ago he had overheard the previous manager, who left to have a baby and then decided not to come back, describe him to the man from the head office as a "permanent fixture." At first George wasn't sure if he liked that description. It made him feel like an old coat hook on which customers could hang their memories of yesteryear. On the other hand it made him feel indispensable: the Rock of Gibraltar of

Crumb and McKenzie. Yes, he was Mr. George Tomkins AR, RoG. There had been so many changes since he first started working there. Mr. Crumb had already retired when George started, and Mr. McKenzie died a few years later and was succeeded by his son-in-law. Eventually the son-in-law sold the business and now they were part of a big chain with a head office in London. But they always kept the original shop name because, as the man from the head office had told the employees, it made the customers feel that they were shopping in a family-run business—a notion that helped create a nice personal atmosphere. Now George was the assistant manager and, despite all the extra responsibilities, was as happy there as he had been when he first started. The current manager was a young man called Nigel, who would usually come to work dressed in black. Nigel insisted that the staff all be on first-name terms. The two girls who now worked there wore short skirts and streaked their hair. One of them had a small tattoo on her ankle. They always giggled when George talked to them. Sometimes, when they came to work on Monday mornings, they looked a bit hung over, but he was sure that they were good girls really. How things had changed since the days of Mr. Lasky and Miss Crisp at the library.

The times of year that George enjoyed the most were around Christmas and the summer holidays. People needed advice on what to take for their holiday reading or what to buy as a present. Giving advice, especially about books, was something he was very good at. When a customer came into the shop he could tell at fifteen feet if they were a P. D. James or a Jeffery Archer. After a while, George had quite a devoted following of customers who would always come in and ask for him by name. After their holidays they would sometimes come by and thank him for his reading suggestions, and he would usually be treated to a little bit of their holiday gossip. It made him feel that he was almost part of their families.

Of course, the book business, along with so many other things, had changed a lot over the years. It used to be mainly detective stories, biographies, and Victorian romances. Now people seemed to be writing books on everything, and everything always seemed to have something to do with sex—or so it seemed nowadays. But then times were changing, and George prided himself on being a man who knew how to change with the times. He remembered how he was one of the first, if not the first, person in the village to change to the *Independent*. He used to take the *Times*, although it was never quite the same after they started putting news on the front page. When Mrs. Snyder, who was one of his bookshop regulars, first quoted a book review from the *Independent* George felt a bit put out. But after a while he decided to investigate the new paper for himself. It was important, of course, to do these things discreetly, so he bought a copy every day for a week when he was in town and read it during his lunch break. It was a little extravagant having the *Times* delivered to his home in the village and then buying another paper at the same time. But then he didn't want to give Mr. Patel, the newsagent, something to gossip about. By the end of the week George had decided to change papers. He planned his strategy very carefully. The next time he went to the newsagent to buy a tube of mints he said, very casually, as Mr. Patel was counting out the change, "Perhaps you could be so kind as to change me over to the *Independent* next week, Mr. Patel." Mr. Patel was obviously a bit taken aback by this unexpected move and could only say, "The *Independent* … yes, Mr. Tomkins," without any additional comments, and Mr. Patel was a great one for gratuitous comments. Just as George had planned: quiet, polite, but incisive—that was the way to do things. Of course, Mr. Patel got his revenge. A couple of weeks later when George was in the store, Mr. Patel said, in a rather loud voice, "Enjoying the *Independent* I hope, Mr. Tomkins?" With Mrs. Rogers and Mrs. Jakes in the store the news was as good as public property. But within a couple of months Dr. Jacobs and the vicar had also changed newspapers, and George acquired the reputation of being something of a trendsetter. One way or another, whether it was changing to the *Independent* then, or his little invention for stopping leaves clogging up drains now, he was always making a contribution to the life of the village, and it seemed difficult to believe that Sir George wouldn't find him as personable as everybody else.

The next Sunday soon came round, and George was at his customary station by the church door next to the vicar's wife when Sir George came out with Lady Rowena in her wheelchair. After a brief but hearty exchange with the vicar, Sir George, who for some reason hadn't noticed George, started to push the chair over the steps. George stepped forward and, with a pleasant smile, put out his hand to steady the chair.

"Quite all right, Tomkins, no need," came the brusque response, and Sir George twisted the chair away and down the steps.

George all but staggered as he followed Sir George out of the churchyard. He felt as though he had been kicked in the teeth. "Quite all right, Tomkins, no need." No need, indeed! Next it would be "Carry on, Tomkins," and "That will be all for now, Tomkins." If he had been impressed by Sir George's appearance at their first meeting, now George saw the man's small cold eyes, the red veins in his cheeks, and the supercilious edge to his smile. The man was not a gentleman: he had no respect for other people. It was war! Quite how he would wage his war with this titled member of the landed gentry he wasn't sure, but win he would. If his Uncle Sidney could stand up to Hitler, George could certainly stand up to Sir George. Yes, on the village green, in the village store, at the Golden Crow, he would fight on. He would never surrender.

Despite his anger at Sir George, the following week passed pleasantly enough and nothing could dull the excitement George felt as Saturday approached. This was his day for going up to Town. These occasional day trips to London were a great source of pleasure, and on the Friday evening he started to make preparations for the next day's adventure. He gave his shoes a brisk polish. These were his "town shoes" with stout soles that were good for walking but with a smart design in a dark-brown leather that made them respectable enough for going into the posh shops. Suede shoes were definitely not appropriate. He then ironed his favorite cotton twill shirt with the light check pattern and put out his wool tie with a quiet red-and-brown weave. Normally, he would wear his blue windcheater: a sensible thing, with all those extra pockets, for an outing up to Town. This time though, just for a change, he would wear his brown tweed jacket. Yes, he would look quite the country gentleman. He then packed his shoulder bag, a blue British Airways bag he had bought at last year's jumble sale, with last week's *TLS* to finish reading on the train, a small pack of Kleenex, and an extra tube of mints. He gave his jacket a good brushing. He was all set for tomorrow. Definitely a bacon-and-eggs breakfast with an extra rasher of bacon for energy.

Of course, these trips were not only for pleasure. There was, he liked to think, their professional side. George liked to look in at the big bookshops to see their holiday displays and new stock. This would sometimes provide ideas for the displays at Crumb and McKenzie. When discussing this with Nigel, he enjoyed being able to describe, in a casual sort of way, what he had seen in some of the London bookshops. Nigel appeared to be impressed by this. "Go up to London often, do you, George?" and George would give a little smile projecting, he hoped, the air of a man with a secret life. But above all, there was just the thrill of being in London itself, not that he would want to live there himself. Yes, London was still the heart of the Empire, even if the Empire didn't really exist anymore. To see the Houses of Parliament, Buckingham Palace and, if there was time, a visit to the Victoria and Albert Museum was somehow very reassuring. His itinerary would always start with a brisk walk across Green Park to Buckingham Palace and then along the Mall past Clarence House. As much as he respected the Queen—and she certainly did a magnificent job—it was the Queen Mother who had his heart. Good old Queen Mum! What with the shocking death of Diana, and the antics of some of the other Royals, where would they all be without her? Walking past Clarence House, come rain or shine, was his personal act of homage. If he had a hat on he would doff it as he passed by the gates, and if he wasn't wearing one he would make a discreet bow as he passed by. Maybe one day he might actually see her as she came out. Once, a big limousine had swept out of the gates when he was about fifty feet away, and he thought he caught a glimpse of a flowery hat; but then a group of Japanese tourists got in the way and he couldn't be sure anymore. To actually see the Queen Mother in the flesh and wave to her would be a moment to remember. Maybe, just maybe, he might even meet her in person. It would probably be on a Royal Visit to the village or to Crumb and McKenzie although, as he sometimes had to remind himself, it was all very unlikely. Nonetheless, she would be introduced to him and would say, "How are you today, Mr. Tomkins?" and he would reply, "Very well indeed, thank you, your Royal Highness." Then she might say, "Such nice weather today," and he would reply, "A perfect day, Ma'am." It was most important to get the protocol exactly right: "Your Royal Highness," on the first verbal exchange and then "Ma'am" for any subsequent exchanges. It really was very important to know these things. If the meeting took place in the village he might even have the opportunity to present her with a basket of his famous home-grown tomatoes and she would say, "Thank you very much indeed, Mr. Tomkins," and he would reply, "An honour and a pleasure, Ma'am." Of course none of this would ever happen, but he so liked the idea that he would sometimes replay the scene in his head and could almost hear the village brass band playing patriotic tunes in the background.

"Thank you very much indeed, Mr. Tomkins."

"An honour and a pleasure, Ma'am."

Yes, if the Queen Mother could address him as "*Mister* Tomkins", then Sir George had to. There was absolutely no excuse.

George finished his rounds of the bookshops at Hatchards. After examining the displays of new books his usual ploy was to ask an assistant for some obscure title or an out-of-print book. This usually necessitated the manager being called in to help. George would then start up a little conversation, casually dropping a few remarks that would reveal, to the astute listener, that he was in the trade himself. He wasn't too impressed with Hatchards' selection this year, and the assistant had been able to answer all his questions easily, if not a little curtly, or so it seemed. He left the store and found himself wandering rather aimlessly around the nearby side streets. Maybe he would take the tube back to King's Cross a little earlier than necessary and give himself time to have a cup of tea and a Kit Kat at the station. George started to feel a few drops of rain and, looking up, saw that the sky had suddenly turned very dark. Within moments, the drops had turned into torrents, and he found himself running for shelter, which he quickly found under a nearby hotel entrance. It was very crowded and people were jostling for taxis. A strong gust of wind seemed to push the little crowd up against the revolving doors of the hotel and before he knew it he found himself propelled into the hotel lobby.

It was as though he had been transported into a different world. In one corner of the lobby a young woman was playing a harp, and in clusters of overstuffed armchairs and settees sat little groups of people having afternoon tea.

A crisply dressed waitress came up to him and said, "How many will there be for tea, sir?"

George was quite taken aback and found himself saying "Just one, thank you very much," when he really wanted to say, "I'm going to get a cup of tea and a Kit Kat at King's Cross, thank you."

Suddenly there he was, sitting in an armchair in what must have been one of the smartest hotels in London, being handed an elegant tea menu as though he were a respected member of the aristocracy. He looked at the menu. There was a selection of teas to choose from: Earl Grey, Darjeeling, Jasmine … finger sandwiches, toasted crumpets, and a choice of cakes. All included at one price. The price! It was outrageous! So that was how the rich spent their money. At that instant he could understand why Mr. Jakes always voted for the Labour party. But what was he to do? He could see the waitress approaching his chair to take his order, and it really wouldn't do at all to say that he had just come in to escape the rain and was on his way to King's Cross to get a cup of tea and a Kit Kat. George could see himself being escorted out of the hotel and the assembled tea-drinkers looking at him pityingly and barely suppressing their snickers.

No, it was time for bold action. He had been in tighter spots than this. He would stay and have tea! He would have to make some economies next week. He would have to do without the piece of salmon he liked to have on the week-ends. Mr. Cheetah, the fishmonger, two shops down from Crumb and McKenzie, would always have it ready for him to pick up on his way home on Friday afternoons. He would have to drop by and say that he was trying a little change of routine for the next week. It might be a little embarrassing, but there was nothing he could do about that. Yes, tea at a smart hotel. It would be an experience. He could tell Mrs. Peterson about it and then reassure her that nobody could beat her lemon sponge cake, "Not even the best hotels in London, I can assure you." And, of course, Mrs. Snyder would appreciate it. She was always going up to London and had probably had tea there herself.

Soon George was drinking tea out of an elegant china cup and watching the world, a completely different world, about him. On the one hand, there was the genteel calm of the tea-drinkers: hotel guests of many different nationalities, smart London ladies getting together for a tea-time chat, well-dressed businessmen indulging in boardroom intrigues over afternoon tea, and a group of veiled Arab women surrounded by piles of Harrods' shopping bags. On the other hand, at the front of the lobby, there was the hustle and bustle of arriving and departing guests and uniformed doormen carrying large quantities of expensive-looking luggage. Thinking of luggage, he suddenly realized that his blue plastic British Airways shoulder bag must have looked a little out of place, and he surreptitiously slid it under his chair. There was clearly a romance about hotel lobbies: a "microcosm of life" as the book reviewers were so fond of saying. George discreetly beckoned to a passing waitress for some more hot water. While he was here he was certainly going to make the most of it. Of course, it would be very impolite to stare at everybody, so he slipped his copy of the TLS out of the shoulder bag and pretended to read it as he peeped around at the exotic new world he had stumbled into. He was having a wonderful time and felt completely at home in these salubrious surroundings. People would probably assume that he was a country gentleman having tea while waiting for his chauffeur to collect him. He was very pleased that he had decided to wear his tweed jacket that day.

After a while, George became aware of the couple on the settee behind him. It would be rather rude to turn round and look directly at them, but when he had summoned the waitress he had caught a glimpse of a blond head close to a grey one—almost certainly an American couple on holiday. The man was probably one of those corporate executive types with a new young wife. Then he heard the woman giggle and the man laugh. There was something familiar about the laugh. By looking at the reflections in the many mirrors around the lobby George realized he could get a good look at them without them seeing him. Incredible: the man was Sir George! What a coincidence! But who on earth was that blond and very pretty young woman with him? Maybe it was his daughter. But as far as anybody in the village knew, Sir George and Lady Rowena didn't have any children. It must be a niece, then. But you didn't put your hand on your niece's knee like that. It was a floozy! Well, well, well. Sir George—member of the so-called gentry, former Tory MP, devoted husband and keen gardener—was nothing more than a good for nothing womanizer having a tea-time assignation in a London hotel while poor Lady Rowena was suffering at home. One should have known from the start that the man was up to no good. By the time George had finished with him, Sir George Stanmark would be very sorry that he had failed to address him as "*Mister* Tomkins." Their war had only begun last week but now a swift and bloodless victory was assured. All that was required was a strategy. He could go over to him and say, "Good afternoon, Sir George. What a surprise seeing you here." But that would be too obvious. Or he could make sure they passed each other in the lobby and give Sir George a conspiratorial wink. But that would be too sneaky. No, he would just walk past him with a cheery, "Good afternoon, Sir George," as though they were casual city acquaintances who often ran into each other at places like that. That was the way to do it: discreet but effective. What a military man might term a surgical strike.

Sir George visibly blanched as George's salutation swept past him, and George could just catch the scoundrel say to his young companion, "Just a friend from the city." Revenge was so sweet and victory was almost complete. Tomorrow, after church, it would be match point. He could hardly wait. It would be game, set, and match, George Tomkins. It would be Tomkins United, ten, Stanmark City, nil; an overwhelming victory. On the train journey home he couldn't stop humming Land of Hope and Glory.

Despite the anticipation of victory, George slept soundly that night, just as Monty had done on the eve of El Alamein.

Standing by the vicar outside the church door the next day he waited for Sir George to emerge. After what seemed like an eternity, the man came out of the church pushing his wife's wheelchair.

"Good morning, Sir George," beamed the vicar.

George's perfect moment of triumph had come. "Good morning, Sir George," he said in exactly the same cheery tone that he had used the previous afternoon at the hotel. He could see his greeting resonate on Sir George's face.

There was the usual hearty handshake with the vicar and an apparent ignoring of Mr. Tomkins. Then just as he started to turn away Sir George said to the vicar, "Sherry as usual, Vicar?" and then, after clearing his throat, "Perhaps you would care to join us too, Mr. Tomkins?"

"It would be a pleasure, Sir George."

NON FINITO

Nicholas was glad he had gone to the restaurant for an early dinner that evening. Fridays were always a popular night. The combination of locals and tourists made for a busy time at the many dining spots around the plaza, and there was already a line of people queuing up at the restaurant's reception desk, hoping for a table. He looked around at the seemingly timeless theatre of a typical holiday restaurant. A romantic young couple toasting each other with sparkling eyes and sparkling wine in anticipation of a night to remember and, in all likelihood, quickly forgotten. Stressed-out parents for whom the family vacation was turning into an endurance test as they tried to keep a semblance of order among their restless and sunburnt children. And middle-aged couples eating in either stony silence or silent communion, and for whom the narrow twin beds in their cramped hotel rooms provided a convenient cover for their state of marital stalemate. At one time or another he had been an actor in all those scenes himself. He smiled to himself at the rather horrible thought that he might yet appear in the scene being played out at the table next to him.

A foursome of two older couples: the two women, oblivious of their husbands, were deeply engrossed in conversation; while the two men, red-cheeked, pot-bellied and equally oblivious of their wives, were engrossed in their food—their last remaining legal pleasure. Like twin pigs at the trough they were sharing a tureen of *soupe de poisson*, and in a well-practiced holy ritual, they took little rounds of toast, carefully spread them with garlic *aioli*, topped them with pyramids of grated cheese, and launched their little boats of gastronomic delight onto the thick, saffron-tinted sea.

Over many years of solo business trips Nicholas had learned how to enjoy eating at restaurants by himself. This was no small skill: it was easy to look foolish or lonely, or both. While eating, he acquired the studious air of one totally absorbed in the task (this could lead the causal observer to think he might be a food critic). While not eating, he would look around with the relaxed air of a man of affairs taking a break from a busy day (this could lead the casual observer to think, correctly, that he was a successful businessman). When the waiter came by, he would engage in light-hearted banter in fluent French (this could lead the casual observer to think he might be a local personality). And at the end of a meal he might savor a brandy—gone were the good old days when one could smoke a cigar—with the air of a sensuous man-of-the-world. Well, that was the idea at least, and despite these little flights of fantasy he suspected that he looked just like who he was: a middle-aged English businessman on holiday in Nice.

After looking at the menu and exchanging a few empty pleasantries with the waiter he ordered the *rillettes*, followed by a steak, and a rather expensive bottle of Bordeaux. Putting aside the copy of *Art & Antiques* he had brought to look at over dinner, he left his table and walked into the restaurant to the men's room behind the kitchen—a near bedlam that resonated with frenetic shouts and clattering dishes, and smells of fish. As he came back outside he crossed paths with his waiter who was striding back into the kitchen.

The waiter smiled at him in a slightly conspiratorial way. "Ah, Monsieur, you did not tell me you had guests this evening. I have seated them and laid their places."

Nicholas was speechless. He had no guests, but he also had no waiter to question further, only the swing of the kitchen doors. Full of curiosity, he walked slowly back to his table to see who his "guests" might be. Sitting at the table was a dark-haired woman and a dark-haired young girl, maybe six or seven years old. The girl was holding a rag doll and leaning towards the woman who was showing her the menu. Madonna and child or Siren sisters? He walked quietly up to his chair and stood there silently. The woman looked up at him with bright, dark eyes and gave him a dazzling smile.

"It was so busy in the plaza tonight. We saw you dining by yourself and Cathy chose you, didn't you sweetheart?"

The little girl looked up with an equally bewitching smile. "No, it was Ariadne who chose you," and she lifted the doll in his direction.

He didn't know which surprised him more: the charm of their little ploy, or the fact that a six-year-old girl would name her doll from Greek mythology. Trying to look at ease, in a stern sort of way, he sat down.

"I know it's terribly wicked of us to do this, but with so many people here tonight and Cathy so hungry, I just decided to break the rules." And looking at him straight in the eyes, "I've never done anything like this before. I hope you'll forgive us."

Nicholas managed, just, not to burst out laughing at this little deceit and kept a straight face. If nothing else, it promised to be an entertaining evening. He smiled back. "Well, what are holidays for without meeting new people? Welcome to my table."

The waiter came over to the table with the approving smile of a Frenchman admiring an attractive woman. "Let me take Madame's order. And, Monsieur, I told the kitchen to hold yours so you can all eat together."

She ordered a salad and a steak, rare (carnivore or maybe opportunistic omnivore, Nicholas wondered to himself), and for the little girl she ordered the *moules*. The waiter poured the woman a glass of wine from the bottle Nicholas had ordered for himself earlier. She smiled at him, "You'll let me buy the wine, of course." After the waiter put down the bottle, she picked it up again and poured a little into the empty glass by Cathy and then topped it up with water. Nicholas could hear the waiter mutter, "*Magnifique*" as he walked off to his other tables. The woman, whoever she was,

was remarkable, but the little girl even more so: dolls from Greek mythology, wine, and *moules*. When his daughter was that age she had a pink bunny called BunBun, and could barely be persuaded to eat anything more than macaroni cheese and drink chocolate milk.

The woman gave another beautiful smile. "Cathy, we are so *rude*." The "rude" was said with a particular emphasis that set the little girl giggling. "You haven't introduced us to this nice man."

Susan. Cathy. Ariadne. Nicholas. The introductions were made and the conversation began. As Susan talked, Nicholas observed her closely. Her age was difficult to judge. She could have been anywhere from her late twenties to mid-thirties. She wasn't wearing any makeup except for a touch of lipstick, and she wore what looked like a tantric medallion around her neck. Her dark eyes were bright, lively, and slightly troubled. Although she beamed attentively at him when he was talking to her, he sometimes had the feeling that she was simultaneously glancing around the restaurant to see if there was anybody more useful to talk to. She and Cathy were from London. They were on holiday for a few weeks. She had seen an advertisement to share a summer rental in Nice with a couple of Australian women. She was a sculptor and was currently exhibiting two of her pieces at one of the smaller fringe galleries in London. She had, of course, noticed his magazine. She loved antiques and wished she were rich enough to collect them herself. When he told her that he was an art and antique dealer, she became particularly animated and displayed considerable knowledge about his specialty: artwork and furniture from the period of the English Romantic Movement, especially the paintings and etchings of Samuel Palmer. In fact, the conversation was fascinating, and the time slipped by rather quickly. This really was a captivating woman. Clearly very knowledgeable in the arts, unusually well-traveled (quite how she managed all this travel as a self-proclaimed impecunious artist, he couldn't quite fathom), amusing anecdotes interspersed with snippets of new-age claptrap, and a beautiful smile. At one point, when she turned her head, her profile—along with her dark hair and eyes—reminded him of Picasso's portrait of Dora Maar. Perhaps it was because that Cubist rendition showed both sides of the subject's face, and Nicholas wondered just how many sides there were to Susan's face. Her manner was warm and vivacious, and at no point did he sense that she was trying to flirt with him. He also had the sense that the appraisal was mutual. She had probably counted every one of his grey hairs and estimated his annual income to the nearest ten thousand pounds. As he sipped his coffee he turned to Cathy, who had spent most of the dinner intently playing with Ariadne and throwing captivating smiles at the other tables and passers-by.

"So, what do you like doing, Cathy?"

"I like having fun."

Susan cut in, "My father was a classics professor at the University of British Columbia." This was the first time she had made any real statement about her otherwise mysterious background. "When I was twelve he was already taking me to chamber concerts and endless museums. That's not the way for a young girl to grow up, so I make sure that Cathy and I always have fun together. Don't we, sweetheart?"

The little girl burst into giggles. "Oh yes, I love fun."

Suddenly Susan glanced at her watch, "My God, the time. We must run." She got up and looking Nicholas warmly in the eyes held out her hand.

"Nicholas, this has been delightful. I do hope you have forgiven us for gate-crashing your private party. Cathy, say good-bye to Nicholas."

Ariadne proffered a hand that he solemnly shook. He watched them walk off together hand in hand, and appraised Susan's hips and long, shapely legs encased in tightly fitting jeans. He wondered where it was they had to dash off to so suddenly.

The waiter came to his table. "Monsieur, *l'addition*."

Nicholas smiled to himself as he paid for all of them. Quite a pair of operators: maybe that's how they ate every evening.

Nicholas was sipping an espresso after lunch and had just asked the waiter to bring his bill. He looked out over the beachfront concession area in front of the bar and considered the slabs of meat, basting in suntan lotion, lying in neat rows on the wooden deckchairs. Some were rare and some were well done, some were lean and some were fat.

Despite the touristy aspects of Nice and the ever-increasing crowds that seemed to converge there every summer, he always enjoyed his brief holidays there and was enjoying his current visit after so many years' absence. At first he had gone there, long ago, with his parents, and then later with his wife and daughter. Although he could easily afford to stay at more exclusive resorts, Nice had a sentimental pull on him. Before this reverie could progress any further, there was Susan standing by his table.

"Nicholas, I am so embarrassed. I don't know what you must be thinking of us. Walking off last night without paying for our dinner and …" with a winning smile, "the wine!"

She was wearing a long sari-like skirt tied around her waist and a black bikini top. Her upper body was lean: flat stomach, small breasts, and all parts appeared to be deeply tanned. Before he could say anything, she picked up the bill the waiter had just put on his table, walked over to the bar, and with a few words of explanation in excellent French paid for his lunch. A quick and rather uncharitable mental calculation on Nicholas's part suggested that Susan had got a bargain: the cost of dinner last night was several times more than his lunch.

"Really, Susan, that was absolutely unnecessary. I really enjoyed your company last night. It was my pleasure."

"No, Nicholas, you must have thought we were a couple of con artists. When we got to our room and Cathy told me I had forgotten to pay, I almost died with embarrassment. Didn't I sweetheart?"

Cathy materialized wearing an almost identical outfit to Susan's. "We were so *naughty*." The "naughty" was said with the same emphasis as Susan's "rude" the previous evening, and Cathy set herself off into a bout of giggles.

"Well, let me reciprocate. Susan, please let me buy you a drink and young lady …" turning to Cathy, "let me buy you an *ice cream*," and he said "ice cream" with the same emphasis as her "naughty." Cathy giggled and suddenly gave him a hug before sitting down. Susan looked a little embarrassed, and there was a hint of sadness in her eyes.

"She's a very affectionate child. She just wants everybody to love her."

"I am sure everybody does."

After the drinks and ice cream they went down to the beach, and two deckchairs next to his miraculously became vacant for Susan and Cathy. After sunning themselves for a few minutes, they disappeared into the changing rooms and both reappeared wearing black, one-piece bathing suits. Nicholas could now see the full extent of Susan's long and well-shaped legs that, combined with the way she carried herself, made him suspect that she had had years of ballet training as a girl. Susan and Cathy went into the water and frolicked around as he sat and watched. They were clearly deeply connected: somewhere between mother and daughter and close sisters. He had noticed that Susan never referred to Cathy as "my daughter" and Cathy always addressed Susan as "Susan." He started to sketch some notes for an article he had been invited to write for *Art &*

Antiques. Eventually they came back from the water, wet and laughing, and Susan wrapped Cathy up in a large beach towel. Cathy immediately fell asleep, and Susan adjusted the umbrella to shade her from the sun. Looking at Cathy lying there strongly reminded Nicholas of his own daughter sleeping on a deckchair, maybe at exactly the same spot, all those years ago.

"You look very pensive, Nicholas."

"Looking at Cathy reminded me of my own daughter sleeping on the beach during our family holidays here many years ago."

"Nicholas, you never told me you had a daughter too."

Too. That was it: Madonna and child.

"Yes, I have a daughter. She's twenty and she's at university in America."

Susan looked at him questioningly, and he found himself telling her more about himself. "I often took my family with me on business trips to New York, and then we would go off and have a vacation in Yellowstone or somewhere. After Barbara saw her first black bear by the roadside, she fell in love with America and always insisted she would go and study there. At some amazingly expensive private school in New England, I might add. But she's happy there and lives quite close to my sister who married an American." For a man who was usually very private he felt he had already revealed a large amount of his personal history in those few sentences.

"And Barbara's mother?"

"She died in a car crash eight years ago."

"Oh Nicholas, that's terrible. That must have been a terrible blow."

"Yes."

She immediately picked up the curtness of his reply and changed the subject. "What are you writing?"

He told her about the article he was writing on the paintings and etchings of the Ancients, a group of followers of William Blake, and they fell into a long conversation about art and design. He was again struck, as he had been the previous evening, at her range of knowledge and originality of thought. The late afternoon sun crept over them like a warm, soft blanket being drawn up over a bed. Cathy stirred, opened her eyes and gave him an angelic smile. "I was asleep," she explained proudly.

"Nicholas, what are you doing tomorrow?"

"Nothing special, Susan. I was planning to spend most of the day here working on my article. Why?"

"I was thinking of taking Cathy for a picnic to Eze tomorrow. Why don't you join us? Do you have a car here?"

"Yes, I always rent a car."

"That's great. If you provide the transport, I'll provide the picnic."

"Picnic, picnic, I love picnics," Cathy chanted.

"I'd love to join you."

The next morning, they drove the short distance from Nice to the bottom of the famous hillside town and slowly walked up its winding streets to the top. They stopped about half way to browse, somewhat mindlessly, in some shops and sit at a café overlooking the sea for a leisurely cold drink. They reached the top and found a spot where they could sit and eat lunch. Susan spread out the contents of her colorful shoulder bag. Out of a plastic box came some miniature cold omelets stuffed with *ratatouille*—something she had apparently made early that morning—and out of another came little rounds of herb-studded *chevre* in extra virgin olive oil. There were black olives, *cornichon*, a baguette, perfectly ripe peaches, a half-bottle of expensive red wine, and the piece-de-resistance: a small bowl of wild strawberries.

"Susan, this is beautiful. You must have spent a fortune ... and the wild strawberries—they're my favorite."

"I knew they were."

"How?"

"Oh, one just knows these things."

He felt guilty about his thoughts of her freeloading after the dinner on Friday night and gently patted her shoulder. "You're quite remarkable, Susan."

She looked warmly into his eyes and smiled. Cathy ate all the sophisticated food with gusto, talked to Ariadne, and sketched pictures of large grinning cats on a scribbling block that Susan had produced out of the bag. The child had a remarkable capacity for entertaining herself as though she were deliberately trying to make space for Susan and him. They talked more about themselves. Her story continued from a childhood centered around the University of British Columbia, to art school in London, her work as a sculptor, and the trials and tribulations of bringing up Cathy. Susan never made mention of Cathy's father and projected that any questions about this were strictly off limits. Nicholas followed her narrative intently, trying to pick up any reference points by which he might estimate her age. Strangely, it was difficult to do so, and even if there seemed to be the occasional inconsistency in the narrative, it all added up to a full and interesting life. He told her more of himself: his very different childhood in a well-to-do banking family, Oxford, an internship at the National Gallery, his art-and-antique business, Barbara. He too kept the topic of his late wife off limits. They were rather like a pair of experienced card players cautiously laying out the cards of their lives one at a time but never revealing their full hand. After about two hours they wandered down again stopping at the same café for ice cream and coffee. This time they talked much less and just seem content to stare out to sea and enjoy each other's presence. As they drove back to Nice she asked him if he wanted to come over to dinner and meet her two "Aussies." He was very tempted, but felt he was getting drawn to her too quickly and told her that he would love to another time but he had to make a very early start the next morning for a trip to Marseilles.

"You never told me you were leaving." Susan sounded quite upset.

"No, no, this is just a short, overnight business trip. I'm visiting an antique dealer who claims to have an unusually good consignment of furniture and clocks from a very wealthy client who's decided to leave France and settle in Switzerland. I've had some terrific pieces from this dealer before and don't want to miss this opportunity."

Susan seemed placated. "Sounds exciting. Cathy and I will miss you at the beach, though."

Nicolas drove the car through the narrow, winding streets of the city to her building. They got out, and Susan pulled a key out of her bag and gave it to Cathy. "Now run upstairs, sweetheart, and surprise the Aussies."

"Surprise, surprise," chortled Cathy as she skipped indoors.

"Nicholas, once again thank you for a lovely day. Drive carefully. All those lunatic French drivers, you know. And come and find us as soon as you get back." She suddenly leaned forward and gave him a light kiss on his cheek, swiveled round, and ran into the building after her daughter.

Although Nicholas had told Susan that he probably wouldn't return from Marseilles until late the next evening, he decided to come back earlier, and by late afternoon he had reached the outskirts of Nice. Realizing that it was an easy detour to Susan's building, he decided to drop by on the off chance that Susan and Cathy might be there. He found a nearby parking spot and walked towards her building. Just as he turned into her street, he heard the roar of a sports car and saw a bright green, open-top Ferrari draw up. Inside were Cathy and Susan, with Cathy sitting in the front. A tall, dark-haired man, probably in his early thirties, dressed in an elegant white suit, jumped out of the driver's seat. Coming round to the other side of the car he plucked Cathy out and gave her a hug. Susan stepped out, sexily attired in shorts and a bikini top. The man put Cathy down, exchanged kisses on both cheeks with Susan and, with deliberate exaggeration for Cathy's benefit, leapt back onto his steed. He quickly roared off and Susan and Cathy waved to him before skipping, hand in hand, into their building.

Nicholas went back to his Renault rental and drove to his hotel. No doubt Susan and Cathy had gate-crashed that man's dinner the night before. Or maybe not. He didn't go out that evening but stayed in his hotel room and worked on his article while intermittently musing about Susan, Cathy, the green Ferrari, and his own experiences the previous night in Marseilles. He had not told Susan that the antique dealer in Marseilles was an old flame who always consummated her deals with him with a night of intense lovemaking. It was a strange relationship: they saw each other at most once a year, and although they both had other lovers, they never lost their spark of sexual attraction. Last night as they made love he had wondered what it would be like to make love to Susan and tried to imagine that the pale, plump legs locked around his hips were the long, lean, tanned legs of Susan.

Nicholas went down to the beach at about ten o'clock the next morning. Cathy and Susan were already sitting at a table by the bar. Cathy ran over to him as he came down the steps from the promenade, gave him a hug, and led him to their table. Susan gave him one of her warm smiles. "Nicholas, lovely to see you again. Please sit down. I've just asked the waiter to bring you an espresso. Tell us *all* about your trip. Don't leave out a thing! Did you miss us?"

Any irritation he felt over the episode with the green Ferrari melted under Cathy's hug and Susan's smile. "Yes, I missed you both terribly," and he sat down and started to tell them a suitably sanitized version of his visit to Marseilles.

The next three days, his last before he had to return to London, passed in a warm glow of sunshine and the company of Susan and Cathy. They spent most of their time together at the beach, had dinner each evening, and after dinner they would walk along the Promenade des Anglais like a little family, with Cathy holding his hand and Susan's arm gently linked to his. There was clearly a strong sense of attraction building up between them. Occasionally their hands would touch and sometimes she would lean against him when he would point to something, or when she would look at what he was reading. These little physical intimacies passed without comment or significant glances, just the occasional warm smiles. The only thing, for him, that marred their time together was an incident when they were walking along the Promenade. The green Ferrari drove past, and the driver blew his horn and exchanged waves with Cathy before disappearing at high speed.

"A friend of yours?" he asked.

"Cathy will wave to anybody. Just some rich guy with a fast car."

Thinking about his recent night in Marseilles and his far-greater deception, Nicholas left the matter at that.

On his last night in Nice, they arranged to eat at the restaurant where they had first met. Susan turned up without Cathy. "She's running a slight temperature, maybe too much sun today, and is staying at home tonight with the Aussies. She's very upset at missing you and told me to tell you that Ariadne sends you a big hug."

Although genuinely disappointed at not seeing the little girl, Nicholas was also excited by the opportunity, at last, of having Susan all to himself. Susan and Cathy together were like a perfect act and he wanted to see how Susan would fare without her best supporting actress. Over dinner, Susan asked him a lot of questions, some quite detailed, about his shop, his flat in London, his cottage in the country, and what it was like to drive his Range Rover. She asked whether he had ever thought of exhibiting pieces of contemporary art and sculpture in his shop as a complement to the paintings and antiques. He hadn't, and said he would consider it seriously. After dinner they strolled along the Promenade. She held his arm rather tightly and leaned against him as they walked. He was still, to his own irritation, very curious about the green Ferrari.

"Susan, I haven't been quite honest with you." He could feel her stiffen. "The other day, I came back from Marseilles earlier than I had said and stopped by your building. I saw you and Cathy in that green Ferrari we passed a couple of nights ago, but when I asked if you knew the driver, you said you didn't."

Susan turned and looked at him straight in the eyes. "Nicholas, I never tell lies. When you were away, Cathy—and you know Cathy—started chatting to this Italian. You know how Italians are: they just love children, and he offered to take Cathy for a spin. That was it. A five-minute run up and down the Promenade. He really was just a rich guy with a fast car. That's exactly what I told you, and that's exactly how it was. He wanted me to go out with him that evening but, of course, I said no." Her eyes suddenly softened and she giggled. "I do believe you're jealous." The tension was broken.

"Yes, I confess I was a little jealous. I'm sorry if I offended you in any way by asking."

She didn't reply but just leaned up against him that little bit closer. They walked down to the pebbly beach and strolled by the sea. At a relatively deserted part of the beach he pulled her into his arms and kissed her. At first they kissed quite gently and then long and passionately.

"Susan, I've been wanting to do this since I first met you."

"I know."

"You know?"

"Of course."

She paused for a moment. "Nicholas, I know this sounds corny, but this has really been one of the happiest few days of my life. This is no ordinary little holiday romance. This is something different. I know you have to go back to London tomorrow morning, but as soon as I'm back home I want to see you again."

She rested her head against his chest and they stood there for several minutes listening to the sound of the water lapping on the beach and, in the background, the slightly incongruous sound of some students playing drums a little further down the beach.

"Nicholas, I must go back to Cathy now. I want to walk back by myself." She took his face in her hands and kissed him gently on the mouth. "Bye, Nicholas. I'll see you soon." She turned and ran up the steps to the Promenade and was out of sight by the time he reached the street.

Eight days later, Susan called him at his London flat in the morning. It was going to be a sunny day, and they agreed to meet by the Serpentine that afternoon. Susan and Cathy were already at their prearranged meeting spot when he got there. Susan was simply dressed in a white blouse and long dark skirt—combination that set off her tan and dark hair to stunning effect. Cathy and Ariadne jumped into his arms and gave him a big hug while Susan smiled at him and brushed her cheek against his shoulder. They rented a boat and rowed around the lake with Captain Cathy and First-Mate Ariadne giving him occasionally suicidal directions that included an apparent attempt to ram another boat crowded with giggling, chador-covered women. After they had finished on the lake they sat on a bench eating ice cream, and Cathy entertained Susan and Nicholas with French-waiter imitations. When Cathy had completed her performance, they talked effortlessly about the projects they were now involved with: an antique show Nicholas was going to next week in Manchester; Susan's latest commission; an exhibition of Fauvist paintings they both wanted to see. Nicholas was very excited about a new acquisition: a painting he was trying to authenticate as an original Samuel Palmer, and he was eager for Susan to see it. He had to leave after a couple of hours to meet a business associate for an early dinner. They almost simultaneously suggested to each other that they go to Greenwich Observatory on Sunday for a picnic.

They took a tour boat along the Thames to their destination. Nicholas had often made that journey: as a boy with his grandfather, who had liked to reminisce about the Blitz and the nights that the London sky had burned red; and then, many years later, with his daughter. It somehow seemed fitting that, after all those years, he should now be making the cruise again with Susan and Cathy. They lay under a tree near the Observatory, eating and talking while Cathy alternately played and dozed. When he and Susan looked at each other, Nicholas could see desire in her eyes and felt himself to be strongly aroused. She had been right on that last night in Nice: theirs was not some standard little holiday romance. He had had enough of those to know. This was something much deeper. At one point, when Cathy ran off after a stray puppy, Susan pressed herself close to him and kissed him on the mouth.

"Nicholas, I can hardly stand it. We must have some time together alone—soon," and then she jumped up and ran after her daughter.

They had to wait until the end of the following week when he had returned from Manchester. Susan was to come over to his flat for a drink and to look at the new painting, and then they would go out to dinner. Cathy would be spending the evening at a friend's house. Susan appeared at his door promptly at seven o'clock. She kissed him quickly, almost embarrassedly, and then seemed to run into his flat and started to admire it. Nicholas had furnished it with spare, modern lines, lightly interspersed with antiques and old paintings, some of which were quite valuable. Susan's eagle eye appraised it all. He poured some wine and they sat together on his black Italian sofa. They talked about Cathy, his trip to Manchester, the commission she was struggling to finish. After about half an hour the conversation seemed to peter out. He kissed the nape of her neck. She seemed to tremble. She put down her wine glass and put her arms around him.

They never made it to the restaurant that evening. They made love for the next several hours. She was very strong and her long legs wrapped around his hips in a way that realized his sexual fantasy during that other night of love making in Marseilles. Her orgasms were slow and deep. As they lay on his bed she whispered, "It's been a very long time, Nicholas. I'm so glad it's you."

"It's been a long time for me too, Susan. I'm glad it's you too."

A little later, after another intense coupling, he noticed that she was still wearing the same set of heavy bracelets on her left wrist that she had worn all the time in Nice, even when she went into the sea. He gently stroked her forearm and started to turn the bracelets around. Although usually a very observant person, he had, until that moment, failed to notice some scars on her wrist that were very well concealed by the bracelets. She could see what he was doing. She gently pushed his hand away.

"That was another life, Nicholas. Please don't ask me anything."

He kept his silence but wondered just how many lives she had had.

Detumescence gave way to hunger, but he had so little food in his kitchen that they ended up sitting on his bed eating toast and marmite and drinking more wine. They chatted and laughed about nothing in particular, and stroked and kissed each other's faces. They still hadn't viewed his new acquisition and they went into his study, both of them naked, to look at it. The painting was of a garden scene with a couple standing under a tree laden with brightly colored fruit. There appeared to be no artist's signature, and closer inspection of the brushwork suggested that the painting of the couple was not quite finished. However, there were striking similarities with one of Palmer's best-known paintings, Garden in Shoreham, in which a single female figure stood under a heavily blossomed tree. But there was no need to explain this to Susan since, as he had already learned, there was little about art and art history and this particular artist that she didn't know. While the likeness of the trees and the overall composition strongly suggested that it was Palmer's work, possibly a sequel to the Shoreham painting, equally important was the fact that the canvas had some scorch marks—the reason why Nicholas had been able to acquire it for a reasonable price. Although the damage reduced the value of the painting, it was a vital clue consistent with the fact that Palmer's son had burned most of his father's paintings after his death. Perhaps this one had somehow survived the bonfire and had been salvaged. An old friend, who was a conserva-tionist at the National Gallery, was also convinced that the painting was a Palmer and thought that it would be possible to repair the canvas and maybe even uncover the artist's signature, albeit with a lot of work. Nicolas wasn't sure if it would really be worth the expense, but there was a charm to the painting—reminiscent of Palmer's famous Magic Apple Tree painting—that made him want to have it done. When he talked about this project with friends or professional acquaintances he usually felt that he was giving a lecture, but not with Susan. She stood by his side, holding his hand, and rested her head on his shoulder as he talked.

"Yes," she said quietly when he finished. "I also think it's the real thing. It would definitely be worth trying to have it restored." Suddenly she looked at her watch. "My God, the time. I must run."

As with the first time she had said that almost three weeks before, he wondered where it was she had to dash off to so suddenly. She quickly pulled on her clothes, kissed him, and raced out of the flat before he even had time to put on his dressing gown.

Susan called him early on Sunday morning and asked him if he was doing anything that afternoon. Cathy would be playing at a friend's house for a few hours, and she wanted to come over to his flat and show him something. Nicholas could scarcely wait. When she arrived, wearing a black blouse and jeans, he was surprised to see that she was empty-handed. He had imagined that she was going to bring her portfolio to show him pictures of the sculpture she was working on. They embraced for a long time at the door and he could feel her breasts pressing through her blouse and his shirt. He offered her some coffee he had just brewed. They went into his kitchen, poured a couple of mugs, and went back to the living room and sat on the sofa.

"So, Susan, I'm bursting with curiosity. What is it you want to show me?"

She blushed a little and slid right up next to him. She suddenly undid her blouse and pulled it open showing him her small round breasts, still tanned all over. "I wanted to show you how much I wanted you," and she flung her arms around him and pushed him down on the sofa. They made incredibly intense love and she seemed to suck every drop of energy out of him. He felt completely knocked out and it was a while before he felt he had the energy to speak.

"Susan that was even more incredible than Friday. You surprise me."

"You're doing wonderful things for me Nicholas, you really are." She lay on his chest and looked him in the eyes. "Being with you, Nicholas, has restored my energy, my drive, and my sense of well-being. You know, I was completely stuck on the last phase of my sculpture. But when I looked at it again yesterday, I knew I could finish it. That was, in part, why I wanted to see you today: to tell you that and …" here she giggled, "to completely recharge myself."

She suddenly looked at her watch and he knew exactly what she was going to say. He mimicked her, "My God, the time. I must run."

She laughed. "I think you're the only person who has ever understood me, Nicholas."

She got off the sofa and pulled on her clothes. "Nicholas, I know this sounds terribly rude, but please don't call me next week. Thanks to you, I'm ready to complete my sculpture. I will be totally absorbed. I get like that, you know. If you call me, I will start to think about making love to you and will lose my concentration. You do understand, don't you, sweetheart?" It was the first time she had called by anything other than his name. "As soon as it's finished, I'll call you and have you over for dinner. I'll cook you a meal to remember."

She called him six days later. "Nicholas, I hated being cut off from you for so long after our wonderful weekend together. It was truly wonderful, you know. As I told you, you inspired me. I've been able to work flat out since then. It's all finished. I'm so pleased with the way it's come out, and I have you to thank for it. Come over tomorrow. Late afternoon. That will give you and Cathy some time together while I prepare dinner. She's been missing you. I'm very glad it's you Nicholas. See you tomorrow."

When Nicholas drove up to her address in Bayswater, he noticed a large black Bentley, with a chauffeur sitting inside, parked on the other side of the street. This wasn't exactly the most fashionable address in London and the car and chauffeur looked out of place. He walked down the single flight of stairs to her basement flat and rang the doorbell. There was a rush of small feet from inside. Cathy threw open the door and flung herself into his arms. He carried her down a dark hallway towards an open door and the sound of voices. He stepped into a large, brightly lit room. It was furnished with a low sofa and huge floor cushions at one end, lots of halogen spotlights, and a large table with an eclectic mixture of modern and old chairs at the other end. Standing at the table, looking over some sketches, were Susan and a man. He was maybe late-fifties, with neatly groomed silver grey hair. He was wearing an expensive double-breasted grey suit, jacket undone, and a thickly striped Jermyn Street shirt with a strongly patterned tie, slightly loosened at the collar.

Susan looked up. She looked uncomfortable. "Nicholas, how great of you to drop by." She gestured towards the visitor, "Nicholas, this is Peter. Peter, this is Nicholas Motcomb, a friend of Cathy and me."

The man, who looked vaguely familiar, smiled at Nicholas and held out a well-manicured hand. His voice exuded an irritating self-confidence. "Nice to meet you, Nick. Susan, I must run along now. The plans look great. Just call me at my office tomorrow to go over the remaining details. I mustn't interrupt your little party."

"Nicholas, I'll just walk out with Peter to his car. There were a couple of things I need to ask him."

Peter strode energetically ahead and ruffled Cathy's hair. "Bye, princess. Be good."

As Susan followed Peter into the hallway, she gave Nicholas a slightly phony smile and gently brushed his hand.

Nicholas felt very confused and uneasy. He definitely knew the man from somewhere. Maybe he had seen him at one of the charity events he sometimes went to. His relaxed and self-confident manner was impressive but disturbing. Susan's phony smile and her "drop by" troubled him even more. However, Cathy was dancing round him with Ariadne and demanding his attention.

"So, Cathy, what have you been doing since I last saw you?"

"I've been playing princess."

"How do you play princess?"

"I drive in Peter's car and tell the nice man in the black hat where I want to go. He took me to Buckingham Palace to see the Queen. Just like a princess."

"Did Susan go with you as your lady-in-waiting?"

"No, she stayed behind and looked at pictures with Peter."

Nicholas felt as though he had been kicked in the stomach, just as he had felt eight years before. He simply had to escape as quickly as possible. He heard Susan unlatch the front door. He quickly pulled out his phone and dialed his home number. In two rings the answering machine came on and he started talking. "Good God, that's terrible. Do they know when? How was it done? Are the police still there? I'll be over immediately."

Susan was able to overhear most of the conversation. "Nicholas, you look terribly pale. What's the matter?"

"It seems as though there was an attempted robbery at my warehouse. It isn't clear if it was successful or not but I have to get over there immediately to talk to the police."

"Oh, Nicholas. That's awful, simply awful. Today seems to be turning into a disaster. I was so happy to finish my work and so excited to be able to see you again after our wonderful weekend together. And then Peter turned up unexpectedly." She could see the sour look on his face. "You must really get to know Peter. He's our guardian angel. He's been so helpful to us and has got me these great commissions …."

Helpful, my arse, Nicholas thought to himself. I'm sure Peter has been helping himself to you quite liberally along the way.

"But I fell behind with the dinner preparations, and now your warehouse has been broken into, and you're going to have to run off, and we've hardly had time to exchange a word."

There was a hint of tears in her eyes and she looked at him with such sincerity that he started to wonder if, yet again, he had misjudged her. But no, not this time. He was sure of it. He picked up Cathy and carried her to the door. "Sorry, young lady. The bad guys are in town. I have to run. Susan will explain it to you."

"Nicholas, you must call me as soon as you can. I'm so sorry today didn't work out."

She looked at him anxiously, almost lovingly, as he ran up the steps into the street and to his car.

Nicholas went back to his flat, poured himself a glass of whiskey, and stared out of the window. Lies, lies, lies. She was a liar. He should know, so was he. The pain in his stomach brought back memories of his shattering moment of truth eight years before: the policeman standing at his front door solemnly telling him that his wife had been killed a few hours earlier in a car crash just outside London. He was asked to go to the hospital to confirm her identity. At the hospital, a police detective had asked to talk to him privately. The man was clearly very uncomfortable. Nicholas remembered every detail of that interview and every word of that conversation as though it were engraved on a stone tablet—the tombstone of his marriage. When the policeman said, "Mr. Motcomb, there was a man in the car with her. Sir, I know this must be a terrible time for you, but we think there might have been an abduction and rape," Nicholas recalled how he had sat there with mouth open, stunned. It couldn't be any worse. The detective had continued in a low voice, "When they got her to the emergency room they found she wasn't wearing any underwear, and there were semen stains and bruises on her thighs. The identification on the man tells us that he was one Toby Morrison, and we are checking our records to see if …" Nicholas was barely able to say the words: "He was my business partner." The policeman had looked at him, deeply embarrassed. They both knew. It was worse than Nicholas ever imagined worse could be.

When Nicholas had got home he ransacked his wife's desk. In her diaries he found little Ts marked on certain days. In her financial statements, he found credit-card charges from London hotels with dates that correlated with the entries in her diaries. His wife and Toby: they had lied to him, possibly for years, with consummate skill. Nicholas had never told a lie in his life. That evening he told his first great lie as he explained to Barbara that her mother was dead. Mummy had gone to collect some antiques and Uncle Toby had kindly gone to help her lift the heavy ones into the car. There was a terrible accident on the way home. Although Mummy would never come home again she would always love both of them from Heaven.

That was a lie he had to tell. Since that day, he had learnt that there were many ways of editing the truth, of cutting and pasting one's life. Sometimes lies were needed to avoid hurting people, to make a more palatable narrative, a more comfortable reality. Sometimes one had to lie to oneself to reduce the hurt. Lies were not necessarily deceitful. An economical use of the truth was, perhaps, an existential necessity. And now there was Susan, looking at him clear in the eye with such sincerity—just as his late wife had done—pretending that Peter what's-his-face was St. Francis of Assisi. He thought back over their many conversations and started to recall more clearly all those little discrepancies in her life's narrative. Maybe he had met his match. The only thing that gnawed at him was the tender way Susan had looked at him when he had run out of her flat.

The next day, he ignored the two messages Susan had left on his answering machine. That afternoon he called Ellen. He had known her a long time. Her daughter was a childhood friend of Barbara's. Ellen was already divorced then and had remained single ever since. They had a simple relationship. Perhaps the only honest one Nicholas had ever had with a woman. They could always talk to each other about whatever was on their minds. When they called each other to meet, it was always understood that they would have sex. He went over to her house that evening. As he lay on top of Ellen he found himself wishing it were Susan who was groaning underneath him. The next few days he was miserable: he kept on thinking about Susan, about Cathy. He missed the little girl's sweetness and energy. He recalled all those long, effortless conversations he had had with Susan. He missed her mind. He missed her body. It was ridiculous. He was behaving like a love-sick schoolboy. He forced himself to remember the little dishonesties between them. But it always came back to Susan, her warm smile, the way she kissed him, the way she challenged his mind. He called her. Instead of getting anger he got sweetness.

"Nicholas, I've been so worried about you."

"I'm sorry, Susan, these last few days, what with the attempted robbery and everything, have been a nightmare."

"I know, Nicholas, they've been hard for me too." Somehow over the phone she was able to communicate that she knew it was the "everything" that was causing him grief.

"Nicholas, are you doing anything this evening?"

"No."

"I want to see you Nicholas. I'll be over in about an hour's time."

She appeared at his door wearing a worn pair of jeans and a University of British Columbia sweatshirt. She looked a little pale and there were shadows under her eyes. She smiled at him uncertainly. All his anger melted away. They walked into each other's arms and held each other silently for a few minutes. Then, without saying a word, they went into his bedroom, undressed each other, and made love. It was more intense than before, quite unlike anything he had experienced. Afterwards, as they lay quietly together he realized that he had fallen in love with her. Love was a word that had been banished from his vocabulary long ago. He certainly knew strong emotions. He knew hate: Toby Morrison had taught him that. He knew anger: he had felt that towards his late wife. He knew protective love: he felt that towards his daughter. But to feel unmitigated love for a woman again? Here was a woman with a wonderful mind and a body to match. It was the combination that one fantasized about but assumed belonged only in the realms of fiction. But here she was, lying beside him in his bed.

"Talk to me, Nicholas. What's eating you up? There wasn't any robbery at your warehouse, was there? What is it?"

"How did you know there wasn't a robbery?"

She smiled. "You should know by now, Nicholas. I just know these things about you."

"O.K. Susan, Peter."

"What about Peter?"

"You're having an affair with him, aren't you?"

He expected her to explode. Instead she just rolled over onto her stomach and looked at him calmly. "Peter really is a guardian angel. He's been a terrific help to my career. He helped me get Cathy into a very good private school. Yes, I let him fuck me sometimes. It makes him feel powerful. But it doesn't mean anything. Don't you understand, Nicholas? It doesn't mean anything."

She could see him shudder, and her voice sharpened. "Don't tell me you haven't been fucking other women, Nicholas. For all I know you were screwing some French bitch when you were in Marseilles." Her voice softened again. "You're such a fool, Nicholas. Don't let Peter upset you. Think about our time together, every wonderful minute of it. Don't you remember all our wonderful conversations? Have you ever been able to talk to anybody else like that? I certainly haven't. When I told you that Cathy had chosen you at the restaurant, it was true. We had seen you sitting in a café the day before and she said, 'Look at that nice man sitting by himself.' And when we saw you in the restaurant the next evening I felt we were just fated to meet. Ridiculous, isn't it? Can't you still feel how fantastic and close our lovemaking is? Have you felt like that with anybody else? I certainly haven't. We're birds of a feather, Nicholas. We both want the same things, we both want each other, but we both have our little deceptions and distortions of how things are. We've needed them to survive the shit in our lives, but don't let them wreck our chance."

Nicholas lay on his back and stared at the ceiling. She could read his mind. They were, indeed, birds of a feather. More than that, they were apples off the same tree. But theirs was no magic apple tree: the roots of their tree had been poisoned by everything that had gone wrong in their lives. It was difficult to know what reality was anymore. To hell with Peter, to hell with Ellen, he wanted Susan and only Susan. But he realized at that moment that more than Susan, he wanted peace. He wanted to stop telling lies. He had always argued to himself that they simplified his life, but all they had done was make it more complicated. Yes, he loved her, but life with her wouldn't give him the peace he now craved. With her, there might always be another Peter. With him, there might always be another Ellen. He somehow needed a clean slate. No more deceptions: by him or on him. He just needed one more lie, his biggest, and then he would be free. He took a deep breath. "Susan. Dear, sweet Susan. I can't tell you how much these days and weeks, even the bad ones, have meant to me. You are truly wonderful and Cathy is the light of the world. But whatever I feel for you, it isn't love."

Susan slid off the bed and silently got dressed. "Nothing ever changes, Nicholas; it never changes," and she left.

WHAT REALLY HAPPENED
TO DORIAN GRAY

All the world knows what happened to Dorian Gray. He maintained his perfect youthful beauty while his portrait, kept hidden in a locked room at his London residence, gradually changed in ways that reflected the ravages of time and his life of debauchery until, in a fit of rage, he stabbed the portrait and was found dead—a withered and diseased corpse—lying by the original portrait. Or so Mr. Wilde tells us. But, of course, there are no such things as pacts with the Devil; the Devil resides only in the hearts of evil men. And no painting changes of its own accord other than to fade with time. There is no magic—it does not exist—and there is no technique of science that can cause a painting to change in the way that was claimed. In short, as Mr. Wilde knew better than most, his account of the fate of Dorian Gray was a pure fiction. Yet some elements of the story are true, including that now famous final scene, but how it really happened is another story. Many decades have passed since those extraordinary events, and all those involved are now gone, except me. Before I die, I need to tell the world what really happened.

The first part of Mr. Wilde's account is true: describing in his inimitable style the completion of Dorian's portrait by the artist Basil Hallwood, and Dorian's first meetings with Lord Henry Wotton who had such a corrupting influence on him. However, Mr. Wilde started to deviate from the true events soon after Dorian met the beautiful young actress Sibyl Vane, with whom he believed he had fallen in love. But those feelings were no more than an infatuation inspired by Sibyl's stage portrayals of romantic heroines. That fateful scene in her theatre dressing room, when Dorian rejected Sibyl because she had acted indifferently in her vain attempt to show him that her love for him was more important to her than the fictional love she acted out on stage, was accurately recorded by Mr. Wilde. But what followed afterwards was quite different from the well-known story. According to Mr. Wilde, Henry Wotton told Dorian that, on leaving the theatre with her mother later that night, Sibyl had gone back to her dressing room, claiming that she had forgotten something. When she did not return, her mother found her lying dead on the floor, having poisoned herself with prussic acid. But in his account of this to Dorian, Lord Henry had been careless with the facts, preferring in his mind that fictitious little scene that appealed to his sense of drama.

So who am I to challenge the authority of Mr. Wilde and question his literary genius? Who could know what really happened on that infamous night and what happened afterwards? The only person privy to the truth was Sibyl Vane herself. I know this because I am the real Sibyl Vane, still alive to this day! Let me explain.

After Dorian had left me sobbing on the floor of my dressing room I did, indeed, think of suicide. As I picked myself up, I noticed a piece of paper that must have fallen out of his jacket pocket. It appeared to be a bill of some kind but, most importantly, it revealed his address—something he had never told me. I resolved to go to his residence and beg him, yet again, to forgive me, and if that failed I would then commit suicide in front of him. How dramatic we young girls were in those days! I did leave the theatre with my mother and then told her that I needed to go back to my dressing room, but beyond that Lord Wotton's account was incorrect. I told my mother not to wait for me, reassuring her that I would have one of the stagehands escort me home. My mother was very angry with me that night for having acted so poorly and so obviously disappointing the fine gentlemen who had come to see me perform, and it was easy to persuade her to go home without me. Knowing her weakness for drink, I suspected that she would go to bed with a bottle of gin and not wait up for me. In this way, I was able to make my way to Dorian's residence without anybody knowing.

When I arrived at his house well after midnight, I found it was dark and quiet. The tradesmen's entrance below street level was unlocked and I crept into the house, assuming that the servants must be asleep in their upstairs' quarters. I had hoped to find Dorian brooding alone in the dark in his drawing room, but there was no sign of him. All I found was an oil lamp on the sideboard—casting a flickering light about the room. I wandered around for a few minutes admiring the beautiful furniture, the wall hangings and the ornaments, and then I saw, propped up on an easel in a corner, his portrait. Holding up the lamp, I examined it closely. It took my breath away: he looked even more beautiful in the painting than in real life. Looking at his portrait in that sumptuously appointed room, I realized that I was probably unworthy of such a fine young gentleman. Maybe he had been right to reject me, but it all seemed so terribly unfair and so terribly cruel of him to have toyed with my affections. Pressing my forefinger to my lips, and with silent tears running down my cheeks, I then touched the lips of the portrait. It was my way of giving him one last kiss. But when I lifted my fingertip away I was dismayed to see that it had left behind the tiniest trace of makeup rouge on the painting. Although it was scarcely visible, I was sure that he would see it and guess that I had broken into his home. In a fit of panic, I took my handkerchief—it was a gift from Dorian that I kept tucked in my bosom—and tried to wipe away that trace of makeup. I thought I had succeeded, but when I stepped back I was absolutely horrified. Far from cleaning away the offending mark, I had completely transformed the portrait. That tiny dab of color had changed the sweet smile of a beautiful youth into the wicked sneer of a cruel man. Most people would probably not have noticed the difference, minute as it was in terms of paint, but to me it was as terrifying as a lightning bolt. It was not so much that I had damaged the painting—I had revealed the true character of the man I thought had loved me. That moment transformed me forever. At the time, I was just a seventeen-year-old girl, innocent in the ways of the world and the wickedness of men. However, I had grown up in the theatre and was fully versed in all the greatest dramas of the stage. In theory, I knew all about the rages of men, how the heart can boil with hate, how the innocent can be deceived, how saints can become cruel sinners. But in that moment all those theoretical emotions became the harshest reality. I knew there and then that a very different life lay ahead of me, and that one day justice would be served.

Looking back on it now, it is remarkable to think how the silly romantic gesture of a young girl—kissing the portrait of her beloved—would have such a transformative effect: not just on me but also on the subject of the portrait himself. As Mr. Wilde correctly recorded, Dorian came back to his house in the early hours, having roamed the streets of London all night. When Dorian examined his portrait, he saw exactly what I had seen and had been equally terrified by what he saw. He, too, was transformed. In his case it set him upon a path of wickedness and debauchery, and little Sibyl Vane was quickly forgotten.

There is still the matter of my apparent suicide that needs to be explained. I left Dorian's house and returned to the now-deserted theatre. It was an easy matter to stage my suicide. Actors do it all the time. Using makeup, I discolored my face and lips, and moistened my lips with a few drops of almond essence. I then pushed over a piece of furniture to make enough of a crashing sound to attract the attention of a policeman passing by the theatre. On forcing his way into my dressing room, he found me lying on the floor, weakly gasping for breath, and an empty bottle, marked Prussic Acid, lying by my side. The bottle, of course, was just a theatrical prop. Smelling my breath and assuming that I was very close to death, the policeman, who was young and inexperienced in proper procedures, had me sent directly to a hospital. On that journey I feigned death and the carriage driver, in a fit of panic, took me to a mortuary instead. My body was left unattended, and such were the horrors of those places in Victorian times, it was an easy matter for me to find the corpse of a young woman of approximately my size and age. I dragged her body to where I had been placed, and put my bracelet on her wrist. When my mother came to the mortuary the next morning to identify the corpse she saw a pale, lifeless hand hanging out from under the sheet covering the face and body. She recognized the bracelet and fainted. That my mother fainted at the sight of the bracelet was enough to convince the officials that the dead girl was Sibyl Vane.

Just before I staged my suicide, I took—stole, if you will—some money from the theatre manager's office. I had few qualms about doing so since he had always exploited my mother and me. Furthermore, I knew that with my apparent suicide he would have scandal enough to deal with and would not want to add to his woes with the report of a theft. I used this money to make my way to Paris and start a new life. At first as a singer at a horrible nightclub frequented by greasy self-made men and then, as I became fluent in French, as an actress. My talent and beauty were not unnoticed and I became the mistress of an elderly Montenegrin count who resided in Paris. In many ways I was more of a companion than a mistress, for all he really wanted was a pretty young thing to keep him company while he smoked his cigar, and to entertain him with recitals of his favorite piano pieces and songs. He had had other young mistresses before me but, as was so often the case, they were vain and ambitious—always wanting to be paraded in public to flaunt their finery and perhaps attract the attentions of an even richer patron, rather than stay at home and play the piano for him. But not me: if I was his little bird in a gilded cage, I knew that eventually I would have the keys to my cage and a whole lot more.

After about a year he had a massive heart attack, but rather than abandon him I nursed him back to health. After that, our relationship changed: he now regarded me as his friend and confidant. His doctors advised him to retire to a country estate he owned outside Paris, and he insisted that I live with him there. In its way, that was one of the most peaceful and contented periods of my life. We went for walks in his lovely gardens and had picnics by a beautiful lake on his estate. He was a cultured man, and I entertained him with recitals of Shakespeare and other plays. This was not only a source of great pleasure for both of us, but also an opportunity for me to hone my skills as an actress. I also became my own, and highly skilled, makeup artist. In minutes I could transform myself from a haughty duchess to a humble young scullery maid. I even became expert at disguising myself as a man and could play the part of anything from a handsome young valet to a querulous old marquis. The count loved it all and, in return, entertained me with his seemingly endless fund of gossip about the scandals and intrigues in the aristocratic families of Europe and England. We became genuinely fond of each other. To him, I may have been like the daughter he never had, and to me he was, perhaps, like the father I never knew. A few months before he died he made me his lawful wife. As a result I acquired a genuine title—I became Countess H.—and a considerable fortune.

It was known in high society that the count had married, but his bride was something of a mystery. Because of our secluded life together very few had ever met me. A German baron claimed that he had met me at an official function in Berlin and that I was a sophisticated, dark-haired woman in her early thirties. An Italian count boasted that he had drunk champagne with me at a ball in Rome and that I was a blue-eyed beauty in her late twenties. A Russian prince asserted that he had conversed with me in Moscow and that I was a pretty young blonde with a most charming smile. An American millionaire said he had danced with me at a Parisian club and that I was a vivacious redhead. And a snobbish English dowager claimed that she had sat next to me at a luncheon at Blenheim Place and that I was a young woman of impeccable breeding.

My title and fortune enabled me to develop a network of bankers and solicitors, and various other agents occupying many different positions in society. They were all well compensated to do my bidding—nearly always through intermediaries. Many a butler and lady's maid in the stately homes of England were unwitting sources of information about the goings-on of the English aristocracy. In this way, I could keep track of Dorian Gray's despicable life over the years. In particular, I knew every single detail concerning the death of my brother, Philip, at Dorian's country estate, Selby Royal. Those familiar with Mr. Wilde's account will know that Philip, on returning to England after a long absence on the high seas, had tracked Dorian down to Selby Royal and had been shot—by accident during a shoot, or so it was claimed—by one of the house guests, Sir Geoffrey Clouston. I had the names of all those who were at the house party at Selby Royal when Philip had died: the Duke and Duchess of Monmouth, the Duchess's brother, Sir Geoffrey, Lady Narborough, and three young dandies who were devoted followers of Dorian.

In his account of Dorian's London life, Mr. Wilde failed to record that the residence adjacent to Dorian's had long been empty. At various times, Dorian had tried to purchase it. He was not only unsuccessful in doing so but also in finding out who owned it. Of course, I was the owner. The house was never occupied save for a deaf old caretaker who lived in the basement, and a secluded back entrance enabled me to slip in and out without ever being seen. When Dorian was away on one of his Italian vacations with Basil Hallwood, I had a secret door made that connected a room in my property to the old schoolroom in Dorian's house where he kept his portrait hidden. It was through a spy-hole in that door that I could observe all that went on in that room.

This brings me to the central theme of Mr. Wilde's famous story: that Dorian had eternal youth and, in a Faustian pact, it was his portrait that aged for him. A pretty tale indeed and, in Mr. Wilde's skillful hands, a most entertaining one. But what really happened is explained by science and psychology, some of which was not fully understood in Mr. Wilde's day. One of the roles I played as Countess H. was that of a patron of the medical sciences, and this enabled me to consult with many leading experts of the day. I quickly observed that nothing makes a scholar happier than to talk at length about his own work to a pretty woman who listens with an admiring look on her face.

Dorian's "eternal youth" was, in fact, not so difficult to understand. His mother, Margaret Devereux, was an exceptional beauty and Dorian had simply inherited her good looks and, by a quirk of nature, an incredibly strong constitution that enabled him to be immune to most diseases, including venereal ones. An Egyptian physician, who at one point in his career had attended an Arabian prince with a large harem, told me of his researches in various middle-eastern brothels and how he had found a number of prostitutes who were seemingly immune to infection—although he could not explain why that was so. Furthermore, Dorian's looks were not quite as perfect as claimed, and over the twenty years between the painting of his portrait and his death at the age of thirty-eight there was some erosion of his beauty. But once Dorian started on his life of debauchery, he also became the most extreme narcissist. Inspired by the work of the French aesthete and sensualist, Jean Des Esseintes, Dorian engaged in investigations of not only perfumes but also rejuvenating lotions and creams. He found a number of preparations that enabled him to smooth away blemishes and wrinkles on his face, thereby maintaining his almost perfect youthful appearance.

However, it was the matter of the transformation of his portrait that was far more complex and fascinating, and it was only after many discussions with some of the most distinguished European psychologists that I was able to understand what Dorian saw. His double life led to the development of a second personality. The outside world saw only a man who was cold, cruel, and calm; but he had another secret personality of extreme nervousness and self-loathing. That one small change I had inadvertently made to the portrait all those years ago had convinced Dorian that further changes were possible, if not inevitable. A clear pattern of behavior emerged: after committing some evil deed he would need to look at his portrait and relieve his self-loathing by a psychological process in which the consequences of his actions were transferred to, and displayed on, the canvas. The changes he saw in his portrait were only in his mind! This remarkable phenomenon helps explain why he felt it necessary to murder Basil Hallwoood. It was a dreadful scene that I witnessed in full. As Mr. Wilde would have us believe, Dorian became so sickened by the changes he saw in the portrait that he blamed all his self-loathing on the painter. When he took Basil into the locked room to show him the picture, Dorian became enraged when Basil insisted that he saw no changes apart from the small one I had been responsible for. Such was Dorian's frustration at this that he felt it necessary to tell Basil all his most hideous crimes, and to explain how their consequences were revealing themselves in the hideous transformation of his face and body in the portrait. After a few minutes Dorian stopped his rant. His other cold and calculating personality took over as he realized that his confessions to Basil could put him in danger. His still-resentful former lover might go to the police or try to blackmail him. So Dorian killed him. Poor Basil Hallwood, he was perhaps the only decent man that Dorian ever knew. I also witnessed the gruesome procedure that Dorian's one-time friend, Alan Campbell, used to dispose of the body.

Soon after the death of my brother, I heard reports of Dorian's overtures to Hetty Merton, a beautiful and innocent girl who lived in a village near Selby Royal. When I was informed of the day that he had left her sobbing in the woods, I knew it was time to administer the harsh justice that Dorian deserved. By then, I knew exactly what his pattern of behavior would be: he would return to London and examine his portrait to see what changes his latest misdeeds had wrought. Perhaps he even harbored the vain hope that spurning Hetty was a good deed and that the hideous decay of the portrait might reverse itself. Once I received word that Dorian was on his way home, I let myself into the schoolroom through my secret entrance and hid behind the portrait. When Dorian saw, in his mind, that the picture was as hideous as ever, he grabbed a knife—the same one that he had used to kill Basil Hallwood—and lunged at the portrait.

At that moment I stepped out from behind the picture. Although eighteen years had passed since Dorian last saw me I was still unmistakable. His crazed look turned into one of sheer terror as he saw what he thought was a ghost. The knife in his hand fell to the floor.

"Dorian, don't be afraid. I am not a ghost. I really am Sibyl, your one true love."

That I also spoke in the voice he recognized as mine terrified him even more.

"You are a ghost from Hell sent to torment me."

"No, I am an angel from Heaven come to be reunited with you. Here, feel my hand. I am real," and I briefly stroked his cheek.

He became calmer and I began talking to him in soothing tones. I told him that after he had rejected me all those years ago, I realized that he was right to have done so. Back then, I was not worthy of him, not ready for him, and that by feigning my suicide I could go away and become that sophisticated and successful woman who would be worthy of his love and affection. The time had now come for us to be together again forever.

"Forever?" he asked.

"Yes, forever. United in death." And drawing on all the most famous tragic love stories in history I painted a picture of an exquisite finale for both of us that would end his anguish and bring us eternal joy. He seized upon this idea, recognizing the aesthetic beauty of such an end: one so grand and sensational that even his mentor Henry Wotton would be stunned into silence. In my hand I held a beautiful crystal vial that had once belonged to Lucrezia Borgia. I could see the gleam in Dorian's eye as he recognized its worth. The vial was filled with a clear liquid, and I told him that it was a gentle and fast-acting potion that would send us both into a rapturous sleep in each other's arms. I removed the sapphire stopper, drank half the fluid, and held out the vial to him.

"Quickly, my love, drink it now so that we have time to embrace."

He snatched the vial from my hand and gulped down the remaining fluid. For a few seconds his faced glowed with pleasure and just as he was about to reach out for me, his body was convulsed with a sudden spasm and he collapsed into one of the old schoolroom chairs that were in the room.

At seventeen I was already an accomplished actress and now, at thirty-five, I was a consummate one. So convincing was my soliloquy of love and redemption that he believed every word of it. By a sleight of hand, I had switched the vial with an identical copy containing a poison made according to my specifications by a renowned Damascene apothecary. The fluid I had just drunk was nothing more than plain water. Dorian looked at me with bewildered eyes and tried to speak, but his jaw was paralyzed.

I held up a mirror to his face so that he could see his reflection. "Now, Dorian, look at all the evil you have lived."

The action of the poison was truly terrible: blood dripped from his eyes, his face erupted in hideous blisters, his hair fell out and that which remained turned white, his insides burned up, and he was wracked with a pain that not even the cruelest inquisitors of old could have imagined possible. Because his jaw was paralyzed he could not even have the relief of screaming as he watched himself in the mirror being disfigured and destroyed. The agony was designed to last for half an hour, but to feel like an eternity. At the end, Dorian fell off the chair and died at the foot of his infamous portrait. His was a withered, wrinkled, and loathsome corpse, precisely as Mr. Wilde had described. To some, my actions might make me seem like a monster no better than Dorian himself. But that was not the case. I got no pleasure from watching his agonizing death. I simply wanted justice to be done, not just for me but for all the others he had wronged. Imitating his voice, I screamed in pain and then slipped out of the room by the secret door. Through the spy-hole I was able to observe all that followed.

At the same time that my cry woke Dorian's servants, a messenger boy appeared at Henry Wotton's residence. He told the sleepy servant answering the door that his Lordship must make haste to Mr. Gray's, where a terrible accident had just occurred. Lord Wotton arrived soon after the police, although Dorian's terrified and bewildered servants had no recollection of having sent a messenger to summon him. Using all the bluff and bluster of his class, Wotton took charge of the situation and quickly persuaded the servants and police that he had promised Mr. Gray, if anything should happen to him, that he would take care of the portrait and return it to Basil Hallwood when he returned from his long absence abroad. Henry Wotton was repulsed by the sight of the corpse: it was not only the horrible scars and blisters and bloodied eyes that shocked him; above all, it was the look of sheer terror on the dead man's face—a look that had been frozen in place by death.

The whole episode was hushed up, the servants and police paid off, and it was announced in the *Times* that Dorian Gray had suddenly collapsed and died of a brain haemorrhage. His hastily arranged funeral was held on a cold, grey morning and attended by no one except Lord Henry.

Henry Wotton had always wanted the portrait. Once it was in his possession he examined it closely. He immediately saw that it had changed in the same subtle way that Dorian had noticed all those years ago on the day he had rejected me. Those sweet red lips that Lord Henry had so admired now exhibited a slight, but unmistakably cruel, sneer. As far as he knew, he was now the only person, apart from the mysteriously disappeared Basil Hallwood, who had seen the original portrait. Recalling his last conversation with Dorian, Lord Henry now suspected that Basil had indeed been murdered as Dorian had suggested, and that it was Dorian who was the perpetrator. There was no mistake: the portrait had changed. Wotton recalled (as he often did) his first meeting with Dorian and how that beautiful and once-innocent boy had proposed that the painting should age instead of him. Such nonsense: yet the living Dorian never appeared to age while the dead Dorian was a repulsive corpse. The seemingly timeless portrait, that Dorian had claimed had been lost, now showed that small change in Dorian's face that was clearly the harbinger of his future life of dissipation. For the first time in his life, Lord Henry Wotton felt fear and he destroyed the portrait.

While Mr. Wilde's famous story ended with that sensational discovery of Dorian's body, I still had much unfinished business to attend to. Some months after Dorian's death, Sir Geoffrey Clouston, the man who had killed my brother, was found dead in his study with a gunshot wound to the head. Apparently he had been cleaning his hunting rifle and it had accidentally gone off and killed him. When his affairs were examined, it was found that he had invested heavily in a bogus South American railroad scheme and this resulted in his family's financial ruin. The Duchess of Monmouth became reckless after the deaths of Dorian Gray and her brother, Sir Geoffrey. She embarked on a foolish affair with an Italian count that left her pregnant. She went away to the French countryside under an assumed name for the last stages of her pregnancy. She died in a most painful childbirth and the baby was stillborn. The midwife who cared for her under the greatest secrecy disappeared. Lady Narborough, who was always hoping for at least a little scandal in her old age, died an ignominious death—she was found to have choked to death on a piece of toast while eating breakfast in bed.

Then there were the three young men who had also attended the house party when Philip had died. They had all been slavish followers of Dorian Gray's whims in fashion—from smoking jackets to tie pins—and eager students of his decadent lifestyle. One fell to his death while hiking on a foggy day in the Alps. He had become separated from his hiking partners who realized his absence only when they heard his scream as he fell. Another broke his back in a riding accident that may have been caused by a faulty saddle buckle. Although the fall did not kill him, he was paralyzed from the neck down, and his family hid him away in a private institution where he died a miserable and lonely death. The body of the third was found floating in the Thames near Wapping docks. An old prostitute told the police that she had seen him at an opium den in Bluegate Fields around the time he had disappeared. One morning, the Duke of Monmouth was found dead with a broken neck at the foot of the staircase at his stately home. Apparently he had tripped over a loose piece of carpeting at the head of the stairs. In truth, the duke was a harmless old fool—qualities that Mr. Wilde would have undoubtedly asserted were the perfect qualifications for being a member of the English aristocracy.

The deaths and disasters that befell all those who had attended that fateful house party at Selby Royal when Philip was killed unfolded over the two years following Dorian's death. To the outside world, they all seemed to be unconnected events, but to Henry Wotton there was an obvious and sinister pattern. He became fearful and had extra locks and window bars installed at his London residence. He rarely went out at night, and when he did it was always with company. Although there were still a few young dandies who were impressed by his wit and elegance, his star had faded. His long association with Dorian Gray had tarnished his reputation. Men who had snubbed Dorian at the London clubs now started to turn their backs on him as well. In short, Henry Wotton had gone out of fashion—a realization that was immensely painful to him. Taking inspiration from some of the French Decadents he was acquainted with, he decided to join the Roman Catholic Church. This not only offered the hope of some spiritual peace—a notion that in his glory days he would have ridiculed with some memorable epigram—but also the opportunity for new aesthetic pleasures: the rituals enacted by the gorgeously robed priests, the stained glass windows, the sacred music, the incense, and the beautiful young choir boys. But before taking his first Communion, he partook of one last night of pleasure at his favorite brothel. He spent the night, at great expense, with a stunningly beautiful new prostitute who gave him such intense pleasure that he determined to go back for one more night of carnal ecstasy before renouncing worldly delights. However, he was disappointed: the young woman had disappeared and the madam could give him no information as to how he might find her. A few days later he started to experience the most intense burning in his groin that quickly became excruciating. His physician informed him that he appeared to have contracted a rare and virulent strain of syphilis. It was one that the doctor had only read about but had never actually seen despite his many years of treating the English aristocracy. Furthermore, from what the doctor had heard, the disease was untreatable in any way, horribly painful, and quickly fatal. Lord Henry never had his Communion. He locked himself away in his bedroom and became demented with extreme pain and disfigured with hideous rashes and swellings. Only one servant, hired from an agency and sworn to secrecy, was allowed to attend him. One morning, Lord Henry was found dead—having slashed his own throat with a jewel-encrusted razor that Dorian Gray had once given him as a birthday present. With his temporary master dead, the servant was dismissed, but when the police tried to find him for further questioning the agency found that his file was missing, and the man could not be traced.

Of course, I had a hand in all those deaths. Some might think that it was a vendetta out of all proportion to the crimes committed: revenge for revenge's sake. But it was not just revenge for Dorian's callous rejection of me and the death of my brother. It was also to avenge the wrongs that had been perpetrated on so many women by that depraved and hypocritical class that Dorian Gray and Henry Wotton represented. In later years, I took it upon myself to continue this work. When I heard of some young woman being abused or misled by her husband I would intervene, albeit in more measured ways. An unfaithful husband, sneaking out of his mistress's house in the early hours, might be set upon by thieves and beaten. If the lesson was not learned other punishments would follow:

investments would suddenly fail, directorships might be denied, an anonymous blackmailer would threaten disgrace, and invitations to Court would cease. There were many ways to teach a married man, anxious for his position in society, a lesson. And as for those spineless young "gentlemen" who might toy with the affections of an innocent girl, it usually took only a light beating, a blackballing at a fashionable club, or the withholding of an allowance to correct bad behavior.

But it was not all darkness. There was happiness and joy as well. Hetty Merton married a tenant farmer, a fine and decent young man. A mysterious bequest enabled him to buy his farm, and while other farmers in the region failed, he prospered and eventually became one of the most successful and respected landowners in his county. An eccentric but spritely spinster called Miss Grayson rented a cottage on his farm for the summers. She became a great favorite with Hetty and her three children, and she organized little plays, based on Shakespeare's comedies, for them to act out on idyllic summer evenings. After a few such summers, Hetty received a letter from the London solicitors, Lewis and Lewis, informing her that Miss Grayson had passed away and had left Hetty's children a generous bequest to ensure, in the words of the Will, their "education and future happiness." When Hetty wrote to the solicitors telling them that she and her children would like to visit dear Miss Grayson's grave she was informed that Miss Grayson had, in accordance with her wishes, been cremated and her ashes scattered off the Amalfi coast. There were no known next of kin to whom condolences could be sent.

The life I have had was not the one I had imagined for myself as that innocent seventeen-year-old girl who was so cruelly mistreated by Dorian Gray. I have lived many lives and acted many parts. I have traveled through far-off lands and had experiences that few can even dream of. I have thoroughly enjoyed it all and have no regrets save one. I only wish I could have met Mr. Wilde in person and told him what really happened to Dorian Gray.

FACE TO FACE

The Central Park Mall is a popular spot for portrait artists to find customers, especially on the weekends and mild weekdays. Like all the others peddling their craft—be they drawers, scribblers, cartoonists, draftsmen, illustrators, charlatans, or true artists—I set up an easel with a few samples of my work. A popular trick, which I am not above using myself, is to show a drawing or two of a celebrity, usually a movie star or singer. Once the subject, even if it is poorly drawn, is recognized, the viewer will subconsciously fill in the details from their mental image of that person. And, *voilà*, they see a convincing likeness of Angelina Jolie.

Two young women walk by, probably in their late teens, probably students. They're both wearing similar outfits: tight jeans, layered tops and short black jackets. A pair of sleek young blackbirds flitting by. They stop and look at my work for a moment, walk on, and then stop again and confer. They come back. How much does a portrait cost? How long will it take? Twenty dollars, fifteen to twenty minutes. I can never say that it takes as long as I need, or tell them about Cezanne who needed at least a hundred sittings. The two confer and then quickly read and send messages on their phones. One of them stays and the other walks on. I invite my subject to sit at the end of a park bench close to my easel. She takes up a demure and, I suspect, well-practiced pose. I tell her to relax and just look slightly past me while I draw. She removes a band from her hair, and with a coy shake of her head, releases a little shower of shiny brown waves—perhaps her best feature. I start with the eyes. They are small and empty. It's like trying to draw a vacuum. And that's the trouble with her face as a whole: her eyes, nose, mouth, chin are small, regular and symmetric, but nothing distinctive. Some might call her very pretty—she certainly thinks that of herself—but to my eye, it's pretty much nothing. She has eyes that see, but she has no insight. She has a mouth that talks, but has nothing to say. Nonetheless, I'm sure young men will idolize her. What I see is the need for a subtle accentuation that hints at what she doesn't have, and I make her eyes and mouth slightly smaller than they are. The casual observer won't notice. Maybe she will, and if she does my opinion of her will improve. But I also do her a favor and subtly high-light her cheekbones. While I'm drawing, she periodically glances down at the phone clutched in her hand to check for existence-affirming messages, and when passers-by pause to watch she strengthens her smile. Within fifteen minutes—I know she will get restless if I take longer—the portrait is almost complete. I also know that she won't like it. Just as I'm about to date and initial it (it isn't worth a full signature) a passing jogger wearing dark glasses pauses to look at the drawing and the subject. I catch a flicker of an amused smile, a flash of red hair peeking out from under a tight-fitting knitted cap, and then she jogs away. A petite, black-clad figure. I would like to draw her. My current subject looks at her portrait for a few moments and pouts.

"That's not me. Look …" and she takes her phone out of her jacket pocket, takes a picture of herself and shows it to me, "your drawing doesn't look like me at all. There's something funny about the way you've drawn my eyes and mouth."

"No," I explain, "the drawing represents who you are more than what you look like."

"That doesn't make any sense," she sounds upset. "A portrait drawing of me is meant to look just like me, just like my photo. And anyhow, who are you to say who I am?"

"I just draw what I see."

"Well, all I can say is that you don't see very well. I'm really disappointed. This was going to be a birthday present for my boyfriend. I don't see why I should give you twenty bucks for something that makes me look like, like …" she struggled to find a damning metaphor, "like a retarded mouse on steroids."

She had, at least, noticed my subtle subversions of her features and was closer to the truth than she realized. But she was also typical of quite a few subjects who don't like their portraits: they kick up a fuss and try to wriggle out of paying up for a picture that doesn't flatter the image they have of themselves. None of this worries me, and I don't need the hassle of an argument in public.

"Well, I'm sorry you don't like my portrait of you. You can have it for free. No charge. All I ask is that you keep it for at least a day before you throw it out, if that's what you plan to do with it."

She relaxes and smiles, clearly believing she had won. Made her point. "I appreciate the gesture. I'll take the picture, and here's five dollars for your time."

I decline the gratuity—she didn't protest too much—and off she goes armed with her free portrait rolled up in her hand and a story to tell her friends. Within seconds she's talking on her phone. Tonight she'll study the portrait and convince herself that it's somebody else. Somebody she doesn't know. But she won't destroy it. She'll hide it away in her closet and then, from time to time, sneak another look at it and compare it with her reflection in the mirror to reassure herself that it isn't her. She'll send her boyfriend a carefully brand-managed photo of herself. As for me, I'll file the photo I took of her portrait in the folder marked Rejects.

About half an hour later, an older couple, probably in their midsixties, walk by with a fair-haired little boy, maybe five years old. They stop, admire my display, and ask to have their grandson's portrait drawn, as long as it doesn't take too long. You know how it is with children, and of course I do. But theirs is an easy assignment. Grandparents who want their grandchild's portrait drawn in Central Park are of the doting variety, and a quick cherubic rendition is easily made and will easily satisfy. I don't know how many times I practiced copying Rubens' famous portrait of his son Nicolas and it is the perfect template for this little guy. He's done in ten minutes. Everybody is very happy and mommy is going to be absolutely delighted with the portrait of her little Jacob.

After that there are no more customers for me or my fellow "artist," Bin Jiang, who usually takes a spot on the Mall about twenty yards from where I like to work. We exchange polite little bows when we pass each other. He was an art teacher in Guangzhou for twelve years, or so he claims. But to me he looks more like an accomplished cartoonist rather than an art teacher and portraitist. To pass the time I start reading the *New York Times*. Out of the corner of my eye I see that Bin has snared a young couple, and after a few moments of gesticulation has persuaded the man to pose for him while his partner watches. A big technical difference between Bin and me is that I always use graphite pencils for my street work while guys like Bin work with a charcoal stick all the time. It's a personal choice. Achieving higher values with graphite requires more work. The repeated pencil strokes need to be carefully calibrated in order to achieve the desired tone and, to my mind, the greater effort is rewarded with a greater insight into the subject. And, also, the resulting portraits are physically much more robust. With charcoal it is far easier to achieve dark tones and facile contrasts, but the product itself is easily smudged. Bin has a nice little scam. After he's sold the portrait he does a little demonstration—practically a mime—of how easily charcoal smudges and what a really bad idea it is to roll up a charcoal portrait. Before you know it, Bin has sold his subject a protective plastic sheet and a cardboard carrying frame for twenty bucks. I can see that he's just done it again. My portraits roll up without risk, and I just offer my subjects a length of protective cardboard tubing for a couple of bucks. Our artistic profit margins are very different.

I suddenly become aware of the jogger who had passed by earlier. She takes off her dark glasses, revealing high cheekbones and the most interesting eyes. They are an unusual blue-brown blend: they could be almost any color you want depending on the setting and the light.

"I really liked the portrait of the girl you were working on when I passed by earlier."

"You did?"

"Yes. You captured her perfectly."

"I did?"

"Yes. She was a total airhead."

We both burst out laughing. This could be love at first sight. I absolutely have to draw her. "Would you like me to draw you?"

She looks at her watch. "I have to run." We both laugh again.

"I tell you what: five minutes, and on the house."

She sits on the nearby bench and takes off her knitted hat, revealing curly red hair. She looks at me with a quizzical little smile. With her pale complexion and red hair she could almost be a pre-Raphaelite. In those few minutes all I can do is capture the smile, the line of the nose and the cheekbones, and the depth of her eyes. As is so often the case with portraiture, less is more. She gets up and looks at the sketch with an approving smile.

"Did I capture you?"

"I believe you did."

I'm about to unclip it from my easel to give it to her when she says, "No, no. I want you to keep it. It'll be something for you to remember me by. Perhaps you'll work on it some more—from memory," and before I can respond she pulls on her hat and runs away down the Mall.

That evening I study her portrait. I have to continue working on it, but there's something in that preliminary sketch that I don't want to disturb. Although I say it myself, those few lines seemed to capture her quizzical smile, her character—even if I don't know who she is or what she's really like. That's the miracle of portraiture: the finest line, the subtlest shading, the tiniest crease around the eyes or mouth, can capture not only a likeness but also the person. Sargent and Ingres could do it like no one else. Sargent's ability to put his subject's faces in the shadows—apparently obscuring the details of their features—yet somehow drawing out their personality, their mood, was the stuff of genius. Maybe that apparent lack of detail inspires the imagination—that highest candle—to complete the details in one's mind, to make a mental interpolation that establishes the essence of a person in a way that a photograph, for all its precision, never can. Maybe it's better to make love in the soft light and shadows of dusk. I decide to copy the original and work on the copy. I don't want to risk losing her.

I run in Central Park nearly every day, although I don't usually run along the Mall—too many people—but I'm glad I did today. I've seen that artist there a few times before, but today was the first time I stopped to look at his work. I really liked his portrait of the airhead. I was chuckling about it for the rest of my run. I hope he'll continue to work on that quick sketch he did of me. All the other artists I've seen in the park are really just cartoonists and, although some of them are quite good, the best they can do is produce a likeness. I should know: I've tried all of them and have quite a collection of their various attempts to draw me. I don't think any of them can capture who I am, but I think this artist can.

I've also spent a lot of time in front of the camera having my picture taken. I quickly gave up on color portraits. They were always dominated by my color: my red hair and my pale complexion. But my hair and skin tone is not who I am. I wanted a picture that stripped my face down to its bare essentials. As much as I preferred the black-and-white photographs that were taken of me, I found myself wanting shots taken with less and less lighting to the point where the details of my face were scarcely visible, just a form in the shadows. But it got to the point where the photographers gave up: they couldn't accept my argument that our true selves are to be found in the dark where nobody can see us. I think the guy who sketched me today understands this. I'm going to start jogging down the Mall more often in the hope that he'll continue to be there. I wonder if he'll work on my sketch some more and if he'll bring it to the park in anticipation of me showing up again.

A few days later, I see him at the same spot on the Mall. He has a customer. I wave to him as I jog by. He waves back. On my return run I see that he's now by himself. He waves me over. We smile at each other.

"Don't tell me you've come by to see if I've worked on your portrait some more."

"Absolutely not. Last thing on my mind," and I sit down on the bench next to his easel. He takes a cardboard tube out of a backpack, removes a roll of paper and clips it onto the easel. I can see by the higher quality of the paper that he must have copied, albeit perfectly, the original sketch. But it's now drawn as though it was a studio portrait with directed light lightly shading half of my face.

"I like it very much. It's very Sargent."

He lights up at the compliment. I think he knows it's genuine.

"I hoped you'd like it, but it needs some more work." He scans my face intently. "I just needed to see your face again to continue."

Just then a couple stop by, compliment him on my portrait, and ask how much he charges. I have the feeling that we would both like to tell them to go away. But, of course, we don't. I get up and say goodbye. As I jog away, I glance back and see him position one of his new customers and start to size up their face. I know we'll both be back.

If that couple hadn't shown up, I think we would have talked for the rest of the day. However, no complaints: I drew both the husband and wife, and they were so pleased with the results that there was serious talk of having me draw their two children and a family portrait. They gave me a business card and invited me to stop by their office the following week to arrange a sitting. I've had commissions like that before.

I would have liked to take a photograph of her, but I sensed that she wouldn't want that and would have been disappointed if I had asked. But now that I've seen her face again I can complete the portrait. I first add a little more detail to the eyes and mouth. It's those little creases at the corners that so often reveal the spontaneity of a smile. I also refine the slight asymmetry of her eyebrows and cheekbones. It's ironic that the accepted norms of beauty, that is beauty of the commercial variety, demand symmetry. Yet it is that very symmetry that homogenizes a face and dilutes its character. As I compare my original sketch of her with this more detailed version it is as though she has stepped into the light. So now comes the crucial step. Taking up a softer pencil I start to shade her face, making it ever darker and, apparently, concealing the details that I had worked so hard to render accurately. You see, that's the thing: stepping into the light exposes the details; stepping out of the shadows reveals the character. With each increase of overall value, the subject's face appears to become increasingly masked; but keep stepping back and the portrait becomes evermore alive until, at a magical moment, the true person, their unvarnished personality, is revealed. I've done this many times before, but I knew I would never achieve the perfection I was looking for until I found the right face. And now I have. I can't wait to show her what I've done.

When I go back to the park a few days later, I find her sitting on the bench where I usually work. She's in her usual black running gear and sipping a cup of coffee. Out of nowhere, or so it seems, she produces a second cup.

"Here, I've brought you a coffee: black, no sugar. I've never known an artist who doesn't drink black coffee."

We both laugh, but there is no need to say anything more as I set up my easel and pin up my masterpiece. She looks at it very carefully and then steps back to the optimal distance. I'm rewarded with a smile that I'll never forget.

"You've captured me better than I know myself. I can't tell you how long I've been looking for somebody who could do this. You have. I can't thank you enough."

"Well, the coffee's a good start," I suggest optimistically. We both study the portrait, each of us taking it in for different reasons.

"You'll take it now, won't you?"

"Of course I will. You still have the original sketch, don't you?"

"I do. It's all I need."

She smiles knowingly. I roll up the portrait, put it back in its cardboard tube, and give it to her. As she takes it she gives me a searching look and then leans forward and kisses me on the cheek.

"Thank you again. Thank you so much. I've got to finish my run now," and she dashes off down the Mall.

I never saw her again, but every time I look at that preliminary sketch I reconstruct her face. Into the light and out of the shadows—it's the face I'd always been looking for. I don't even know her name.

MEASURE FOR MEASURE

The haughty administrative assistant, exuding the power of an imperial gatekeeper, gave a frosty smile and pointedly glanced at her gold watch. "Just in time, Dr. Rance. The provost is waiting for you."

Just in time, he mused: he thought he was exactly on time. He had even set his watch to the second that morning using the National Institute of Standards clock. Maybe the "Just in time" was a ploy to make him feel insignificant—a typical upper-administration tactic. But still, if the truth were known, he was a little nervous. It was, after all, his first university tenure committee. He had been appointed to one two years before but had become violently sick after eating a rather dubious-looking piece of meatloaf for lunch on the day of the committee meeting. He had never forgotten that. Apart from the humiliation of having to call the Provost's office to explain his absence, it had reminded him of one of the important lessons of inner-city dining: never eat anything whose ingredients you can't identify.

Well, into the *sanctum sanctorum*. The provost and executive vice-president for Academic Affairs, Quentin

Steele, was sitting at the head of a polished cherry-wood conference table with three chairs on either side, of which four were already occupied.

"Ah yes, Dr. Rance. Welcome," he said with an affable, but surely bogus, smile. "Let me introduce you to the rest of the committee. Everybody, this is …" taking a quick glance down at a file on the table, "Alexander Rance from …" and taking another quick glance down at the file, "Mechanical Engineering. Alex, please meet your fellow committee members: Shlomo Epstein, Chemistry; Julian Holter, Political Sciences; Frank Hegstein, Physics; and Naomi Cantor, Program for Comparative and Feminist Literature."

Shlomo Epstein, sitting on one of the two chairs next to the provost, gave Alex a friendly little wave. He was big man on campus with a joint appointment at Tel Aviv University. He was always appearing in the *University Gazette* in some story about yet another big grant he had been awarded or some International Conference where he was giving the keynote address. Overall, he must have been one of the biggest individually funded researchers in the Faculty of Science: a fact that he didn't let his hapless department head forget for one minute; and, when necessary, the dean of Science and even the provost himself. Julian Holter gave Alex the raised eyebrows and sardonic "Greetings" treatment. He was wearing what appeared to have become the uniform of the Arts and Humanities: a baggy black suit and black shirt done up at the collar without a tie. Another campus operator: always at the center of Faculty Senate business.

Frank Hegstein, who was rather ostentatiously writing equations in a notebook, looked up briefly, made a sort of snorting sound, and went back to his calculation. The man was reputed to be a brilliant theoretical physicist. Definitely a bit eccentric, but sometimes he seemed to be trying a little too hard to look the part. Naomi Cantor just gave a tight-lipped little smile that, to Alex, reeked of disapproval of both him and all the rest of the engineering faculty, if not men in general. Now hold it Alex, he said to himself, you're being too judgmental again. She might be a really fun person when you get to know her. In fact, looking at her now, she's got a nice pair of ... Hold it, hold it; stop thinking about sex again. You're at a tenure committee meeting, for God's sake. Somehow it seemed natural that he should take the vacant seat at the end of the table and not the empty one next to the provost.

The provost looked at the clock on the wall and the vacant seat next to him. "We're just waiting for Milton. He's been doing another interview for ABC and warned me that he might be a few minutes late."

Milton. There was no need to say, "Milton who?" They all knew who was being referred to: Milton Barr, director of the Institute of Strategic Affairs and International Relations, acclaimed expert on world events and now, with the fast-moving international situation of the past few weeks, a TV personality and darling of the university administration. Alex fumed inwardly: God, how he hated that man. The media always needed an expert, and now Milton's moment of glory had come. At the beginning of the crisis he was on the TV news almost every night holding forth knowledgeably about the dramatic changes in the world order that nobody, let alone all those self-proclaimed experts like Milton, could have predicted a few months before. But there he was, shamelessly offering platitudes as though he were handing down the Ten Commandments.

"So, Professor Barr, what is your analysis of the situation right now?"

"Yes, well, this is clearly a very critical moment in what is a very fast-moving situation. I think the key now is whether the right moves to the left or, perhaps more significantly, if the left moves to the right."

"Thank you, Professor Barr, for that most valuable insight. It has been a privilege to have you on our program tonight."

Milton had obviously been such a smash hit with the media that he had gone from "Expert," to "Resident Expert" with, apparently, a handsome little contract to be on hand for nightly comments. During those dizzying few weeks he had traded in his tweed jacket for a double-breasted designer suit and a collection of fashionably patterned silk ties.

There were bustling sounds in the office outside, and then Milton walked in wearing his new uniform. Quentin Steele rushed forward enthusiastically to greet him. After a warm handshake and pat on the shoulder, he conducted him to the vacant seat next to him and gushed, "Milton, your fellow committee members: Shlomo Epstein, Julian

Holter, Andrew Rance, Naomi Cantor, Frank Hegstein. Great interview last night, by the way."

The hero of the hour gave an almost pontifical wave to the table and a conspiratorial wink to Shlomo Epstein. The two of them were currently cochairs of The Presidential Task Force on Strategic Planning for Excellence in the New Millennium. They were obviously relishing that most delightful of academic roles: importance without responsibility.

Quentin Steele sat down and leaned back in his chair. "Well, people," he said, giving the "people" a slight emphasis and a little smile of political correctness in Naomi Cantor's direction, "as you know, we're here to consider the tenure case of Lilith Jackson-Carter. Obviously, I don't need to tell you what a critical moment this is for this fine young scholar. Of all the university service we ask of you—and I know sometimes we ask a lot from you—this is undoubtedly the most important. Absolutely the most important. In addition, it is, of course, the most confidential, yet one where we maintain the highest standards of academic integrity and fairness. Yes, scrupulous fairness. I think all of you, perhaps with the exception of ..." and with a paternalistic little smile toward Alex, "Arthur here, are familiar with our procedures. Procedures, I might add, that have proved to be very successful and are much admired by other institutions. I am, of course, here in an *ex officio* capacity only. It is a wonderful opportunity, for me as provost, to keep in touch with the careers of my best and brightest faculty. And, of course," giving another little smile in Alex's direction, "I am able to give any advice on procedural matters should that be necessary. Ms. Jackson-Carter is to be considered for tenure in the Department of Sociology. She was hired by that department as an assistant professor six years ago and was promoted, in recognition of her excellent progress, to associate professor without tenure, two years ago. She also has a joint appointment in the Program for International Gender Issues."

Alex giggled to himself. Program for International Gender Issues: PIGI for short—couldn't be more appropriate.

"A program," continued the provost, "set up by Milton. A real inspiration, I might add, and one that has attracted many accolades. You will all note, of course, that Ms. Jackson-Carter is, well ... Ms. Jackson-Carter, and it goes without saying that our great institution must be a model of a diverse faculty. Actually, dare I say it, we already have a good record in that regard, but then there is always room for improvement. In fact, Naomi, perhaps you could bring us up to date on our body ... I mean ethno-gender diversity metrics."

"Well, Quentin," Naomi seemed to hiss rather than speak, "the record is better than it was a few years ago, but it is still highly unsatisfactory. In the school of Arts and Sciences alone, there are only six tenured women faculty of whom only one is African American, two Hispanic, one gay, and still no Indigenous Peoples. However, Lilith does represent significant diversity: she is one-sixteenth part Cherokee and one-eighth part African American."

Jesus, thought Alex, I wonder what makes up the remaining thirteen-sixteenths? It was as though Naomi Cantor had read his mind. Giving Alex a sharp look, she hissed: "And frankly, the record in Engineering is appalling. There are no tenured women faculty there at all."

I don't think I want to like you after all, Alex thought to himself. But with uncharacteristic quickness he shot back, "I know the record is very bad, but we ..." the use of the "we" was a stroke of genius, he thought, "are still up against some rather reactionary forces."

"Antediluvian, more like," chipped in Julian Holter.

"Yes, indeed," intoned the provost. "Important issues. Issues that I take with the utmost seriousness. But, as we sit around this table this afternoon, weighing up all the facts, there is one criterion that we must have above all others. All these issues of color, charm, and flavor," and here he gave a little smile in Frank Hegstein's direction hoping that the brainy physicist would appreciate his erudite quip, "have to be secondary to our primary criterion of standards. Yes, standards of excellence." Quentin Steele leaned back in his chair and looked up at the ceiling as if receiving a divine communication. "At Arcadia University we have a long tradition of great scholarship, and in making our tenure decisions we are continuing a covenant ..."

Alex also looked up at the ceiling. In his mind's eye the provost had acquired a long pair of gray donkey's ears and was standing up on his hind legs braying "standards, standards," while all the other donkeys around him were nodding their heads from side to side in approval. For Alex, nothing was more tedious than academics on the subject of academic excellence. When he heard academic administrators talk about excellence, Alex felt like throwing up.

After a few more minutes on the divine topic of standards, the provost looked up at the clock and stopped his monologue. "However, I have already said enough. The case should now be considered by you, the appointed committee. Milton, you're the chair. Lead on, MacMilton," and he gave a little smile as the group politely tittered at the Shakespearean allusion.

Milton summarized the case prepared by Lilith Jackson-Carter's department that they had all received in green folders embossed with the university seal and marked Strictly Confidential.

"Well, perhaps we can follow my usual procedure for these committees …" thus spoke the decorated veteran of many a tenure committee, accompanied by an approving smile from the provost, "and go around the table and ask each of you for your opinions. Naomi, why don't you go first?"

"Well, Milton, as I see it there can be little doubt that Lilith is very deserving of tenure. Her record of scholarship, teaching, and service is outstanding. However, I just wanted to say a few words, to clear up any misunderstanding, about the article listed in her CV that was recently rejected by the *Deconstructionist Review*. The assistant editor of that journal, a dismal male chauvinistic wimp I might add, clearly had it in for her from the word go. Lilith's landmark article, The Penile Delusion, published in *Voice and Gender*, was critical of a recent survey of Third World sexuality published by two Yale professors—both men, of course—who turned out to have been friends of the assistant editor at the *Deconstructionist Review*. So, obviously, they got on to him and made sure she wouldn't get published."

"Obviously?" queried Frank Hegstein to whom little was obvious if it wasn't a seventeen-dimensional cosmic super-string.

"Obviously," retorted Naomi.

Next came Julian Holter's turn. He emphasized Lilith's membership of multiple committees, and highlighted her invited testimony to the Presidential Committee on Campus Diversity that he had recently chaired—a role that seemed to give him orgasms of self-importance. In addition, she was the secretary of a national monitoring group, although exactly what was being monitored Alex couldn't work out. Of particular note was the fact that she had given testimony to a subcommittee of the State Legislature on "Women in the Workplace."

At this point, Quentin Steele couldn't resist butting in. "I have to say that both the president and I thought her invitation to testify was a great credit to the university."

As the discussion proceeded around the table, Alex tried to form a picture of what the tenure case really was, albeit in a field he knew nothing about. In terms of scholarly papers there seemed to be just ten, with titles he didn't understand, in journals he'd never heard of. There was the vitriolic penis article in *Voice and Gender*; the article that wasn't published in the *Deconstructionist Review*; four moderately well-cited papers that were all coauthored with her dissertation advisor; and four internal reports for the Program for International Gender Issues—all of which Milton Barr was very enthusiastic about.

Lilith had advised only two graduate students: one had just completed a master's degree, and the other was doing some sort of fieldwork at a commune in upstate New York. The teaching record, which Naomi Cantor described as "excellent," consisted of a large freshman class on Gender Issues in the World Today, and a graduate seminar on New Methodologies in Socio-Psychological Analysis of Prejudice, for which the enrollment was "large." In Lilith's department, "large" apparently meant anything more than five students. However, closer inspection revealed that these were the only two courses she taught each year. The norm in Alex's department was two large-enrollment classes per semester. Fortunately, Frank Hegstein again took on the role of the Neanderthal scientist and queried this apparently light load. This was quickly quashed by Julian Holter who explained that teaching in Lilith's field required new interdisciplinary methodologies that were sensitive to social justice and equality issues in the classroom; and that the preparation for such classes was far more intensive than the usual rote learning in the sciences and engineering.

Shlomo Epstein was uncharacteristically quiet—no doubt preoccupied with his plans to get the university to build him a new Chemistry annex—and merely said, with what Alex swore was a subtle wink to Milton Barr, "Looks like a fine case to me."

Finally, it was Alex's turn. Something was really bugging him about the whole business but he knew raising the issue would undoubtedly land him in a heap of trouble. But gathering together his courage he began. "Provost ..."

The provost gave Alex an encouraging little smile. "Adrian, please. It's 'Quentin'."

"Quentin, this is obviously more of a learning experience for me, but I wanted to ask you a procedural question. I'm almost embarrassed to bring it up."

"Please, Alan. Please go ahead. Everything has to be on the table in a committee as important as this."

"Well, reading the university regulations and procedures on tenure," Alex could see Julian Holter give a patronizing little smile and Frank Hegstein look aghast at the thought that anybody would waste their time reading university regulations, "I noticed that the rules expressly bar from tenure committees any faculty from the same department as the candidate. As I understand it, Ms. Jackson-Carter has a joint appointment with the Program for International Gender Issues. This is in the Institute for Strategic Affairs and International Relations, of which Professor Barr is the director, and I was wondering if ..." The provost frowned; everybody frowned; storm clouds gathered above Milton Barr's brow. Oh boy, Alex thought, I'm really going to get it now.

Suddenly the Provost's frown cleared and a beam of sunshine appeared. "Yes, indeed, Anthony, very conscientious of you to point that out. If only more faculty took the university regulations so seriously. But the point is that Ms. Jackson-Carter's position in the Program on International Gender Issues is a *nonbudgeted* one and, accordingly, this avoids the conflict of interest issue that you were no doubt worried about. Julian, you're the expert on these matters, isn't that so?"

"Quite so, Quentin. The Faculty Senate Subcommittee on Process and Procedures that I cochaired last year explicitly identified that situation as one in which that particular conflict of interests issue is not an issue."

"Thank you, Julian. Indeed, in this case we have the best of both worlds: an inside expert, very expert, opinion," and here there was a soothing smile toward Milton Barr, "without any conflict of interest. Well, Milton, I think we now need your expert summing up of the case."

"Actually, there is little to say. She is a first-class scholar with a first-class record and if there aren't any further points to be raised," this was accompanied by a threatening look in Alex's direction, "I suggest we vote on it. Those in favor?"

Shlomo Epstein, Milton Barr, Naomi Cantor and Julian Holter immediately raised their hands. Alex, sensing that this was not the time or place to make his big stand, quickly followed suit.

"Those against?" and everybody looked at Frank Hegstein who did not raise his hand.

"Frank, are you voting or not?"

"Abstaining."

The provost quickly cut in. "Well, a five out of six vote in favor of tenure looks pretty good to me and now I can say, after the fact of course, that I consider this to be an excellent decision that will be of great value to the university. So, people, thank you very much for your efforts. I, and the president of course, really do appreciate it. And, Shlomo, perhaps you could stay behind for a few minutes to talk about the space issue and your proposal for a new building."

Quentin Steele accompanied them to the door of his office and into the waiting area outside. He warmly shook them all by the hand and patted Alex on the back. "Well, Aiden, er ... very good. Good luck."

Why, Alex thought to himself as he walked away, do senior administrators always pat you on the back and say "Good luck" like some World War I general about to send you over the top to be shredded to pieces by a hail of enemy machine-gun fire? As he walked back to his office, Alex reflected on the committee meeting and was very unhappy as he thought it all through. The whole tenure case seemed like a farce to him. With a record like Lilith's you'd be lucky to get hired as an adjunct instructor in his department, let alone get tenure. Alex recalled with some bitterness how they had made him sweat it out for the maximum seven years before he was first put up for tenure and how the anxiety was compounded by the fights that went on between rival factions of the department's senior faculty as to whether he should even be considered for tenure.

Obviously, Lilith's case was a whole different game of institutional politics, and the provost's pious platitudes about the primacy of standards were so much claptrap. But then, there wasn't really any reason to expect anything better from a senior administrator. Recalling that little wink from Shlomo Epstein in Milton Barr's direction, Alex thought he had a good idea of what was going on. The thing that arrogant shit Milton didn't know was that Alex knew a whole lot more about him than he could have suspected. Alex's wife, Madeline, who had kept her maiden name of Barber, worked on the research staff at the Institute of Strategic Affairs and International Relations. There was no reason to believe that Milton would have made the connection between the two of them.

There was no shortage of gossip about Milton. According to Madeline, the women in the Institute had nicknamed him "Mr. Goodbar." The man was a shameless womanizer and a total hypocrite. While he preached about women's rights, he also assumed that he was above the rules and tried to seduce everybody in his empire—be they student or secretary. It wasn't clear how far he ever got with his prey, and most of the women who worked at the Institute quickly learned to keep their distance. However, there was little doubt that he had had affairs with two graduate students over the past four years. With that little wink from Shlomo Epstein, Alex couldn't help but wonder if Milton was having an affair with

Lilith Jackson-what's-her-name, and had rammed her tenure decision through the committee. But then, that was just speculation. Maybe Milton hadn't been screwing her, and she really was a great scholar in the making and did deserve tenure. However, Alex knew that he would have to keep his sex-for-tenure theory to himself. Although Madeline was often scathing about Milton she was also very supportive of women faculty, and Alex knew she would dismiss, with a laugh, his hypothesis as the typical, male chauvinistic prejudice of an engineer: "Oh really, Alex. You engineers …" But it wasn't as though Madeline was a feminist. Far from it: she just wanted women to succeed at the university. And, in truth, precious few had to date.

Ah, yes, Madeline. Alex often felt how lucky he was to have her. They had now been married for sixteen years. At college, Alex had been shy and awkward with girls and it was only by chance that he had met Madeline on a hike. She was a bit on the thin side and hid her face behind large, rather nerdy glasses. However, Alex quickly discovered how smart she was, her wonderful smile and sly sense of humor, and she seemed to be the only person who understood his jokes. Their relationship quickly blossomed, but within a few months of the first time they had sex she announced that she was pregnant. He could never quite understand how that had come about—he was sure he had read the instructions on the packets of condoms correctly. With both of them coming from rather conservative families, marriage seemed like their only option. Their first few years of marriage were pretty rough: Alex was very preoccupied with graduate school, and their daughter Miranda had been a temperamental infant. They were tired, frustrated, and poor. It wasn't a good time. But somehow they had survived. Madeline went back to school and got a doctorate. But to Alex, the most striking thing was the way she had changed: it was the proverbial ugly duckling turning into a beautiful swan. Madeline filled out, the glasses were traded in for contact lenses, and suddenly Alex discovered that he had a self-confident and very attractive, if not sexy, wife that his colleagues would eye jealously. God, what dismal wives some of them seemed to have. They were often snobbish, or bitter, or both—often because they had let their own academic careers be subsumed by their husbands'. By contrast, Madeline was able to do her own thing and still retain that sly sense of humor that had attracted Alex to her in the first place. She still laughed at his jokes; but every now and again he sometimes had the feeling that she was laughing more at him than his jokes. Madeline and Miranda were very close. They did aerobic workouts together in front of the television—something Alex was ashamed to admit he found to be quite a turn on—and they seemed to have all sorts of little in-jokes between them. Sometimes at dinner he would feel as though he was being tolerated as a mildly amusing, but not always totally welcome, houseguest.

Well, maybe Lilith Jackson-Carter did deserve tenure, but Alex really resented the way it had been done. In fact, he was beginning to despair about the Institution as a whole.

It was obvious that the way you got what you wanted was either to press the right political buttons like that ambitious slimeball Julian Holter, or that publicity hound Milton; or to buy it in the way that big operators like Shlomo Epstein did. Alex had yet to see a dean not cave in to a faculty member with big grants. The ordinary, hard working faculty like himself simply didn't have a chance.

Alex's bitter mood had only been exacerbated by a recent inspection of the Administration section of the university's directory. It seemed as though there was an administrative Moore's Law in action with the number of bureaucrats doubling every couple of years. But it wasn't just their increasing numbers that infuriated Alex; it was the ridiculous inflation of their titles. The vice president for Research, a hapless bureaucrat who always pleaded poverty when asked for matching funds, had been promoted to senior vice president for Research, and then to senior vice president for Research and Invention. What it was they were inventing, other than excuses to hire more assistant vice presidents for Research and Invention, Alex couldn't fathom. And then there was the vice president for Strategic Initiatives position, whatever that entailed. A year ago it had been rebranded as the vice president for Strategic Imperatives and Sustainability, and just last week, to great fanfare, further inflated to senior vice president for Strategic Imperatives, Sustainability, and Globalization. Worst of all were the seemingly infinite number of provost positions: assistant associate provosts and associate assistant provosts breeding like rabbits and validating their unjustifiable existences by inventing evermore productivity and evaluation metrics that the faculty had to satisfy. It was enough to make Alex want to commit institutional arson.

In fact, this past year had not been going at all well for Alex. Having been spun out as an assistant professor for seven years, his department had now kept him as an associate professor for another seven. He thought he might have had a chance of promotion this year, but the nonrenewal of his research grant had really worked against him. The department head was giving him a hard time, the other senior faculty were openly sarcastic, and the dean, after all these years, still didn't seem to know who he was. His most recent paper had been rejected by the journals, and one of his two research students had suddenly quit. Things at home weren't that great either: Madeline seemed somehow remote and was often out late working on her latest research assignment. Maybe he was just going through a midlife crisis. He still felt that he could make his mark somehow, on something, but quite what and how he didn't know.

A few days later, Alex received a phone call from the provost's office. "Dr. Rance," it was the same patronizing administrative assistant who had greeted him at the tenure committee meeting, "I have an important message for you from the provost."

If it's that important, Alex thought to himself, why isn't the old bastard speaking directly to me himself?

"As you know, the president recently set up the Strategic Planning for Excellence in the New Millennium committee with Professors Barr and Epstein as cochairs and the provost, of course, as *ex officio* chair. They feel it is very important to have a special subcommittee on Space Allocation, and the provost would like you to serve on it. Your fellow committee members will be Mr. Frank Caprini from Facilities Management and Professor Herbert Becker from History. The provost wanted me to assure you that the report of this subcommittee will be taken very seriously and you will all be asked to present it, in person, to the Strategic Planning Executive Council—which is made up of Professors Barr and Epstein, and the provost himself. There will be a briefing session in Mr. Caprini's office, in the Glukerman annex, next Thursday at 2:00 p.m. Thank you. Good-bye."

Alex was initially speechless and then very angry. The bastards didn't even ask him if he would be willing to serve on the committee. They just told him that he would. It was clearly their revenge for his comments on the Jackson-Carter tenure committee. And what revenge! Space issues were so poisonous. There had been a previous Space Committee about four years before. Alex had known the professor in Anthropology who had taken the brief seriously and exposed an extraordinary amount of space hoarding and wastage. Everybody hated him and gave the poor guy the cold shoulder at the Faculty Club, while those seemingly permanent members of the Faculty Senate had a wonderful time trying to out-do each other in expressions of moral outrage and demands that the president and provost convert their palatial offices into community-outreach centers. Of course, nobody gave up an inch. In the end, all that came out of it was that a few rooms used by janitorial services were given over to the library for book storage. And now Alex was going to be put through the same miserable time-wasting exercise. Whatever ideas he might come up with, nobody would listen to them. Epstein wanted a new chemistry annex and Barr wanted a new building for his Institute. Both claimed, of course, that these extensions of their empires were for noble teaching purposes. No doubt, both would get what they wanted. Epstein was proposing to raise half the money from industry and ask for matching funds from the university, while Barr would raise his half from wealthy alumni. Either way, both endeavors would provide great photo opportunities for themselves and the president. The matching funds would, in the end, come out of the pockets of poor hacks like Alex in the form of yet another year without a pay raise and no maintenance on his teaching laboratory. But what could he do? Phone back and say he was too busy to serve on the subcommittee? He didn't really have any choice. As usual, he would just have to do what he was told.

When Alex arrived at the briefing session in Mr. Caprini's office, all he found was Caprini's assistant, who introduced herself as Rita. She was rather pretty in a plump sort of way that was accentuated by her tight-fitting jeans.

"Oh, it's so sad, Mr. Rance. Mr. Caprini was rushed into the hospital on Monday for bypass surgery. So young to have a bad heart. Must have been the stress, you know."

"Where's Professor Becker?"

"Oh, he's not here either. I called his department today to make sure he knows where to come, and they told me he's away on sabbatical or something."

"So it's just me?"

"Oh, I guess so, sir," but seeing the anger on Alex's face, she added, "but maybe it'll be fun."

Fun! It was an outrage! How was he going to have fun! So much for "strategic planning": those idiots were appointing faculty who weren't even here to serve on committees that couldn't do any good.

Rita handed Alex a very big cardboard tube and a huge bunch of keys. "Here are all the building plans and a set of master keys. And here's a tape measure. See, it's got a little clip to put it on your belt … neat don't you think? Maybe you'd also like to have this clipboard?"

Keys, tape measure with a belt-clip, clipboard: they were kitting him out to look like a fucking janitor. Maybe the whole thing was a set-up to humiliate him.

As Alex walked back to his laboratory, he was seething. It was all too much. If he had had another job to go to he would go tomorrow. But he didn't, and he was stuck with this wretched assignment. But maybe there was a chance for revenge. Over the last few years, the student body had become much more militant and the student newspaper much more outspoken. This time an exposé of space wastage could find a more appreciative audience and make a few people squirm. Alex had noticed how senior administrators—always with an eye on the next job—were rather sensitive to the negative publicity of student criticism. One highly publicized sit-in, and their chances of an upward move to another institution were seriously hurt. As far as Alex could tell he was doomed to stay as an associate professor forever, so there didn't seem to be too much to lose.

The next day, Alex went to the Chemistry building to begin his space analysis. As he walked past the men's restroom on the ground floor, an irate, white-haired professor stormed out and, on seeing Alex with his keys, tape measure and clipboard, shouted:

"Can't you people ever get these goddammed urinals fixed properly?"

"Sorry, nothing to do with me," and walking calmly by, Alex left his spluttering assailant behind.

Alex spent several hours in the building checking out all the rooms and reluctantly concluded that they were using all their space as efficiently as they could. In some cases there was definite overcrowding, especially in the rooms allocated to graduate students. All that was left to inspect was the basement area, although it was not included in the building plans he had been given. He went down a flight of stairs and came to an old wooden door, with a papered-over window on which there was a yellow radioactive warning sticker and a No Admittance sign. After trying a few master keys, Alex was able to open the door and found himself in a short wide corridor with a pair of swing doors at the end. He pushed them open and turned on a bank of light switches. As the fluorescent lights flickered on, a vast subterranean laboratory was revealed. It was very dusty, and bits and pieces of old equipment were scattered on some of the benches. As he walked through the lab Alex saw, along one of the walls, a series of doors that opened into small, empty offices. At the end of the laboratory was another pair of swing doors. These, too, opened into another, slightly smaller laboratory, also with an accompanying set of offices. It was incredible: the whole area must have taken up most of the basement and was totally unused. It could easily be converted into at least two classrooms, a medium-sized teaching laboratory, and a suite of offices for graduate students.

There was the sound of a slamming door, quick footsteps, and a strong voice boomed out, "Who the hell are you, and what the hell are you doing here?" It was Shlomo Epstein.

Staying calm, Alex walked casually toward Shlomo. "Hi, I'm Alex Rance, Space Allocation Subcommittee."

Trying hard to get a grip on himself Shlomo replied, "Ah yes, Rance ... but you really should have asked my permission to come down here. Radioactive chemicals, you know."

"I'm so sorry," Alex lied, "I tried to find you but you weren't around."

Epstein's tone became friendlier. "Well, as you can see, Alex, these are my nuclear chemistry labs. I'm actually in the process of starting a new nuclear chemistry group. I'm expecting a big grant from the Department of Energy any day now. In the meantime some radioactive materials are being stored down here. The whole area is quite unsuitable to be used for anything else, of course."

You liar, thought Alex. I know full well that nobody is funding nuclear chemistry at the moment, and that you are not allowed to store radioactive chemicals in a laboratory area like this. You're a goddammed space hoarder, and I've found you out.

Shlomo's tone became very chummy. "You know Al …" Alex noted that he had progressed from Rance to Alex to Al in the space of just a few minutes, "I think you were quite right to bring up that point about conflict of interest at the tenure committee we were on last week. I felt a bit uneasy about it myself. Next time I see Quentin, I'll suggest that he look at that issue again."

Shlomo gradually propelled Alex out of the basement and out of the chemistry building. He shook Alex's hand like a long lost friend. "It's been great seeing you again, Al. Say, why don't you drop by our departmental party next week. We need to see our friends from Mathematics more often."

That night Alex was in high spirits. Madeline always seemed to respond to good humor and they made love for the first time in over a week.

Over the next few days, Alex worked tirelessly on his space analysis discovering more and more wastage and hoarding.

Finally he got to the building that he was really looking forward to inspecting. He had been saving it for last: the Institute for Strategic Affairs and International Relations. From what Madeline had told him, Milton Barr had a suite of offices that took up the entire top floor. As Alex got out of the elevator he was confronted by a large plaque proclaiming: Institute for Strategic Affairs and International Relations. Milton J. Barr, Director. Underneath was a large, framed photograph of the opening ceremony from a few years back, with Milton, an assistant secretary of state, and the university president beaming into the camera. There was a hallway with plush carpeting and contemporary posters on the walls. Alex walked down the hallway, through a door marked Reception, and found a room looking like the lobby of a small, exclusive hotel. A young woman, probably a student-worker, was standing in attendance behind a marble-topped counter decorated with a vase of roses.

"I'm here to see Professor Barr."

"I'm afraid he's in Washington today."

"Maybe I could speak to his personal assistant. I'm Professor Rance. Milton and I …" Alex loved the sound of the "Milton and I" … "are working on the President's Strategic Planning Committee, and I need to go over some data."

The young woman was impressed and ushered him into an adjoining office area. There were three secretaries, each working at their own large desk. One of them stood up. "I'm afraid Sheila, Professor Barr's chief personal assistant, is out today. Is there anything I can help you with?"

Alex explained that he was the chair (but not the only member) of the Space Allocation Subcommittee and needed to check "Milton's space." Somehow the "Milton" and the use of the Presidential Strategic Planning mantra all worked their magic. He was told to help himself and that nothing was locked.

As Alex walked down the main hallway he came to a large room that was obviously some sort of waiting/reception area with a combination of overstuffed modern furniture and antique pieces, and oil paintings of famous alumni. In one wall there were two doors: one led into a small, modern kitchen and the other into a beautifully appointed restroom. The next room was marked Executive Office. It was a plush secretarial area with just one enormous desk where, no doubt, the absent Sheila held court. That room led into a short hallway. On each side was a door marked Conference Room, and at the end was a door marked Milton J. Barr, Director. Alex first looked into the two conference rooms. Each was about the size of a small classroom that could easily seat twenty people. In the center of each room was a long, mahogany conference table with five chairs down each side and an imposing high-backed chair at one end. On one wall, in both rooms, was a whiteboard that looked pristine clean. In fact, both rooms were essentially identical; the only difference was that one had a large cocktail cabinet and the other an impressive array of audio-visual equipment. And finally, the great man's office. Alex gasped as he stepped in. It was fabulous. It had huge windows offering splendid views of the city, and the most beautiful office furniture he had ever seen. One unmarked door opened into a small restroom that even had a shower cubicle. Another door was marked Briefing Room. It was furnished like a lounge, with a stylish chrome and glass coffee table, a couple of leather armchairs, and an enormous sofa. Briefing Room, my ass, Alex thought. I know what goes on in here: debriefing more like. He checked the floor plans. The conference rooms were marked as Seminar Rooms, and the Briefing Room and restroom weren't on the plans at all. As Alex took the tape measure out of his jacket pocket, he dropped his pen and it rolled under the sofa. Bending down, he swept his hand under the sofa to retrieve it. He also swept up a scrap of paper that, without even looking at it, he absentmindedly stuffed in his pocket.

Alex finished his measurements and, with some glee, sat for a moment on the great Milton's executive desk to take stock. It was an amazing exhibition of extravagance and wasted space. If the student newspaper could get a look at it; or even better, one of the city papers, the university would have a lot of explaining to do—especially in these budget-cutting times. Alex left deep in thought trying to work out how best to use his latest discovery.

At home that evening Alex was emptying out his jacket to go to the cleaners. In one pocket he felt a scrap of paper, and was just about to toss it away when he felt that it was slightly greasy. Looking more closely he saw that it was a piece of a condom wrapper. It didn't make sense: he didn't use them. Madeline had had her tubes tied years ago. Then it did make sense, perfect sense! It was that scrap of paper he had swept up from under Milton's sofa in the so-called Briefing Room. So that piece of snake-shit was bonking somebody in his office, maybe even Lilith Jackson-Carter. If only Alex could catch Milton in the act or, at least, make sure that Milton knew that he knew, he might be able to get his revenge. It was quite simple: he had all the master keys and he was, *de facto*, chair of the Space Allocation Subcommittee appointed by the provost, no less. Alex had the perfect excuse to go anywhere he wanted at any time. One evening, he would go back to Milton's lair and see if he could catch the bastard in the act.

A few days later, after working late in his office, Alex walked past the Institute and saw lights in the top floor windows. He decided to go up there right away. As he walked up to the main entrance he noticed Madeline's bike in the rack outside. Suddenly he had a most horrible thought that chilled and shamed him. Would Madeline let that shit get his hands on her? She had recently said that Milton wasn't really that bad, and she had seemed somewhat remote of late. No, no, no. It simply wasn't possible. He was getting paranoid. Madeline was presumably researching in the Library next door.

When Alex stepped out of the elevator at the top floor he found that the door marked Reception was unlocked. Nobody was around, but all the lights were on. Heart pounding, he walked through the reception area, the waiting room, the executive office, and into the hallway leading to Milton's office. The door was slightly open, and the lights were on. Alex sidled up to the door and saw that nobody was in there either. Maybe the janitors had just been through and had forgotten to turn off the lights. As Alex stepped in, he heard a sigh and a giggle coming from the Briefing Room. He could see light under the door. My God, Milton was there. He was doing it. He was caught—*in flagrante delicto*. Realizing that an awkward scene might ensue, Alex quickly took the tape measure and clipboard out of his briefcase and struck his best Space Allocation Subcommittee pose. At that moment, Milton Barr, looking flushed and slightly disheveled, stepped out of the Briefing Room. He froze at the sight of the intruder.

"Who the hell are you, and what the hell are you doing here?"

"Hi, I'm Alex Rance, chair of the Space Allocation Subcommittee. I was just stopping by to take a few last-minute measurements before my presentation to the provost on Friday."

Alex could see a slight flicker of recognition on Milton's face. The man was clearly very agitated.

"You have absolutely no right to come barging in here without my permission. Absolutely no right at all. Apart from the fact that this is a private office, there are confidential documents here. I simply can't have anybody barging in here. You know Rance, I've a good mind to call ..."

At that point the Briefing Room door opened again, and out stepped a very pretty young woman. Her face was flushed, and she was doing up the buttons of her blouse. Alex's heart jumped. Thank God it wasn't Madeline. At that instant he also realized how relieved he was that it wasn't Lilith Jackson-Carter either. But, my God, he thought, I've got you. I've absolutely got you.

Milton's faced was suffused with guilt and embarrassment. But quickly turning to the young woman he said, "Ah yes, Ms. Kennedy. Thank you for coming by to show me your results. If you call Sheila tomorrow, she can set up another appointment to finish our discussion. Goodnight."

The girl looked confused and crestfallen as she left. Alex felt rather sorry for her. She looked only a few years older than Miranda and was clearly very upset at having been dismissed like that. Milton's tone suddenly softened.

"Well, you're obviously taking your assignment very seriously, Alex." Looking toward the door, Milton continued, "And there's another person taking their work seriously. Working full-time and still writing a thesis. She can only come by in the evenings to discuss it with me. I'd rather be at home by now, but one has to respond to such dedication, don't you think?"

I think you're screwing her and holding the implicit threat of no graduation over her head if she doesn't comply, Alex thought as he replied, "Oh, absolutely."

Milton gently propelled Alex out of the office, through the many rooms of his empire and toward the elevator. His tone was now very friendly. "You know, Al, I only just realized the other day that you must be married to Madeline Barber. You must be very proud of her. She is one of our top researchers and," with the air of one man of the world confiding to another, "a damned attractive woman."

You lecherous bastard, thought Alex as he smugly replied, "Oh yes, Madeline is great—in every sense of the word."

As the elevator door started to close, Milton held it for a moment. "You know, Al, we're having a little reception here next week. Why don't you and Madeline come by. We don't see enough of our friends from Physics here. Bye, now."

As the elevator went down, Alex leaned against the side and caught his breath. Incredible: Epstein and now Barr. The two biggest operators on campus, and he had both of them by the balls. Well and truly, if not almost literally, by the balls. If he could play his cards right, he would get something out of it. It was time that the likes of himself struck back. That night he went home on an absolute high. He made such passionate love to Madeline that she was a bit taken aback, but she seemed to enjoy it all the same. She snuggled up to him as he went to sleep. "I don't know about you, Alex. You're full of surprises these days."

Alex could hardly wait for his presentation. He put a lot of thought into how to make his case. It would have to be done very subtly. He couldn't directly accuse Epstein and Barr of space hoarding in front of the provost. He would have to lay out the evidence in a diplomatic, but indirect, way so that they would all know who was guilty without anybody being directly accused.

The three great men all seemed in a jovial mood as Alex walked into the provost's office. Quentin Steele greeted him warmly. "You know, Adam, I have to say how much I appreciate your heroic efforts in doing this space analysis. It was rotten luck that Caprini had a heart attack, and most inconsiderate of Becker to suddenly go off on sabbatical like that. You had to carry the can all by yourself. It's dedication like yours that makes our great university tick. I'm really looking forward to hearing your report. The floor is yours."

Knowing that the provost's attention span was very short, Alex gave the briefest of background histories and summarized the current space statistics. Emphasizing the need for more classroom space—this getting an approving nod from the provost—he went on to say that he would now illustrate the problem by describing the difficulties faced by the Chemistry department and Institute for Strategic Affairs and International Relations. Just as he was about to move in for the kill, Shlomo Epstein interrupted.

"Forgive me for butting in here, Alex. Quentin, I wonder if you would permit me to say a few words?"

"Certainly, Shlomo, certainly."

"I think Alex has hit the nail on the head. Some departments, even mine, are not necessarily making the most efficient use of their space. Some of my old chemistry labs are not being used at the moment. They were being held ready

334

to start up a new nuclear chemistry program. However, I've just heard that the Department of Energy won't be funding this project." Noticing a little frown on the provost's face, Shlomo quickly added, "But they are going to give me $3 million for a catalysis lab instead."

"Splendid, Shlomo, splendid," beamed the provost.

"Well, it seems to me that those old labs should be put to good use. Like any experimentalist, I am loath to give up valuable laboratory space, but now is the time to set an example and make sacrifices. They could be refurbished, at reasonable cost, and turned into two classrooms, a medium-sized teaching lab, and offices for graduate students. Now it doesn't solve the problem in the long-term, but for the next few years during these difficult times, I really think it might make all the difference and save the university a lot of money."

The provost was ecstatic. "Shlomo, this is a splendid gesture and a splendid example. Simply splendid."

At this point, Milton Barr joined in. "I entirely agree with Shlomo. Now is the time for leading faculty like us to set a good example. I'm planning to convert two executive conference rooms—frequently used for briefing State Department officials—into classrooms. Again, this won't solve the long-term problem, but I feel it can make all the difference to my own Institute's space problems for the next couple of years."

Quentin Steele, sitting between Shlomo and Milton, put his hands on their shoulders. "Gentlemen, you are princes among men. With men like you at the helm, our great university is assured of a great future. I thank you both profoundly, and I am sure the president will too." Suddenly he looked up at the clock. "Goodness, I must run now. Time to meet the trustees." As he all but skipped out of the room, he patted Alex on the shoulder. "Another fine piece of work, Ari. Good luck."

Alex left the room in a daze. The bastards, those slick bastards. He had had them on the ropes, and just as he was about to deliver the knockout blow, they had turned the tables on him. Now they were fucking heroes. As always, he thought to himself ruefully, he had blown his big chance. Instead of saying, "I am sorry to report serious space hoarding and Drs. Barr and Epstein are the prime culprits," he had to try to do it in a clever way, and it had all backfired on him. Associate Professor Alexander Rance you are a total failure. So much for making your mark—you were simply out of your league.

For the next few days he was very glum. For Madeline, after his previous bursts of passion, this sudden change of mood was rather disconcerting, and she kept on asking him if he needed to see a doctor. Actually, you are married to a total failure, he thought to himself as he reassured her that he was merely preoccupied with a difficult research problem.

About a week later, Alex was sitting in his office reading the self-serving *University Gazette*. The front page had the headline "Strategic Planning Breakthrough." There was a long article about how Professors Barr and Epstein had solved the space-shortage problem by giving up some of their own space. There was a long quote from the provost stating what a superb example the two of them had set and how he, and the president, now expected all faculty to do likewise. Also on the front page was the headline "Two Faculty to be Honored," followed by the news that the Board of Trustees had voted to award the University Medal of Honor—which the article described as the Nobel prize for university service—to Drs. Barr and Epstein in recognition of their "outstanding and selfless contributions to the life of the university." Alex felt sick to his stomach. It was more than he could take. He had absolutely had his fill of the endless hypocrisy and corruption at the institution. He would resign and become a high school teacher.

There was a knock at the door and his department head, Peter Howarth, came in.

"Can you spare me a minute, Alex?" he asked in an unusually friendly tone.

"Of course, Peter. Come in."

Making himself comfortable in the one empty chair in the room, Peter said, "You know, Alex, I was talking to the provost a few days ago. He was enthusing about your great work on the Strategic Planning Committee. He then said that he'd noticed in your file that you had been an associate professor for seven years and asked if there was any reason why you were not being promoted to full professor. Actually, I was testifying to the Strategic Planning

Committee, and Shlomo Epstein and Milton Barr were both there too. I didn't know that you guys were all such great buddies. Quentin was very insistent about your promotion, and although ..." and here Peter's voice hardened for a moment, "I won't have outsiders meddling in the way I run my department, Quentin is difficult to resist when he gets so enthusiastic. However, I think he's right: it really is time that you became a full professor. You obviously have a way with these big shots and you should be more involved in the running of the department." As he got up to leave Peter continued, "I don't know about you, Alex. You're full of surprises these days. Perhaps one of these days I will have to consider handing the reins over to you."